Love
Without Limits

DIANE GREENWOOD MUIR

Cover Design Photography: Maxim M. Muir

Don't miss any books in Diane Greenwood Muir's

Bellingwood Series

Diane publishes a new book in this series
on the 25th of March, June, September, and December.
Short stories are published between those dates
and vignettes are written and published each month
in the newsletter.

Mage's Odyssey

Book 1 – Mage Reborn
Book 2 – Mage Renewed

Journals

(Paperback only)
Find Joy — A Gratitude Journal
Books are Life — A Reading Journal
Capture Your Memories — A Journal
One Line a Day – Five Year Memory Book

Re-told Bible Stories

(Kindle only)
Abiding Love — the story of Ruth
Abiding Grace — the story of the Prodigal Son
Abiding Hope — the story of the Good Samaritan

You will find a list of all published works
at nammynools.com

CONTENTS

CONTENTS
NOTE FROM DIANE
CHAPTER ONE 1
CHAPTER TWO 11
CHAPTER THREE..21
CHAPTER FOUR...31
CHAPTER FIVE 41
CHAPTER SIX..52
CHAPTER SEVEN..64
CHAPTER EIGHT 75
CHAPTER NINE 86
CHAPTER TEN...97
CHAPTER ELEVEN 109
CHAPTER TWELVE 120
CHAPTER THIRTEEN 132
CHAPTER FOURTEEN 143
CHAPTER FIFTEEN 153
CHAPTER SIXTEEN 164
CHAPTER SEVENTEEN 174
CHAPTER EIGHTEEN 186
CHAPTER NINETEEN...197
CHAPTER TWENTY...207
CHAPTER TWENTY-ONE 217
CHAPTER TWENTY-TWO..227
CHAPTER TWENTY-THREE 239
CHAPTER TWENTY-FOUR 250
CHAPTER TWENTY-FIVE 262
CHAPTER TWENTY-SIX 275
THANK YOU FOR READING!...287

NOTE FROM DIANE

It's difficult to write a character who is growing up and coming into themselves. I want to stay true to the personality they've developed along the way. Much like you and I, every stage of life causes changes in the way we look at and experience the world. Hopefully, with good guidance along the way, we become better for it.

I grew up with parents who encouraged me to be the best at whatever I did. They were pragmatic about mistakes and failures, but that didn't mean I stopped trying. My father wanted me to become a concert pianist. The day I told him that career wasn't a choice I wanted to make was hard on him. He had consistently encouraged me toward excellence. Since he was a busy man, we went through one period where he set a tape recorder on the table beside the piano with instructions to record the piece I was practicing for contest five 'perfect' times. Egads. But I did it.

The funny thing is that one reason I didn't want to become a concert pianist was because of the many hours I'd sit alone in a practice room. I couldn't imagine eight hours a day by myself, practicing the piano. Now, I crave eight hours of alone time in order to clear my mind and prepare it for the writing that I am desperate to take on. So many stories to tell and the only way to do that is when I'm by myself.

You'll meet a new character in this book. Bailey is the name of one of my fabulous nurses who answers a million questions. When I told her that my questions led to a plot in a book, we knew her name would be used. I love my new friends.

The team that supports my writing with everything from photography to design work, proofreading, and editing is filled with friends who mean the world to me. Thank you to: Carol Greenwood, Alice Stewart, Eileen Adickes, Fran Neff, Max Muir, Lisa Burton, Nancy Quist, Linda Watson, Amanda Kerner, Rebecca Bauman, and Judy Tew.

Spend time with us at facebook.com/pollygiller.

CHAPTER ONE

The problem with having a child active in the music program was having a child active in the music program. Things never slowed down. Next year would be worse, but this year was busy enough with both her oldest boys involved in band and choir.

While Noah participated in musical events, Elijah was part of them. He didn't miss a beat. If there was something going on, he was there. Tonight's jazz band concert had been yet another in a string of concerts that filled the last two months of the school year.

Polly and Henry hadn't brought their other kids to Boone for the concert since tomorrow was a school day. Noah and Elijah would be home late enough as it was. They could have waited to bring the boys home, but Elijah begged and begged to go out with his friends. Luckily, those friends included Miles Gorham, who often drove the boys back to Bellingwood after these types of events.

Tomorrow afternoon was another busy one with spring baseball heating up. Elijah had to be part of that as well. He could have chosen differently, but he was a good ball player, and his coach was willing to work with the practice schedule to ensure Elijah had an opportunity to play. Polly refused to say out loud how nervous she got at the idea of her piano-playing boy using those precious fingers to catch hard-thrown baseballs. If Elijah wasn't worried, she would remain calm.

"What are you thinking about?" Henry asked.

"Elijah's fingers."

He chuckled. "The only thing I refuse to allow him to mess with is a saw. We can repair most injuries. We might be able to save a lost finger, but I'd rather not tempt fate. No saws for that boy."

"I'm okay with that. One thing to worry about is enough."

"When is Noah going to get his driver's license? He's old enough."

Polly shook her head. Noah's sixteenth birthday had come and gone last November. Even though she'd tried to convince him to take the driving test, he had expressed no interest. Elijah had pressed him. No response. The boy didn't want to drive. His friends were driving, and Polly trusted them with her sons. Miles Gorham and Graham Birdsong were both excited at the freedom they experienced. Noah didn't care.

"I have no idea," she said. "Maybe you should talk to him."

"I have. He acted like I was an alien asking him to submit to body probes. What has him so nervous?"

"The responsibility. If Noah moved to a large enough city where he could walk to his job and cars weren't required, he'd be happy."

"If Noah could do his job from the privacy of our library, he'd be happy," Henry responded. He turned toward their street. "How many kids do you think have made it into their rooms?"

It was only eight-forty-five. While Delia and Gillian had eight-o'clock bedtimes, the rest of the kids were safe until nine o'clock.

Henry pointed at the house. Every single light was on. The foyer was lit up as were the living room and the kitchen. That was all they could see from the street. "Looks like we had a party."

"Poor Lexi."

"She probably started it."

Amalee drove into the slot she used in the garage and waved at

Polly. Teresa, Zachary, and Kestra waved, too and Polly smiled as she got out of Henry's truck.

"How was your evening?" Polly asked as they ran to greet her. The four Ricker kids had grown more and more comfortable with Polly, Henry, and everyone else who was part of this big family.

"It was fun," Kestra said. "We had fried chicken for supper."

"With black-eyed peas and rice," Zachary said.

"That sounds tasty," Polly said.

The kids continued to go to their home church in Boone every week. Sometimes others in the family went with them. Everyone was always welcome. Polly would never take that away from the kids. It was the last connection to their former life. Their grandmother's home had finally been sold and the money from that sale put into a trust. The woman's belongings were in storage. The kids could take all the time they needed. Their memories would be preserved as long as Polly had anything to say about it. They'd each chosen pieces of furniture, paintings, and special things to put into their rooms. A beautiful landscape from their grandmother's living room hung in the hallway upstairs. Amalee had chosen a small side table with a pretty lamp to set under the painting.

"How was the concert?" Amalee asked.

"It was good," Polly said. She let her arm drop to her side, knowing that Kestra would take her hand.

Sure enough, the little girl slipped hers into Polly's. "Did Elijah play good?"

"He played very well."

"He always does," Teresa said. The girl had a bit of a crush on Elijah. Since he'd started working with her on the piano, she'd given herself over completely to his teaching. When he wasn't practicing, she was. They'd moved the electric keyboard to the basement so when there was too much going on upstairs, he could hide out in his room and play. At least he used headphones when Noah wanted to sleep.

"Are we going to have ice cream tonight?" That was from Zachary.

Polly laughed. "I hadn't thought about it. Should we?"

"I think so," he said. "When Noah and Elijah come home, we should celebrate that they had a good concert."

"Did you hear that, Henry? We should celebrate with ice cream tonight."

"I heard it," Henry said with a laugh. He put his hand on Zachary's shoulder. "What if we don't have any in the house?"

Zachary's eyes grew big. "We don't have ice cream? We always have ice cream."

Henry looked at Polly, as if she would know whether they did or not. She shrugged and shook her head, which caused him to stop in his tracks. "Zachary," Henry said, and paused. The little boy looked at him, wondering what was coming next. "Zachary, if we don't have ice cream to celebrate, the house might fall down around us. You and I should probably do the manly thing and go out to hunt and gather."

That also confused Zachary. "Hunt for ice cream? Can't we find it at the store?"

"Back in the old, old, old, old, days," Henry said, "Men went out to hunt for meat. They gathered grains, fruits, and berries to ensure their families had plenty to eat."

"I'd rather be a hunter/gatherer than barefoot and pregnant," Amalee said. "I don't mind cooking, but it's not my favorite thing to do."

Polly chuckled. "I'm with you, Amalee. It's a good thing there are plenty of people, both men and women who don't mind taking care of the home."

"You take care of this home," Teresa said. "You and Lexi."

"And you and your brothers and sisters all help. So does Henry," Polly said. "If I had to do it by myself, you'd come home from school and find me in a babbling puddle of goo on the kitchen floor."

"I've seen it," Henry said. "It's not pretty. Anyone else want to ride with me and Zachary?"

The boy's shoulders fell. He had been looking forward to a trip with Henry.

Polly kept a tight grip on Kestra's hand. She'd felt the girl try to pull away. "No," she said, "we'll go in and alert the troops that tonight is a party night. We'll be ready when you return. You boys go be boys."

When they got inside, no one was in the kitchen, which was generally the gathering spot for the household.

"Where is everyone?" Polly asked. She didn't yell because who knew what child was finally going to sleep. Delia and Gillian should be upstairs, but if they'd given Lexi too much trouble, they might still be floating through the household.

"It's just us," Cassidy said, coming down the hall.

"Who is just us?"

"Me and JaRon. We were watching a movie. Caleb is in his room and Lexi is upstairs with Gillian."

"Delia?"

"I helped put her to bed. She didn't want to go to sleep. Said she missed you." Cassidy shrugged. "Obiwan is with her. I made him go to her room."

"Smart move. I'll run up and say good night."

"Where's Zachary?" JaRon asked. He and his new roommate had become friends – probably closer than he was with Caleb, who was in the process of establishing his own idea of independence within the family.

"Shopping with Henry. It seems that we're having a party tonight to celebrate Noah and Elijah's concert."

"Do you mean ice cream treats?" JaRon asked in hushed tones.

"I do," Polly whispered back. "If you all can hold your horses, I'm going to check upstairs and then I'll be back for the party." She headed for the back steps.

Before she got to the top, she stopped and sent a text message to Lexi. *"Zachary and Henry are bringing ice cream treats if you're still up and want to spend time with us. No big deal."*

Caleb's door was open, and he waved at Polly as she walked by. He was propped up in his bed, reading a car magazine, his dog Angel tucked in next to him. For a boy who hated reading, once they found something that interested him, he much preferred spending time in his room. They'd brought in a bookshelf for him, something no one ever expected. The piles and stacks of magazines were neat and organized. He didn't read a magazine once and then set it aside. When he was out of new things to read, he went back and found old ones to dig into.

Obiwan stood in the door of Delia's room, his body vibrating with joy at seeing Polly. He was such a good boy. No noise, no barking, just a full-body wiggle.

When she got to the room, she saw why he hadn't left. Delia was on the floor beside her bed, piles of clothing around her. The two bottom drawers of her dresser were open and empty.

"Well, well," Polly said.

Delia looked up in shock. "Not my fault."

"What's not your fault?"

That question received a perplexed look. Delia pointed at the piles. "This."

"Did Obiwan open your dresser and take out your clothes?"

"Yes," Delia said.

"Interesting. Do you think we should fold these things back up and put them away?"

"He'll just take them out again."

"Do you think we should leave them in piles on the floor?"

"No," Delia declared.

"What should we do with the clothes?"

"I don't know." Delia flung a pair of pants into the pile, obviously frustrated.

"Honey, I know you opened the drawers and pulled out the clothes. Obiwan doesn't have fingers to open drawers. Will you tell me why you are upset?"

"Don't know," Delia said, her lower lip stuck out in a pout.

"If I help you clean this up and lie down in your bed with you for a few minutes, would that help you feel better?"

"Maybe."

"Did you miss me?"

Delia stood up, then wrapped her arms around one of the piles and lifted it toward Polly. "Sorry."

"I know. Why don't you put your pants in one pile, and I will fold your shirts."

It didn't take long before the clothes were put away. Delia stood in front of her bed. "I don't want to go to sleep."

"I understand."

"Everybody was gone."

"Everybody was busy."

"I want to be busy. I don't want to be alone."

"Oh, honey, I'm sorry you felt like we left you alone. You know we'll always come back, don't you?" Delia's old behavior was to cover herself with blankets and pillows – to hide from the world until it made sense again. Polly knelt in front of her and said, "I'll lie down beside you for a few minutes. I'm sorry you were scared of being alone. That's something I need to notice from now on."

With a deep sigh, Delia climbed into bed and moved all the way over. They'd pushed her bed against the wall so she could surround herself with blankets and pillows if necessary. Polly drew blankets over her daughter and then lay down beside her, turning so they could see each other. Obiwan jumped up on the end of the bed and draped himself across Polly's legs.

"He wouldn't let me leave my room," Delia said.

"Because he knows it's your bedtime. He also stayed close because he knew you were upset. Now, he's just glad that you're doing okay. What did you do at Grandma Marie's today?"

"James had to take two baths."

"He did? What happened?" Polly chuckled. Marie always had something going on out there with the four children she cared for. She wanted grandchildren and she had them. Delia, Gillian, James, and Lissa were active and busy, and Marie wouldn't have it any other way.

"He went outside and found mud. I wanted to play in it, too, but Grandma said no. James had fun, even if he had to take a bath."

"And the second bath?"

"Lissa poured juice on him."

"She did?"

"It was a accident. She cried. He got another bath. Grandma said it was a good thing she has a washing machine, or she'd run out of clothes for us."

The number of times Delia and Gillian came home in different clothes than they'd worn to Grandma Marie's house was nearly the same as there were days in the week.

Polly closed her eyes and breathed slowly in and out. When she peeked at Delia, the little girl yawned and snuggled into her pillow. This wouldn't take long. Delia was much like the rest of the kids. Unless her schedule was messed up for a reason, she fell asleep and woke up at the same time every day.

When Obiwan moved to the floor, wagging his tail, Polly knew that it was safe for her to leave the bed. She made sure Delia was tucked in, then stood in the doorway watching for a few more moments before turning off the light. Closing the door, Polly took a breath. That had been easier than she expected. What she hadn't expected was to discover how difficult it was for the little girl to have her family spread out in the evening. Had Polly been at home, it wouldn't have been so hard. She needed to plan better.

She stopped in Caleb's doorway. "Henry and Zachary picked up ice cream treats. We're celebrating Noah and Elijah's concert. Do you want to join us?"

"Okay," he agreed and set the magazine on his bedside table. "Will you let me get a job when I'm in high school?"

"We'll talk about it," Polly said. "What's on your mind?"

"I'd rather work than go to school. Somebody said something about doing that for school credit."

"It's not a bad idea," Polly agreed. "Ask more questions. Your classes are already set for first semester. What are you thinking?"

He shrugged. "If I could work at Woody's Garage, that would be awesome."

"What if they don't have a job for you?"

"They do. I asked. It's only a few hours a week, but at least I'd be working. School doesn't have anything that I want to learn."

Henry and Caleb had pored over the school catalog. There was nothing on automobile mechanics available. If Caleb couldn't work, it was going to be a long four years. She knew better than to encourage him to enjoy his high school years. He was going to struggle the entire time. He wasn't an extrovert unless he was in an environment that made sense to him. He had trouble learning, though he had learned to work through much of that. She and Henry spent hours with Caleb at the dining room table, showing him how to get through his schoolwork. He didn't want to participate in extra-curricular activities. He wanted to get through school as fast as possible and start working.

"You're going to be fine," Polly said. "It won't be easy, but your dad and I are with you every step of the way."

"I know." He put Angel on the floor, then stood and stretched. His muscles were thickening. Polly and Henry's budget for school clothes was not inconsequential. Luckily, her kids didn't mind thrift store finds. The way they moved through sizes was incredible. It wouldn't be long before Caleb would finish growing. She could see the man he was going to become.

"Let's get some ice cream," she said, hooking her arm around his. "I want you to know that I'm proud of how hard you've worked these last couple of years. Your grades are acceptable, you have worked to be active with the family, and you are finding things that you enjoy doing. That's what I want for all of you."

"I still think about how I nearly screwed it all up."

"Don't think for a minute that you won't mess up again," Polly said with a laugh. "That's the way humans learn. You'd think we'd figure it all out, but we don't. The thing to remember is that no matter how badly you screw up, we still love you and will be there to help you get through it." With a quick hug, she said, "I really do love you."

"Me too, Mom."

Polly moved so he could go down the stairs in front of her. She didn't need him to see that his last words had brought tears to her eyes. Caleb wasn't one for affection, either physical or verbal.

The family's noise came from the dining room. They walked in to find Elijah standing at the end of the table describing some event from the day.

Henry pointed back at the kitchen. "In the freezer," he mouthed.

Polly opened the freezer drawer and pointed. "You pick," she said to Caleb. "Do you want a glass of water, too?"

"Yeah."

CHAPTER TWO

Hoping to find the main part of the house empty when she got home after working at the hotel on Thursday, Polly breathed a sigh of relief when she found no one there. Because Lexi was so awful at taking time off, Polly and Henry tried to insist that she choose one day of the week. She had chosen Thursdays, though more often than not, she worked anyway. After the holidays were over, Lexi and Polly sat down with a list of Lexi's clients and worked out the days they were most likely to order. Fridays were big days because the weekend was coming, but since Thursday evenings downtown were generally buzzing, most people didn't order. Thursday was Lexi's day for herself.

The morning with June Livengood at the hotel had been filled with gossip and stories of people around town. June had been a live wire today. Nothing important had been shared, but she had plenty to say. By the time Polly was ready to go, she found herself anxious. The woman had jabbered without stopping the entire time Polly was there.

The dogs were happy to see her, and she opened the patio door for them to go outside. The little ones had finally been trained to the invisible fence. Since the back yard was so large, they had plenty of room to run and play.

Polly looked out over the fence to the cemetery beyond. She hated to admit how peaceful it looked. She'd said that once to Sal, who worried that Polly was yearning for an early grave. No, it was a quiet space that few people bothered with unless they were visiting a loved one.

One by one, the dogs came back inside, and Polly made a decision. She wanted to take a walk. It was a beautiful day and there was no reason to stay inside. She'd find something to eat for lunch when she got back, but right now, she needed quiet.

She slipped out the patio door, crossed the yard to the gate, and passed through the hedge separating their property from the cemetery. The monuments and gravestones were as familiar to her as the rooms in her house. Polly turned to the right and headed east. This path would take her past Andy and Len Specek's home.

Warmer temperatures helped bring signs of spring. Trees had finally leafed out. The cemetery was a glorious place during the summer when the beautiful old trees spread their canopies of leaves over the grounds.

The house just west of the Specek home had been empty for the last six months. Andy had mentioned two weeks ago that a new couple had moved in, but she didn't know anything about them. In a small town like Bellingwood, not knowing what was happening in a neighborhood was no fun. When Polly lived in Boston, people came and went in complete anonymity.

"Polly!"

She looked up to see Andy standing in the doorway of her back deck. "Hi there. I assumed you would be at the library."

"Not today. Do you have a minute?"

Polly looked down the sidewalk. Her walk wasn't as important as she'd thought it was. "I do. How are you?"

"She's a pip. That's how she is." Beryl's head popped up over Andy's shoulder. "I saw you coming and sent her to beckon you inside. I brought treats, though since I wasn't prepared for you to pass by, I didn't bring coffee."

"I have coffee," Andy said. "It might not be Sweet Beans, but it's pretty good."

"I've had plenty of coffee." Polly walked up the steps to the deck. "Spent the morning at the hotel."

"How is June?" Beryl asked. "How is her mother? Her aunt?"

"They're the same," Polly replied. "Tell me more about the treats that you brought. I haven't eaten lunch yet."

"Would you like something?" Andy asked. "I have chicken and dumpling soup, or I could make you a roast beef sandwich."

"That's okay," Polly said.

Beryl scoffed. "Let the woman make lunch. If you don't, I will refuse to allow you access to treats."

"Soup," Polly said with a nod. "Chicken and dumplings sounds wonderful."

"You know Len will be grateful to you for finishing it," Andy said. "He took a serving to work this morning and said he was tired of leftovers. It seems we live on leftovers."

"I'd live on your leftovers," Beryl said.

"You don't eat enough anyway." Andy shook her head. "No matter how Lydia and I try to keep food in your house, you end up throwing too much of it away because you just won't eat it."

"I'm busy. You know how hard it is for me to break away from my work when I'm in the middle of a creative moment. The last thing I want to do is stop to cook."

"We've done the cooking."

"I still have to heat or reheat food. I have to make a decision as to what sounds good to eat. I have to divert my brain power to paying attention to something other than what my heart tells me to do."

Polly looked at Andy and shrugged. "I've seen Rebecca get like this. She's talked about how Andrew doesn't want to do anything when he's focused on writing. She has learned to put food in front of him and walk away. If he eats it, then great. If not, she replaces it until he does."

"I need Rebecca in my life."

"Rebecca needs to be less of a keeper and more of a do-er,"

Polly said. "Sometimes I worry that she will spend her life boosting Andrew's career and allow hers to languish."

"That girl has too much talent to allow it to languish," Beryl said.

"Her problem will always be that the busyness of the world will supplant her need to create," Polly said. "Her most creative times have been when the two of you work together and she's freed from worrying about making money or doing what she thinks needs to be done. It's easy to let her get away with it, too. I love that she is willing to watch the kids or help with household tasks. Until right now, I don't think that I realized how much she needs me to release her from those things so she has time to be creative." Polly huffed a quick laugh. "That's why her room is always a mess. The time it would take her to clean it up is better spent inside her mind or with pencil to paper."

"After all these years with me, you're just now applying what you know to your daughter?" Beryl asked.

"Some days I feel as if I will never give my children all they need," Polly said. "I think I have it all figured out and then I learn something new."

"At least you're learning," Andy said. "Some of us just raised our children the way we were raised. It didn't occur to us that we could do it differently or be better."

"Your kids are fine," Beryl said with a frown. "Don't do that to yourself."

"But they are the same. They didn't learn how to make different choices. Did Bill really want to be a farmer? I don't know. It's all he was ever expected to do. Even Amy. She's a nurse. She's a very good nurse, but when she was young, she loved to make art. We didn't encourage her to be an artist, we encouraged her to get a job. Not a career, but a job where she could make a living, especially if she didn't marry a man who would allow her to be a stay-at-home mom."

"She loves her life," Beryl said. "You have to stop this. Amy loves caring for people. She loves being a nurse."

"But would she have loved being an artist?" Andy asked.

14

"Ask her. Stop beating on yourself." Beryl wildly waved her hands at Andy. "Or I'll do the beating for you. I'm good at beating up my friends."

Andy shook her head. "I tried to give Polly a compliment and now you are threatening to beat me."

"You took a swipe at yourself," Beryl said. "You can only operate with the knowledge and skills that you have at the time. When you learn more, you do better. You're already doing better with your grandchildren. I hear you encouraging them to live big lives."

"Time to heat the soup," Andy said, and walked away.

"That's telling her," Polly said.

"You started it."

"I know. Sorry. What are you doing here today and why isn't Andy at the library?"

"Miss Joss has another person working there now. You'd know this if you ever went to the library. Too good for public services?"

"You're on a roll," Polly said.

"That's because Andy has something in mind for me and I don't know what it is yet. You showed up before she told me."

"Something difficult?"

"Who knows? Did you hear that she has new neighbors?"

"I did. Have you met them?"

"Met him. Didn't like him at all."

Polly blinked. "That was quick."

"He's arrogant. Didn't want to waste any time with old ladies. Like we were going to intrude upon his life. Buddy, you just moved to a small town in Iowa. Everyone is about to know everything about you. If you plan not to get along with us from the get-go, you're going to have a miserable time here."

"Maybe he won't spend much time in town," Andy said from the kitchen.

"Who knows," Polly said. "Now, I'm still interested in those treats you brought."

"One-track mind," Beryl said. "I didn't expect to see you today, but I bought those black and white brownies you like so much."

"Those are my favorite."

Andy walked back in, carrying a tray with a steaming bowl of soup, a basket of crackers, a cup of coffee, and a thick slice of buttered toast. "I didn't know if you'd like something more, but this is Sylvie's sourdough, and it tastes wonderful with the soup."

"Mmmm," Polly said. "I feel odd eating in front of you."

"We'll eat treats," Beryl said. "And drink our own coffee. And find out why my friend has brought me to her house on a Thursday afternoon. What's up with you, Miss Andy?"

"Maybe I wanted to spend a few minutes with my friend," Andy said.

"We all know better. You're making me nervous."

Andy sat down, took a sip from her coffee, then reached for a napkin from the center of the table. "You're right. I had an ulterior motive." She took a muffin from the Sweet Beans box and broke it into pieces.

Before Andy had a chance to take a bite, Beryl snagged the napkin filled with muffin bits and pulled it away. "You don't get to eat until you tell me what has you all in a knot. What could you possibly ask me to do that would be so stress-filled?"

"She has rules about treats," Polly said in an aside to Andy. "She always wins, you know."

Andy nodded. "I'm supposed to ask if you would consider donating a painting to the library's permanent collection. And then, to top it off, I'm to ask if you would help me arrange the artwork we already own into a type of gallery in the basement. Joss and I have it to the point that we can use that front room for something other than storage. Since we have some really nice pieces and Bellingwood is your home, and you are such a famous artist ..." Her voice trailed off.

"That's all?" Beryl asked. "Of course, you ninny. I'll donate whatever the library needs. If you wanted to auction off one of my paintings to raise money, I'd donate something for that. Why have you never asked before?"

"Because you're so busy and, honestly, it's never come up. We've acquired paintings over the years from donations and as part of collections that come to us, but until I started digging them out, no one knew the extent of what we had."

"You know some of it will be exquisite and some will be garbage, right?"

"I know," Andy said. "I've already identified some garbage, but I want you to look at it before I put it back in deep storage. Joss and I also talked about hosting a summer art show." She nodded at Polly. "Ask local artists to display their work."

"For sale?" Beryl asked.

"I think so. Maybe leave it all up and when everyone is in town for Bellingwood Days, we'll sell the pieces that artists want to sell."

"I want to be on the board," Beryl said.

Andy frowned. "What board?"

"The library board."

"Trust me," Andy said, "you do not want anything to do with those old nincompoops. The hoops Joss has to jump through to get anything done are enough to make a sane person crazy. I refuse to be on the board."

"Nothing will ever change if all you ever do is invite the same people to do the same thing," Beryl said. "If I'm donating paintings, I want to be on the board."

"It doesn't work that way."

"It can."

"It will only make you angry. You don't have time for a picayune little-town library board."

"I will make time. Give me one year and I will clear out the worst of the low-hanging fruit. Give me two years and we could rebuild the library board into something that resembles an assembly that makes intelligent decisions."

"You don't have that kind of power."

"But I scare the crap out of people because they never know what's going to come out of my mouth next. And they don't know that I have friends who would love to be part of the library's growth."

"What friends?"

"There's one," Beryl pointed at Polly.

"Leave me out of it," Polly spluttered around a mouthful of soup. "I don't do boards or committees."

"Nan Stallings and Alistair Greyson," Beryl said. "JJ Roberts, Doug Randall, and Josie Riddle."

"Josie from Sweet Beans?"

Beryl nodded. "Young blood. People whose children and families actively use the library. People who see that the library is the lifeblood of a community."

"Doug Randall?" Andy asked. "He doesn't have children."

"But his business is right across the street."

"She's right," Polly said. She wiped away a dribble of butter that had escaped her mouth. "When Caleb was lost, he spent time at Boomer's. Then he discovered that he loved car magazines. You and Joss and Miss Bethany at the school library added magazines to the stacks so he would have something interesting to read. Comic books and car magazines. For a boy who was never going to be a reader, Caleb spends alone time in his room with his nose stuck in things that have words. He reads all the words. He may never love to read fiction, but at least he's reading. His world opened up because of the library and the comic book store."

Andy chuckled. "You know the thought of Beryl on the library board will give Joss a stroke."

"I'm so stinking tired of listening to people who have lived in Bellingwood all their lives refuse to accept that others might have something productive to offer. My brothers were the worst. They wanted everything to remain the same. It didn't matter that having things remain exactly as they always were meant that the town was dying." Beryl shuddered. "I listened as two old guys – older than me – ranted and raved about how the new young people were destroying all the good things about Bellingwood."

"Don't tell me," Andy said with a sigh.

"Don't tell you what?"

"You went off on them."

"No. I was with Lydia. She made me promise to stay quiet. I sent scathing looks their way, but no one noticed."

"Not every old person feels that way," Andy said.

"But the ones who do are mouthy and no one stops them from speaking their vitriol all over the place."

"Getting into it with them changes nothing," Andy said. "You can't change their minds. All it does is make you look like a fool."

"I'd feel so much better, though," Beryl said. She put one of the cheesecake brownies on a napkin and pushed it toward Polly. "Look at you sitting there all quiet and stuff."

"It's safer. You don't get all het up too often, but when you do, it's pure entertainment," Polly said. "Besides, I was eating. Thank you, Andy. The soup was wonderful."

"With warmer weather coming, my soup-making days are about to come to an end," Andy said. "I'm ready for fresh vegetables and fruits and salads and all the wonderful things that grace my table during the summer, and I will welcome soup season back this fall."

"Listen to her," Beryl said, shaking her head. "She's such a wonder."

"What did I say that has you making fun of me this time?"

"All the traditions you have. It's sweet. It is so anti-Beryl, but it's perfect for you. Isn't that the best thing about having crazy friends? You get to see how differences enrich the world."

"You are my crazy friend," Andy said. "And thank you for reacting positively to me asking for a donation. I was nervous about it."

"Why? I'm your best friend."

"And I hate the idea of using that relationship to talk you into doing something you might not want to do."

Beryl put her hand on top of Andy's. "I give you a lot of trouble about a lot of things, but you are one of my very best friends. If I didn't want to donate a painting, I'd tell you. I want to do this, not only for you, but for the library, too. Honey, I get requests every day to donate my paintings. Some I agree to, most I don't. If all a person can do is send a message asking for a donation, I will say no." She huffed. "Or I'll ignore the entire message. I do a lot of that."

"How many of those do you get a day?" Polly asked.

"Between that and my stalkers, way too many," Beryl said, her face tightening.

"You have stalkers?"

Beryl shrugged. "I have one that refuses to leave me alone. It doesn't matter that I never respond, I get regular emails. Sometimes daily."

"Is it someone local?"

"I don't know," Beryl said.

"Do you keep the emails?"

"No!" Beryl exclaimed. "Why would I want to keep them? They creep me out."

"For evidence. What if this person does more than send an email?"

"Give me a couple of weeks," Beryl said. "I can rack up at least fifteen or twenty emails from the person."

"You should," Andy said. "Why have you never said anything about this?"

"What am I supposed to say? Someone adores me to the point of being creepy? That sounds weird."

"Do you know if it's a male or female?" Polly asked.

"I'd say it was a female, but that's hopeful thinking. The idea of a man stalking me this way would keep me up at night. I don't want to talk about it."

"Please keep some of the worst emails," Polly said. "If you told Aaron, he'd say the same thing."

"He knows. When it started a few years ago, I asked what I should do. He told me to ignore them, and they'd go away."

"But they didn't," Andy said.

"And I've gotten very good at ignoring the emails. I don't even bother opening them anymore. I don't want to know what creepy thoughts are in this person's head."

CHAPTER THREE

Even though they'd spent the morning together, Beryl wanted more of Polly's time, so there they were, standing in Andy's driveway beside Beryl's car.

"Let me at least drive around the block with you," Beryl said. "I'm not finished talking, but Andy didn't need to hear the rest of this."

"What do you mean?" Polly asked.

"I mean, she's worried about the new couple that just moved in next door. She won't say anything."

"Andy never would. I'm glad she talks to you."

"And to Lydia, but Lydia will try to fix the problem. Andy doesn't want anyone to fix it, she only wants someone to listen. Accusing a neighbor of abusive behavior is never a good way to start a relationship."

"She's that worried?"

Beryl nodded, then pointed at the passenger side of the car. "Get in. Please?"

There was only one person Polly didn't like riding with. Beryl was that person. She'd never had an accident, at least as far as

Polly knew, but riding with Beryl was worse than teaching her kids how to drive. She rode up on other drivers' back ends, she took corners either too wide or too narrow, and she waited much too long to turn in front of traffic and would sit and wait for a ridiculous amount of time.

But Beryl was looking for more conversation, so Polly steeled herself and walked to the other side of the vehicle. The drive should take less than five minutes. Surely, they'd live through the next five minutes.

"What do you want to do about Andy?" Polly asked. "Or do you just need someone to talk to? I can be that person." She chuckled. "Sometimes I forget that people need me to listen and not offer advice."

"You're pretty good at advice. Maybe I am looking for that."

Polly was doing her best not to grip the handle on the door. She clasped her hands together in her lap as Beryl turned onto the highway. Getting through the cul-de-sac had taken more time than expected.

"What can I do?"

"Keep an eye on them. I know you walk through the cemetery." Beryl shook her head and Polly flinched when she threw her hand up in the air. They were about to turn off the highway and Polly wanted Beryl to pay attention. "Maybe if we talk to Andy more often, she won't get herself involved. I'm terrified that she'll walk into a situation where she gets hurt."

"By the neighbor?"

"You know how she is. Andy never tells anyone about the good things she does for people. I don't know if she even tells Len. She just wades in and offers her help."

Polly nodded. Andy had found a way to take care of Stephanie and Kayla Armstrong long before anyone else in town met them. She'd been there for Wyatt Post's mother before she died, offering assistance in different ways. The woman wasn't afraid and maybe she should be sometimes.

When Beryl pulled into the Bell House driveway, Polly stopped herself from sighing in relief. Rebecca had made it a policy that if she and Beryl ever went anywhere, she drove. Whether it was her own car or Beryl's car, Rebecca was the driver.

"Do you want to come in for a minute?"

"I should go home and work, but I don't want to," Beryl said. "Do you have time for me?"

"Of course I do. Come on in."

"We should share pictures of the kids' trip to New York City," Beryl said, taking out her phone.

It had been a few weeks since Rebecca and Andrew's spring break vacation to the Big Apple. They'd had a great time. Drea and Chloe came down from Boston for the last two days of the trip and rented a suite at a hotel in the East Village. Before that, the kids had stayed in a tiny apartment in Manhattan, the home of the brother of one of Andrew's college friends. The apartment was empty during spring break because the brother was meeting the whole family in New Orleans. He rather liked the idea of someone staying in his home while he was gone.

Andrew and Rebecca hadn't been able to get over the intensity of life in the city. Though both went to school in moderately-large Midwestern cities, Iowa City and Des Moines had nothing on the east coast. Everything moved faster. While some people were as rude as they came, others were polite and helpful.

They were fascinated by street vendors, and Rebecca couldn't wait to announce that she'd been pickpocketed. All she lost was a five-dollar necklace that she'd purchased for Cassidy, but the realization that she'd experienced something stereotypical of New York City was more fun than the actual purchase.

The kids had done all the touristy things they could find, from the Empire State Building to Battery Park, Ellis Island, and the Statue of Liberty. They'd shopped at Macy's and found the largest Barnes and Noble bookstore they'd ever seen. Rebecca dragged Andrew to museums nearly every day and they still hadn't had time to visit all she'd wanted to see.

Rebecca was so fascinated with the city that she couldn't wait to return. Andrew was exhausted from the trip. This had been the first time he'd traveled without his family, and it was an eye-opener for him. He felt protective of his girlfriend, and worried whenever they were out too late at night. The pressure to keep Rebecca safe had almost been too much, though he'd never admit that to her. He had admitted it to Polly one afternoon when Rebecca was wandering the depths of the Guggenheim and he was exhausted, standing in front of a painting by Pissarro. They'd already been to the Metropolitan Museum of Art and while he loved seeing classic pieces of art, Andrew wasn't as entranced with their reality as was Rebecca. He would have been perfectly fine looking through the catalog while in the comfort of his favorite chair.

On the other hand, Rebecca came back fully energized and ready to face the rest of the semester. She had taken so many photographs while in the city that she wanted nothing more than to sit with her pencils and paints, lending her eye and talent to the canvases in front of her.

Polly and Beryl walked into the house. When they made it to the kitchen, Lexi looked at them, guilt written across her face.

"What are you up to?" Polly asked with a grin.

"Nothing. Why?" Lexi swallowed.

"Because you look like the cat who ate the canary." Beryl frowned. "My cats would probably eat a canary and then I would have to vomit. Why did I have to visualize that idiom today?"

"No one is in the house, and I wanted an ice cream sandwich," Lexi said. "So I had an ice cream sandwich. I shouldn't feel guilty, should I?"

"Only because you haven't offered one to me," Beryl said.

"And me," Polly echoed. "How's your day?"

"Quiet. I don't know what to do with myself."

"Get out the ice cream before you go any further with your self-deprecation," Beryl said.

Lexi laughed and walked back to the refrigerator. She opened the freezer and took out the box. "I have to hide these in the back. Delia has figured out how to open the freezer."

"That will be a problem," Polly said. "Ice cream treats need to go into the big freezer now. You're tired of relaxing?"

"I think so. Will and I are taking Gillian to a movie tonight. I don't want to sit in the apartment upstairs all evening and I know you'll be mad at me if I do any work to prepare dinner."

"Yeah," Polly said in an aside to Beryl. "We don't like it when she acts like family and tries to clean up or anything. The girl works too hard."

"What are you two doing here?" Lexi asked. She stared at Polly. "How did you find Beryl?"

"I took a walk and ended up at Andy's house," Polly said. "Have you paid any attention to her new neighbors?"

"They only moved in a couple of weeks ago, right?" Lexi asked. "The wife seems nice enough, but I don't like her husband. I saw them at the grocery store the other day. He was hovering over her like he wouldn't let anyone near them. This is Bellingwood. She's safe enough."

"Not for him," Beryl muttered.

"What do you mean?"

"Andy is pretty sure he's abusing her."

Lexi nodded in understanding. "That makes sense. She flinched when he lifted his arm or got too close. I didn't think much of it, but now that you say something, I should have recognized what she was feeling."

Polly shuddered. "I hate knowing this or even thinking about it. How am I supposed to look at him without getting involved?"

"That's why I'm worried about Andy," Beryl said. "She'll get involved and then she'll be in way over her head."

"You aren't worried about me getting involved?" Polly asked with a laugh.

"If you do, there will likely be a dead body and you'll kick the meanie man's hiney until his only hope is to straighten up and fly right."

"It *is* your reputation," Lexi agreed.

Polly put her hand out and waited until Beryl realized she was waiting for the ice cream sandwich wrapper. After dropping them both into the trash can, she said, "We're going to the office. Beryl wants Rebecca's New York City photos."

"I can't imagine making that trip," Lexi said. "That's not true. I can imagine. I wonder if I'll ever travel like that. Do you really enjoy it, Beryl?"

Beryl flung her arms out and cackled. "It's the most fun I have. Well, other than sitting quietly in my studio with a paintbrush in my hand. I love seeing new places and experiencing new ways of life. Those thoughts fill me up and give me new perspectives on the art I create. I'd hate to create in a vacuum. Once Rebecca started traveling with me, it only got better. Not only was I exposed to new images and perspectives, but I experienced those things through someone else's eyes. Rebecca gets excited with every new adventure."

"How that girl lives without letting fear dictate her life astounds me," Lexi said. "You and Henry did a great job with her. I want to give that same sense of confidence to Gillian, but I don't know if I have enough to make sure she doesn't turn into me."

"Thank you," Polly said, nodding. "I don't know if it was us as much as it was her mother. When things got rough, Sarah Heater didn't hesitate. She made a change and made it exciting. When she was dying, she didn't lie around and feel sorry for herself, she made sure that Rebecca was ready to face whatever was coming, no matter what. Rebecca figured most of it out by herself. All we did was support her. Rebecca only needed to hear that she was making good decisions, even if I wouldn't have made the same ones. She's a smart girl. So is Gillian."

"You're going to be here to help me not be scared to let her do her own thing, right?" Lexi asked. "Please?"

"I don't know what you're talking about, Miss Lexi," Beryl said. "You started your own business and are making a go of it from what I hear. People love your cooking. You had an idea, you tried it, and when it worked, you made sure to be consistent. That's what makes the difference between success and a dream. If all I ever did was visualize the paintings I wanted to create, I'd never have the life I have now. I had to consistently work every day at my job. I don't get to have artist's block. I insist on consistency. That's one thing I've tried to instill in my students.

You can have talent out the ears, but if you don't do the work, no one but you will ever know how amazing you are. And you, Miss Lexi, are amazing."

Lexi blushed and turned away, but quietly said, "Thank you."

Beryl swatted Polly's arm. "I've embarrassed her. Let's get out of here before her blushing blows her head off the top of her body."

Once they got to the office, Beryl dropped into the chair beside the glass door leading to the small back porch. "I could spend time here watching the world go by."

"I don't sit in that chair for that very reason. The worst is when I end up in the rocking chair on the porch. I get nothing done."

"It's very peaceful."

"Except when the kids and dogs are all outside playing."

"Even that would be peaceful." Beryl drew in a long breath. "I miss Rebecca."

Polly had taken her seat behind the desk. "I understand. I do too, but the two of you have a special bond."

"Not like mother and daughter," Beryl said. "It isn't even like a mentor and student. In some ways, she is an extension of me. All that exuberance for life is inspiring. When I'm tired, she shares her energy and I see the excitement ahead of us. We need to travel again."

It had been difficult the last couple of years. Rebecca was focused on having enough money to get through the school year. She had made it clear that she didn't want to rely on Polly and Henry for everything. The trip to New York City had been a Christmas gift for Andrew and Rebecca from their parents. Otherwise, they couldn't have afforded it.

"She'd like that," Polly said.

"I want to hire her this summer."

"To do what?"

"To work for me."

"I understand, but to do what?"

"She'll clean the house, cook my meals, help me in the studio, do whatever I want. A personal assistant. I will teach her how to set up meetings with gallery owners and how to write contracts to sell my paintings. Even though she's learning a lot in college, it's time for her to learn the practical side of my life. What do you think?"

"I think it's too good to be true. So will Rebecca."

"I should have done it last year when she was frustrated while looking for a job. But she didn't say anything, and I wanted her to have the opportunity to experience a big life."

"You give her a big life."

"I will pay her as well as any other job, but I also intend to pay for any trips we take. We haven't discussed where we'd like to go, but now's the time. She's going to end up marrying that Donovan boy and then I'll lose her to married life."

"I doubt that," Polly said with a smile. "She'll never quit you. And that Donovan boy will let her live her life the way she wants to live it, or we'll find him upside down in a snowbank in the middle of July."

"She'd be the girl who could find one," Beryl said. "Do you think they'll live near here?"

Polly leaned back and closed her eyes. "That's a good question. It's what I would like, and Sylvie would be content to have both her boys nearby. What neither of us knows is what the kids think their lives should look like. If I had my way, they'd move into the house."

"They could move into my house," Beryl said with a small smile. "If Andrew is successful with his writing, he'd be a quiet roommate. Other than the keys clacking on his keyboard, everything happens up there in his brain. He probably wouldn't even know it when Rebecca and I left to tour the world."

"If they want to live in Bellingwood, we'll make it happen," Polly said. "I don't know what I'd do if she lived too far away. I tend to clutch my babies close, even though I know they should be allowed to soar."

"They can soar while living near us," Beryl declared. "And that's all I have to say about that. Now, one more thing. I can't go to her opening night."

"For the art show at Drake?" Polly asked. "Okay."

"I feel awful. I'd like to think I can get everything done in time to be able to go with you all, but I know me. I'll be working late."

"That's okay."

"It's really not. I want to go down one of the days the show is open, but I feel sick that I can't be there for her. I haven't talked to Rebecca about it yet."

"She'll understand," Polly said. "She knows your work ethic. It's one of those things that has kept her going all these years."

"Will you take pictures for me?" Beryl asked.

"Of course. I'll even take some video. Beryl," Polly said quietly, "you can't worry about it. Rebecca will be caught up with everyone else who is there. Wouldn't it be awful if you forced yourself out of the studio only to stand off to the side while Rebecca did her thing, not having time for you? She's going to have plenty of people around."

"It's just that it is the worst day of the entire month for me to leave my studio." Beryl wasn't finished beating herself up. "I will go down another day and I'll be there for the closing of the show. Maybe I can take her out that night for an after-party."

"You need to talk to Rebecca," Polly said. "She will understand. She'll also be annoyed that you are so worried and don't trust her to understand."

"Whoa," Beryl said, throwing her body back against the chair. "That hit me right between the eyes."

"Good. Our girl is a smart young woman."

"I'll send her a text to call me tonight or tomorrow," Beryl said. She put her hands out as if to stop more questions. "I know everyone thinks if I would just get to work right now, I'd open up that evening ..."

Polly interrupted her. "Stop trying to explain yourself. You have a structure for work that fits you. You don't need to apologize for it. You should never have to explain your process to anyone. This is your life, your business, and you get to make decisions all by yourself. If someone doesn't understand, that's their problem, not yours."

"You make too much sense," Beryl said. "You know there are only a few people who understand my life. My family never did. Even Andy and Lydia have trouble sometimes, though they try."

"Sometimes I'm too pragmatic for my own good," Polly said. "Most of the time, though, it works for me. I don't know where I got it other than my father. He wanted people to know that they were accepted for who they were, not who he wanted them to be. It made his life more interesting and our lives more fun. I never felt like I had to be a certain type of person for him to be happy with me."

"And this is why we love you. I wish I would have known your father," Beryl said.

"He was an amazing man."

"Do you miss him?"

"Not like people expect," Polly said. "He gave me everything I needed. Would I like him to be able to see what I've done with my life? Yes. Would I like our kids to know how wonderful he was or to have him be friends with Henry? Absolutely. But if he had lived, my life would be much different. I'm happy and have no regrets. His life filled mine while he was alive, and memories of him fill me now." She huffed a laugh. "See? Pragmatic."

CHAPTER FOUR

Low-key was the best description Polly had for the art show opening reception at Drake. Polly and Henry hadn't planned well with regards to dinner for their family. It took everything in her to keep the kids from ravaging the refreshment table. The kids had looked at every piece of art at least three times and were long past finished with being in polite company. That wasn't a surprise. After a long week of school, Friday evenings were generally spent doing something more fun than dressing up and being good.

Rebecca's instructors raved about her talent and commitment to her craft. She had submitted five pieces to the show, and all were hanging in a prominent location. Polly was proud of her girl.

"She's pretty good." Ray Renaldi put his hand on Polly's arm as they stood in front of a landscape that Rebecca had painted from a photograph she'd taken while touring England. "You should be proud."

"I'm very proud," Polly said. "Thank you for coming with us."

"How could I say no?" he asked. "You needed me."

She really did. Their large family no longer fit into the Suburban. When they traveled, it had become a caravan. Lexi,

Marie and Bill, Ray, and Henry all drove to Des Moines, their cars filled with family. Heath and Ella, Hayden and Cat, along with Sylvie and Eliseo, Lydia and Aaron, and Andy Specek, had come down separately. Andrew had also found a ride to Des Moines so that he could be part of Rebecca's opening night.

Rebecca was surprised to see such a large group of her friends and family attend the art show, but Polly wasn't. If Rebecca had been concerned that Beryl wasn't there, she didn't say a word. In fact, she assured Lydia and Andy that Beryl was coming on a day when she and Rebecca could wander through the show by themselves.

Andrew broke away from Rebecca and strode over to Polly and Ray. "Could I talk to you for a minute, Polly?" he asked.

She nodded. "What's up?"

"I'm coming home this weekend with Mom and Eliseo. Would you and Henry have any time for me? I want to talk to you about something."

"About what?" Polly lifted an eyebrow. "Does Rebecca know?"

"No!" he said and then wilted in on himself when his words were louder than expected. "She can't know. Not yet. I want to surprise her with something for her birthday, but I need your help."

"Help with what?"

Andrew rolled his head on his neck. "Please. I want to talk to you and Henry at the same time. I'm only here asking for a time to come over to your house."

"I shouldn't keep pushing, right?"

"If you love me, you'll stop."

"Let me talk to Henry. Text me if I don't get right back to you. I'll give you a time when you can come over. This is a good thing, right?"

"It's a birthday present. It's a good birthday present."

"How is Rebecca going to feel about you coming back to Bellingwood without her?"

"I told her that I'm working tomorrow and Sunday because they need someone at the coffee shop. Mom's going to let me take my car back to Iowa City for the last two weeks, so that means I can stop in and see Rebecca on my way back to school Sunday afternoon."

"Are you working at the coffee shop?"

"I would never lie," Andrew said with a grin. "I called and told them I was available. They always need extra help on the weekends."

"Pretty good job you have there."

"It's nice," he said. "I make more money editing papers for people, but that money goes toward my school. The coffee shop money is for fun."

"I'm glad you can have fun, then."

"How much longer?" Cassidy asked with a touch of a whine in her voice. She was holding onto Agnes' arm, having dragged the woman across the room to Polly.

"Yes," Agnes added, using the same tone of voice. "How much longer?"

Polly gestured for Ray to join them. Cassidy, Agnes, Teresa, and Amalee had ridden down with him. If they wanted to go home now, that would be fine. In fact, anyone who had a ride and wanted to leave could go back to Bellingwood. Even though tomorrow was Saturday, keeping the kids out too late made for a rough weekend.

"Mom!" Elijah came her way, pushing Bergie Mansfield's wheelchair as fast as he could. "Look who's here."

"Hi, Bergie," Polly said with a smile. The boys hadn't seen much of each other during the school year. Both were involved in school activities. Bergie looked as happy to see Elijah as her son was to see his friend. "Where's your mother?"

Bergie turned and pointed to the entrance. "She stopped to talk to Henry. We were late and wanted to get here before you left." He poked Elijah's arm. "Guess who got to drive the van?"

"No way," Elijah said, sending his mother a scathing look. "All the way from Ames?"

Bergie nodded. "I'm getting better at city driving, but four-lane highways are easy. I pulled over before we got to Des Moines, since it's a strange city. Mom thought she'd do better than me trying to find the right building. She was right."

"Mom won't let me drive except around parking lots right now," Elijah said. "How am I ever going to learn if I don't drive on regular streets?"

"When you prove to me that you're paying attention, you can drive on the street," Polly said.

"Whatever." He rolled his eyes, then laughed. "She wasn't impressed when I tried to run over a traffic cone."

"Where did you do that?"

"In Boone at the high school. I was there late for a rehearsal and since the lot was empty, I begged and begged. Then I screwed it up."

"Not really," Polly said, rubbing his shoulder. "You were doing fine until you were distracted by your friends who drove past us."

"I can't do that," Elijah said. "Or I'll never be able to drive."

"You gotta think about it like you're practicing the piano," Bergie said. "Total focus until you know it so well, you don't gotta focus no more." He shot a grin at Polly. "Right?"

"If, by using bad grammar, you are attempting to distract me, it worked." Polly smiled as Eve Mansfield walked toward them. "Thank you for coming down this evening. Have you talked to Rebecca yet?"

"Not yet. After Elijah sent a text to Bergie about the show, I thought it might be nice to come see you all. I talk to Henry nearly every day, but I haven't seen you in months. I'd tell you that we should have lunch together, but until one of us sets a date and time, those are just useless words."

"I'm the worst," Polly said. "If I see you when I'm out and about, I'm all about spending time with you. Otherwise, I'm as bad as Elijah. Distractions are my downfall."

"Mine, too. Henry keeps me on my toes, though. It's nice being part of something as exciting as these projects. Sal Ogden is a lot of fun, too. They didn't have to keep me on board after I donated the land."

"Everything I hear from them is that you've offered many great suggestions."

"Maybe growing up as Frank Mansfield's daughter wasn't all bad." Eve shuddered. "Yes, it was. I learned everything I know using my own brains. And I've learned a lot more these last two years. It's been really something."

"You're pretty smart, Mom," Bergie said. "How else could you have raised me into such a brilliant young man?"

"And this is why I love him." Eve patted her son. "Wander with Elijah, then come find me." After the two boys were gone, she said, "Bergie misses spending time with Elijah. We are so close, why doesn't it happen more often?"

Polly laughed. "Because that would require us to schedule things. We're bad at that, remember?"

"Is 'Jah doing anything this weekend? I'd love to take him home with us. We could bring him home tomorrow afternoon."

"Elijah would love that."

With a nod, Eve said, "It's one of the reasons we came down. If I was ever going to make it happen for those two, I needed to dig in and drive. I'm glad to see Rebecca's show, but you know me. Bergie's happiness will always push me to do things."

Polly gave her a quick hug. "Elijah is practicing madly for his recital, but that's far enough off that he has plenty of time to prepare."

"He and Bergie have talked about doing something together," Eve said. "They've chosen the music and Bergie has been practicing. Maybe they can work on it this weekend."

"Do you have a piano?"

"A keyboard, but it will be enough, don't you think?"

"If you stayed for dinner tomorrow after bringing Elijah home, the boys could have the living room for a time."

"It's not like we have busy social lives. I'm either working or we're at school for something Bergie is involved in."

"No kidding," Polly said. "Most evenings are shot, especially at the end of the semester. I'm looking forward to summer break. I'm looking forward to Elijah getting his driver's license."

"What about Noah?"

"The boy doesn't want to drive. He just doesn't care about it. We're going to work on that this summer. He's sixteen. He's been through a driver's education course. He's a good driver, but he doesn't care. His buddies have their licenses and one or the other of them will drive back and forth to Boone. Now that Amalee is part of the family, she drives, but she's graduating this year, so we'll be back to no high school driver unless Noah gets pushed into it."

"And you're pushing?"

"A little bit." Polly laughed. "One thing he doesn't want to deal with is managing a car. Paying attention to upkeep and all that. I haven't yet told him that all he'd have to do is talk to Caleb and the car would be in pristine shape all the time. The other day, I heard Caleb talking to Henry about something that sounded off in Lexi's car. Sure enough, she needed something or other fixed. I didn't pay much attention, but I did tell Caleb that he should always let us know if one of the family's cars needs attention."

"He loves it that much, huh," Eve said. "I could have used a mechanic when I was living on my own in Wisconsin. We've found a garage in Ames, but I only have one vehicle. If I have to give up the van for any period of time, Bergie has no good way of traveling anywhere. When he's ready to drive, we'll have a second vehicle." She shook her head. "Am I ready for that?"

"Polly," Henry had snuck up beside them. "Delia's close."

She chuckled. "To a meltdown?"

"Noah has done all he can do. She's tired and grumpy."

"Did Lexi already leave?" Polly asked.

"Yes, with a carload."

"We're running out of children. Are you okay with Elijah spending the night at Bergie's?"

Henry smiled at Eve. "That would be fun for them."

"They're coming over tomorrow for dinner," Polly said. "And Andrew wants a few moments of our time this weekend. I told him that I'd find out when you'll be around."

"What's that about?"

"Something with Rebecca's birthday."

"That's next week," Henry said.

Polly nodded. "Who knows what he's up to. I thought we'd just go down to Des Moines and take her out for dinner. She'll be jammed up with studying for finals."

Eve touched Polly's arm. "I'm going to wander through the show, then take our boys back to Ames. We have extra clothes for Elijah to sleep in. Anything else he needs; we'll make it happen. Thanks for letting me ask at the last minute."

"That boy needs all the excitement he can find," Polly said. "Thank you. We'll see you tomorrow." She turned back to Henry. "I'll tell Rebecca we're leaving. Let's stop at McDonald's on the way out so we can keep tummies from rumbling too badly."

"I'll round up the kids who are still here and fill the Suburban. We'll meet you out front."

The party was beginning to break up. Polly's friends and family had all taken off, so it was easy to spot Rebecca. She was talking to Cathy South, her roommate.

"Are you leaving too?" Rebecca asked.

"Pretty soon. Delia's about to fall apart."

"I can't believe you brought her along."

"This was a full family outing."

Rebecca laughed. "You had to bring extra drivers. I love that Ray came. He sent video to Drea and Jon. Can you believe it?"

"He's a good guy. How do you feel about the opening?"

"Overwhelmed."

"By what?"

"By everyone showing up. It's only a college art show. Not the big-time or anything."

"Imagine what they'll do when you hit the big time."

"I hope I can at least make a bit of a living with my art," Rebecca said with a sigh. "I don't know what else I want to do with myself. I don't think I'd be a good teacher. I don't want to teach in a school. Maybe college, but then I'd have to get more degrees. Am I ready for that?"

"Honey," Polly said. "Tonight is not the night to worry about your future. Tonight is a chance to celebrate your present." She took cash out of her pocket. "Why don't you and Cathy go somewhere to celebrate."

"Pizza," the two girls said together as Rebecca took the cash from Polly. "And coffee. We know just the spot."

"Celebrate, then. We'll celebrate again when we come down for your birthday dinner next week. Will you join us for that, Cathy?"

Cathy looked at her roommate and Rebecca nodded. "Duh," Rebecca said.

"Looks like I will. Are you bringing everyone?"

"Just me and Henry. The rest of the family can party with Rebecca when she comes home for the summer."

"Did Beryl talk to you?" Rebecca asked.

"About what?"

"Working for her?"

Polly nodded, then realized she'd spent a lot of time standing here with the girls. "She did. Why don't we talk about it all tomorrow after you are awake and fully caffeinated. Henry is waiting for me. We're going to feed the kiddos and take them home."

"I'm sorry," Rebecca said. "I just miss you guys."

"Only two more weeks, and you'll see us on Thursday for dinner. You choose where we're going."

Rebecca threw her arms around Polly and held on tight. "Thank you for everything. I love you."

The words were a bit unexpected, but Polly continued to hold her daughter as she said, "I love you, too. We are so proud of you. Not only your amazing work that's hanging here today, but because you are who you are. You are everything that you are and it is wonderful. Call me tomorrow."

When Rebecca finally released her, Polly gave Cathy a quick hug. She knew how difficult it was for a young woman to not have her mother around to give hugs. Cathy was coping just fine, but it was still a loss.

By the time Polly got outside, the lights were on inside the Suburban and Henry was turned in his seat. She opened the passenger door in time to hear him say, "Delia, she's here. Stop whining."

Delia didn't often get scolded by Henry, so she looked at him in surprise.

"I'm here," Polly said. "And we're going to McDonald's. How does that sound?"

Delia clapped her little hands together. "Ice cream?"

Rats. Delia remembered where they had gotten ice cream one time. Only one time was all it took.

"Ice cream later," Polly said. "First, a hamburger."

"Cheeseburger," Delia said, correcting her. "No pickles. No onions. No mustard."

"I remember," Henry said. "I hope you boys know what you want. I never remember who gets what."

"Is Rebecca going to be famous?" JaRon asked. "She had the most visitors there tonight. There were two students who didn't have anybody, so I talked to them. Their families live too far away to make the trip. One of them asked me to follow him around with his phone and video him."

"Did you?" Polly asked.

"Of course. He was kind of sad, but his stuff was interesting."

"Which one was that?"

"All that wire frame sculpture stuff. Kind of weird, but he was proud of it, so I acted interested."

Polly laughed. "I love you, JaRon. You are a good kid. What did you think, Caleb?"

"Rebecca's art was the only stuff that made sense to me," he responded. "Noah told me that sometimes art is about how people look at the world differently. He showed me pictures of Picasso on his phone. Right?"

Noah said, "You got it. Picasso was weird, though. It was a whole movement called Cubism. Picasso kind of invented it. All abstract stuff with fragments of the image placed on the canvas. We have some art books in the library if you want to look at them."

"Not so much," Caleb said. "That stuff is weird. I like Rebecca's paintings. I can even understand Ms. Watson's paintings. Those have, like, real animals and other things in them. That makes sense."

Polly caught Henry's eye and smiled. Their kids were discussing things at high levels. Caleb didn't realize how far outside his box he was thinking.

"Do you spend time looking at art books, Noah?" Polly asked.

"Sure," he said. "I want to know everything. I don't like everything, but I want to know what it's about. That's why I pay attention to Elijah when he wants to talk about composers. I want to know that stuff too. I don't want to play it, but I like listening to it."

"I like some of it," JaRon said. "It's relaxing. When I get a phone, I'm going to ask Elijah to program it for me."

"We need to take them to more museums," Polly said quietly to Henry.

"Not me," Caleb said, leaning forward. "I heard that. Unless it's a car museum. Then I'll go."

"You should search for automobile museums in the region," Henry said. "I'd take you."

"Can I go, too?" Noah asked.

"Me, too," Delia said. She pointed at the golden arches when Henry turned into the parking lot. "I'm starving!"

"Let's see what Caleb can find. Okay, boys. Do you know what you want to eat?" Henry asked.

CHAPTER FIVE

One thing Polly loved about Saturday mornings was having her children at home. The older kids all had places to be. It was funny how they were up and ready to go earlier on Saturday mornings than when they had to go to school. They worked just as hard, but it was something they loved.

Amalee had found a job at the grocery store. Sometimes, she took Caleb and Elijah and either dropped them off at the music store and the garage, or if they were late, parked behind the grocery store. It was only a few blocks from there to their jobs.

Henry usually took Noah to the barn at Sycamore House since both were up early.

Even as the older kids spread out through town, Saturday mornings were relaxed. JaRon and Zachary were in the living room playing video games, Cassidy had spent the night at Agnes' house, Teresa and Kestra were upstairs in their room, and Delia was in Lexi's apartment watching television with Gillian. Lexi's Saturday mornings were spent on the sofa in her living room with a cup of coffee, her laptop in place as she planned menus and shopping lists.

That meant Polly was alone. She'd had one cup of coffee and felt pretty good. It was strange not to have anything pressing. Polly had come awake in the middle of the night and spent at least an hour wondering what it was that Andrew wanted to talk to them about. He was coming over after his shift at Sweet Beans ended later today.

Rebecca wanted to talk to Polly, but she wouldn't wake up until late morning at the earliest. She'd texted Polly in the middle of the night after getting back to her dorm room with Cathy. They'd gone out with some of the other artists and had a wonderful time, but the text came in after two o'clock this morning. Knowing the two girls as she did, they'd stayed up even later debriefing the night. As Polly thought about it, Rebecca wouldn't be awake until early afternoon.

"Obiwan," Polly said to the dog lying beside her on the sofa in the kitchen, "what do you think?"

He looked up when he heard his name. Tail wags against the sofa back told her he was waiting for whatever came next.

"Since the rest of the animals are hiding around the house, maybe you and I should take a walk. We don't get to do this by ourselves very often."

Obiwan jumped to the floor, his tail wagging like mad. Polly's walk on Thursday had been interrupted by Beryl and Andy. Though the cemetery was busier on Saturdays, it was still early enough that even Charlie Heller wouldn't be there yet.

She took her lightweight jacket off its hook. The weather was beautiful, but the night's chill hadn't lifted. Polly laughed to herself. When her kids wanted to wear shorts to school in early spring, she'd allowed them to suffer once or twice. They usually corrected their own behavior. Elijah was the worst culprit. That boy was contrary just to be contrary.

Polly sent a text to Lexi that she was going to be gone before walking down to the family room. Dogs and cats were curled up beside the boys who were in the middle of a shoot-em-up game.

"I'm taking a walk with Obiwan," she said. "I shouldn't be long. If you need me, I'm in the cemetery."

JaRon laughed and paused the game. "Not many moms announce they're going to hang out in the cemetery."

"That's funny," Zachary said. "I've never heard anyone say those words – if you need me, I'm in the cemetery."

Polly ruffled the hair on his head. He was such a good kid. Both boys were good kids and they had become good friends.

"I wish we were going out to Grandma and Grandpa's house today," JaRon said.

"I know, but Grandpa is busy with Mr. Seafold, which means that Grandma is taking notes and keeping them on track."

JaRon shrugged. "I know. I can't wait for them to finish the plans and start the work. It's going to be so cool, Mom. Do you think they'll have it done for this year?"

Bill and Ben were planning a holiday fun center to be built across the road from Ben's log house. Bill had put most of the work they would usually do on the model train set on hold since he intended to move it in its entirety to the main building once it was constructed.

"I don't know. Even when they have their ideas sketched out, it will be another year before the whole thing comes together."

"I miss working with Grandpa."

"I was just getting started," Zachary said.

Polly smiled at them. "This summer you won't have an opportunity to be bored and miss him. He'll have you working like mad."

"I hope so," JaRon said.

"Obiwan and I will be back in a bit," Polly said. "I love you boys." She slipped out of the room and closed the door, ensuring the rest of the menagerie wouldn't follow them. "Come on, bud. It's just us today."

Polly opened the sliding glass door and waited for Obiwan. He sprinted to the back gate, knowing what was next. That dog sometimes knew her better than Henry.

As soon as they passed through the hedge separating the cemetery from the Bell House property, Obiwan stopped moving. He sniffed the air, then looked up at her.

"What are you doing, bud?" Polly asked. "You know the path I take. Go on."

With that encouragement, instead of walking ahead, he took off at a run.

"Obiwan," Polly called out. "What are you doing?" He never left her side. Other animals, people, or normal distractions didn't bother him. Then Polly's heart sank. He did leave her side for one thing. She picked up the pace. What had he found today? It had been a long time since Obiwan was involved in one of her events. She didn't know what else to call them.

He paced in front of the gate leading to Andy's new neighbor's home. When he whined to be let in, Polly put her hand on his head. She didn't want to trespass, especially if there was trouble in the household. Henry would not be happy if she got herself into trouble.

Then she heard a moan. The sound set Obiwan off and he whined again, this time, pawing at the gate. Polly opened it and he pushed past her, running toward the house. He stopped at the patio, standing over a lump on the pad.

When Obiwan nosed the lump, Polly heard a feminine whimper, then another moan. She was already running. The woman who comprised the lump was bleeding from two places. A hole in her left leg and another near her left shoulder.

"I'm Polly Giller. This is Obiwan. He helped me find you." Polly took out her phone and started to tap out 9-1-1 when the woman's trembling right hand stopped her. "Ethan. Find Ethan."

"Is he inside?" Polly stood. She didn't know what to do next. This woman needed her help. She took off her jacket and laid it across the young woman's torso, then crept toward their sliding glass door. She could see into the kitchen and saw where the woman had come from. Blood pools were in direct contrast with the immaculately clean bright white floor.

Polly opened the door and called out, "Ethan? Are you in here? Ethan?"

She didn't receive a response from inside, but the woman continued to whimper out his name, asking Polly to find him.

More blood was on the floor of the dining room, another very clean room. Blood had been smeared on the table and on the back of an ecru chair in the corner. The living room had more blood, this time, some of it leading toward the stairway. As she followed the trail, she stopped, glad that Obiwan stayed outside. It was as if he knew he wasn't needed inside the house. A young man had fallen face first trying to go up the steps. Blood was everywhere. On the banister, the wall, the steps, him. Everywhere. Polly didn't count the number of wounds in his body. If he had lived through that, she'd be surprised.

Instead of going up the stairs, Polly put her hand through the banister rails. She could reach his ankle to check the body. Not only did she find no pulse, but the body was already cooling.

Rather than call the 9-1-1 operator, she swiped through her address book to Aaron's number and waited for him to answer.

"Good morning, Polly," Aaron said. "To what do I owe the pleasure?"

"If you find this stuff pleasurable, I should have a talk with your wife," Polly replied. "I need an ambulance and crime techs at the house next door to Andy and Len's house. A woman has been shot. She's still alive and is outside with Obiwan. A man is dead on the stairway inside the house."

"I'll be right over. Let me round up the troops." Aaron ended the call. If someone was alive, he wouldn't waste time chatting.

Polly grabbed a blanket from the sofa, then stopped in the kitchen and opened drawers until she found dish towels. She didn't care about blood at this point. All she cared about was ensuring the woman lived until the ambulance arrived.

When she got back outside, Polly's heart leapt. Obiwan had curled himself around the woman, offering his warmth. He was going to require a bath when they got home, but she didn't care.

"You are such a good boy," Polly said, choking back tears. How did he know? She'd often thought that loving pets were nothing more than furry receptacles for God's angels to reside.

After pressing the dish towels against the two open wounds, Polly draped the blanket across the young woman and Obiwan.

"Ethan," the young woman moaned.

"I found him. I'm sorry, but ..."

Before Polly finished the sentence, the woman said. "He's dead."

"Yes."

"Good." With that word, the woman took in a heaving breath. "It's over."

Polly didn't know what to say to that. "Do you know who shot him?"

"No," the woman said. "He shot me when I tried to run away. Who would do this to me?"

"I don't know, but I do know the sheriff. He'll find out. Can you stay awake until someone gets here?"

"I will. I tried to go back inside, but ..."

Polly tucked part of the blanket under the woman's head. "I understand."

"Afraid."

"That the shooter was still there?"

"Uhhh. I hoped someone would find me. The fence is high."

Polly understood that random thoughts traveled through your mind when you were under stress. She only hoped that the ambulance would arrive soon. Then she heard the siren wailing through town. "They're coming now," she said. "Soon you will be in better hands than mine."

The young woman tried to move, and her right hand came out from under the blanket. "Thank you for finding me. I'm so weak."

"Of course you are. You've lost blood."

"I tried to stop it, but I couldn't."

"You did just fine. You're still here. What's your name?"

"Bailey," the woman said with a sigh. "Bailey Jenkins."

"Is Ethan your husband?"

"Hell. He's really dead?"

"He's really dead. At least the man inside on the stairway is dead."

"Blonde?"

"In red shorts and a black t-shirt," Polly said.

"That's him. Unbelievable. I will live through this, and he won't. I win."

"You did?"

Bailey's eyes fluttered. "So weak."

The siren had come to a stop.

"Bailey, I need to unlock the front door for the paramedics."

"Okay. Come back, please."

"I will and I'll bring help."

Polly darted through the open patio door, past the bloody smears and into the living room. She opened the front door just as Adam Masterson and his partner, Joan, were coming up onto the stoop. When they got inside, she pointed at the body on the stairway. "He's gone," she said, "but there's a woman on the patio out back who needs you. Two gunshots that I can see. She's doing okay, but she's getting weaker."

"Show us," Adam said. He glanced at the body and said to his partner, "Check to be sure."

Polly led him through the house, and he glanced at Obiwan who was still wrapped around the woman.

"Her name is Bailey Jenkins," Polly said. "Obiwan, help is here."

He looked up at hearing his name, then slowly moved away from the woman. She moaned again. "So warm," she said.

"We'll keep you warm now," Adam said. "That's a good dog right there."

"He's something else," Polly said.

Adam's partner came out and the two of them checked the woman thoroughly before lifting her onto the gurney. She moaned and whimpered as they did, tears flowing freely.

Then she put out her hand to Polly. "My family."

"You have family?" Polly asked, suddenly terrified that there were kids in the house.

"In Boone."

"The sheriff will contact them for you."

"The office. Second drawer on the right," Bailey said. "Houseman."

"I'll tell Sheriff Merritt," Polly said. "Your family will know where you are as soon as possible."

Tab Hudson was the next person through the back door. She stopped Adam and looked at the woman. "I'm Deputy Hudson. Once they get you settled at the hospital, I'll stop in to see you."

"Okay." Bailey sagged back onto the gurney and Tab nodded for Adam and Joan to go ahead. Then, she turned on Polly. "What do you have to tell me?"

"So much," Polly said. "Is Aaron coming?"

"I'm surprised he didn't arrive before me," Tab replied. "I was on my way out the door when he called and diverted me. This is kinda close to your house. What are you doing here?"

"I took a walk with Obiwan."

"And why, exactly, does Obiwan have blood on his fur?"

"He wrapped himself around the young woman to keep her warm."

Tab shook her head. "I will never understand how animals are so intuitive. Did Adam have a problem with it?"

"No. Obiwan kept her warm while I went inside and found her husband's body."

"You've met them?"

"No, she told me who he was."

"Does she know who the killer was?" Tab lifted her eyebrows. "I'm kind of hoping this might be an open and shut case."

"She said that she didn't, and I believe her. You'll hear her relief at the death of her husband. You might want to talk to Andy Specek next door. Apparently, she's been worried about these two. They just moved in, and she heard loud explosive fights."

"Mrs. Specek said something to you?"

"No, she wouldn't. Andy told Beryl she was worried, and Beryl mentioned it to me. She was annoyed that Andy hadn't called Sheriff Merritt."

"We'll stop in and talk to her today, then," Tab said. "Tell me what you know."

"Bailey Jenkins. The husband's name is Ethan."

Polly stopped talking while Tab took out her notepad. Once

her friend started writing, Polly continued. "I didn't ask what time it happened."

"Weird that no one heard anything," Tab said.

"I thought so, too. Andy and Len don't sleep all that heavily. Bailey wants you to call her family."

"She has family close by?"

"Apparently, in Boone. Last name Houseman. She mentioned something about a drawer in a desk in the office. Maybe there's an address book."

"Deputy Hudson?"

Polly recognized Allen Dressen's voice coming from inside the house.

"Out here," Tab called back. "You start inside. I'll be right there." She chuckled. "This should wake up the neighborhood."

Polly pointed at the back gate. "If it does, we have an entirely different problem on our hands. Charlie Heller won't be happy if the dead start walking around and make a mess of his cemetery."

"You're twisted up there," Tab said, tapping Polly's head.

Both of them looked up when the back gate opened.

"Zombies," Polly whispered. "You woke them."

Aaron Merritt opened the gate and took in the scene. "Did we get to the woman in time?"

"On her way to the hospital," Tab said. "I'll interview her when she's stable and settled in a room. Sounds like she has family in Boone."

He frowned. "Really."

"Houseman?" Polly said. "Her married name is Jenkins."

"Terry Houseman," Aaron said. "Has anyone called them yet?"

"How do you know that?" Polly asked. "More than ten thousand people live in Boone, and you know that name?"

"Terry works for the city. I didn't know his daughter and her husband had moved back to the area. Did he do this?"

"Her husband?" Tab asked. "Polly thinks he's the dead man on the stairway inside."

"Did she do this?" Aaron's eyes grew wide. "She's a nice girl, but maybe he pushed her too hard. Ethan Jenkins was a real piece of work. They should never have gotten married, and she should never have let him move her away from her family. There was nothing her family could do about it, though. He had her under his thumb from the day they met. If I'd had my way, he'd have been in jail. She never said boo to us about any abuse."

"Did you talk to Andy?" Polly asked. "She was worried about them."

"I was just over there. Since we were taking up space in the cul-de-sac, I let her know what was going on. She didn't say anything to me."

"Ask her," Tab said. "Polly tells me that she heard fighting."

"Andy Specek wouldn't tell me anything unless she was certain," Aaron said. "The more likely scenario is that she'd get involved and try to protect her neighbor. Then I'd have to rescue more than just one woman. At least when Lydia helps out, she tells me what she walks into. Not Andy. She just keeps walking in and telling no one."

"Not even Len?" Polly asked.

"Not if she's afraid he'll stop her." Aaron huffed a laugh. "Once you showed up, Polly, Andy's adventures with people in desperate need became fewer and fewer. She's more likely to give money to pay bills than wade into a difficult situation. But if one of those showed up next door, she wouldn't hesitate. I hate to say it, but I'm glad this is over before she got involved."

He looked at the dog who was patiently waiting beside Polly. "Do I dare ask why Obiwan is bloody?"

"Obiwan kept Bailey Jenkins warm while Polly found the dead body," Tab said. "I want an Obiwan to ride in my car with me."

"I don't know if anyone could find another dog like Obiwan," Aaron said. "I'm certain he ended up in Bellingwood because Polly needed extra protection from the world. The things I've seen this dog do over the years astound me. I'm glad he's yours, Polly."

"Me too."

"The blood is Bailey's?" Aaron asked. "He didn't get into anything else?"

"Obiwan didn't enter the house," Polly said. "I went inside

when she asked me to find Ethan. Obiwan stayed to keep her warm." Polly put her hand on her head. "They took my jacket because I'd wrapped that around her. I don't care about it, but I don't know what was in the pockets. Could you check on that for me?" she asked Tab.

Tab nodded. "Bailey is going to ask about you. What do you want me to tell her?"

Polly patted her back pocket, then shook her head in frustration. "Give her my business card. They are in one of the pockets of the coat. She can call any time. If she wants me to come to the hospital, I'll be there."

"Another of your rescues?" Aaron asked. "You're pretty good at it."

"Whatever I need to do, I'll do," Polly said. "And you won't give me any trouble about it. Right? Right."

CHAPTER SIX

Very few things pushed Henry over the edge, but when he saw the blood on Obiwan's coat and all over Polly's clothing, he pursed his lips. "That's a lot of blood. Are you hurt? Is Obiwan hurt? I saw the emergency vehicles and got worried. Should I have come down to find you? What's going on?"

"We're good," Polly said, looking down at herself. How had she managed to get so much blood on her clothes? "There's a young man who isn't okay, and his wife is in the hospital. Obiwan and I need only a shower. You're home early."

"When sirens tear through town before I finish breakfast, I feel it is important to check on my wife."

"But you were able to finish breakfast, right?"

He chuckled. "I don't often give up my breakfast. Yes, I finished. I brought home half of my chicken fried steak for you."

"Have you seen any other family members up and about?" Polly glanced at the clock. It felt like she'd been out of the house for hours, but it had only been forty-five minutes. She was surprised that Teresa and Kestra were still upstairs.

"Talked to the boys in the family room. The dogs wanted out. I left them in there since I didn't know what was happening with you. Have you fed any of the kids?"

She shook her head. "Let me take Obiwan upstairs and then we'll roust the troops."

"I'll come with you."

Polly lifted her eyebrows. "To help me shower?"

"If you want, I could do that. I could also help dry Obiwan off when he comes out." Henry shook his head. "Better yet, I could help dry you off."

"Come on, Obiwan," Polly said and made a mad dash for the back steps. No matter what insanity she faced beyond the walls of her home, this man could settle her like no one else. The three of them raced upstairs and down the hall to their bedroom. Once inside, Henry closed the door. While Polly carefully stripped off her bloody clothes, he started the shower. There was baking soda in the cabinet beside the washing machine. Polly rinsed her clothes in cold water, treated them for a few minutes, then tossed them in the machine. It was already half full. She loved having a washing machine in their bathroom. Most of their clothes didn't need to be sorted and they generally just tossed things in, waiting for the next load to go through.

"It's ready for you," Henry said. "Obiwan?"

The dog went back and forth between them with a pained look. He didn't love baths. Showers were easier, especially if he took one with his favorite humans. It was also easier for Polly to wash him down while she was in the shower. He reluctantly followed her in and sat down, just outside the streams of water.

"You can't sit around in a bloody coat," Polly said.

"You are planning to tell me why he's covered in blood," Henry said.

"Because he's a good boy," she replied and took down one of the shower heads.

Obiwan accepted his fate and soon the ordeal was over.

When she released him, Henry was waiting with a large towel. Showers with dogs were fairly standard. Han had enough hound in him that he generally took on a good smell before anyone realized how long it had been. Towels and dog shampoo were always close at hand.

While Polly got dressed again, she explained the morning's events to Henry. She'd told him a little of what Beryl's concerns had been the other day regarding Andy and her new neighbors.

"Ethan Jenkins," Henry said. "I don't know that name. I do know a Houseman. Terry. He works in the assessor's office."

"Of course you do. Aaron knows him, too."

"And the Houseman girl was happy about her husband's death? Did she do it?"

"And shoot herself in the process?" Polly asked.

"Maybe it was a shootout. They both had guns."

Polly chuckled. "No one in the neighborhood heard anything and if they were both shooting, I should have seen guns on the floor. There was nothing."

"Tab doesn't think she did it."

"I don't know what Tab thinks, but I have trouble believing Bailey murdered her husband."

"Are you getting involved?"

"We'll see," Polly said. "Don't be surprised if I do."

"How about I start breakfast for the masses."

"We don't have many masses here for second breakfast," Polly said with a laugh.

"Whatever we make will be eaten."

"That's the truth."

Obiwan followed Henry out and Polly went back into the bathroom to start the washing machine. The girls weren't in their bedroom, and she smiled to herself. They'd found their way to Lexi's apartment and the television.

Knowing that Lexi was awake, she sent a quick text. *"Do you have three of my girls in your apartment?"*

"Still in their pajamas," Lexi sent back.

"Tell them we're about to make breakfast. If they want food, it's time to get moving. You too, Missy. Not to get moving, but you know you're welcome."

"I should get moving," Lexi sent. *"I've been a slug long enough.*

Oops, the television just turned off. Now I have to explain. See you in a bit. Thanks."

Polly was used to talking to people face to face, but sometimes texting worked just fine.

JaRon and Zachary, along with all four dogs and enough cats that Polly didn't bother counting, were in the kitchen with Henry.

"How many?" JaRon asked, a stack of plates in his hand.

"Nine," Polly replied. Even with many of her family out and about, the number of people at this meal was large.

Zachary smiled. "I have a big family."

"Yes, you do," Henry said. "I've decided we're having pancakes and sausage. If anyone wants eggs, they'll have to beg."

"But," Polly set a little whine in her tone.

Henry looked at her. "Really?"

"Nope. Just kidding. I'd be fine with toast and jam."

"Mom!" JaRon said. "Don't give him any ideas. He's making pancakes."

"Do you want to help me?" Henry asked JaRon. "I think it's time you learn my secrets. You too, Zachary. The two of you want to feed your families the good stuff when you live on your own."

"That won't happen for many, many years," Polly announced. "I'm not letting anyone move out until they run away."

~~~

"I'm here," Andrew texted to Polly. *"I didn't want to knock or ring the doorbell, because, you know, dogs."*

"I love you. Come on in," she sent back. Polly didn't know where Henry was. He was in the house, but it was easy to lose family members in this big place. She was in the kitchen finishing another cup of coffee while talking to Lexi about plans for dinner. With Eve and Bergie coming, they wanted to fix something nice.

"Hey," he said quietly at the door.

"Hey, yourself," Polly replied.

"It feels weird to walk in without Rebecca. I didn't know what to do."

"You can always walk in," Polly said. "You're as much a part of my family as anyone."

He gave her a knowing smile and bent at his knees to rub Obiwan's head. The dog had been through a lot that morning and had stayed close to Polly. "I heard you both had quite the morning."

"I guess we did."

"Have you heard anything about the girl that you found?"

"Not yet," she said. "Did you know them from high school?"

"Older than me. Older than Jason, too. Hayden would have known them, though I think they were a year or two older than him."

"Early thirties."

Andrew nodded. "Is Henry here?"

"I just need to let him know that we're ready. Are we ready?"

Lexi chuckled. "What's this about, Andrew?"

"Rebecca's birthday."

"Really," she said. "You need an appointment with her parents to schedule a birthday celebration?"

"We can't have it while we're in school, so yep, I want to set up a time."

"And you need Henry for that?"

Andrew shot her a look. "You have a lot of questions."

Lexi chuckled. "I have a big imagination. Maybe not as big as yours, but I have thoughts."

"I'm ignoring all of those thoughts until I have reality in my hands," Polly said. "Head to the office, Andrew. I'll find Henry. We'll be there in a minute."

He took a deep breath, shot Lexi another look, and walked away. Obiwan picked himself up off the floor and followed.

"That's interesting," Lexi said.

"What?"

"Your dog just followed Andrew to the office. Given Obiwan's need to care for stressed out people ..." She let her words trail away.

"Poor kid. Henry terrifies him."

"I've watched Henry do it on purpose. It's almost mean."

Polly cackled. "It's fun. And a little mean." She sent her husband a text. *"Andrew's in the office. Where are you?"*

"Scaring the crap out of him in the office," Henry texted back. *"You might want to hurry. He's going to bolt."*

"That's fabulous," Polly said to Lexi. "I just sent Andrew into the hands of death. Henry was already in the office."

"That's why Obiwan followed. He's protecting one or the other of them. I'm going to round up JaRon and Zachary. Chocolate sheet cake with homemade ice cream will keep them busy while I work on the rest of the meal."

"Thank you," Polly said.

"First, I'm going to find the girls."

"They were upstairs with Kestra and Teresa. Delia's room is destroyed, but we'll pick it up later."

"The girls will pick it up sooner if I have anything to say about it," Lexi said.

"Tough mom." Polly chuckled. "You do you. I'll do whatever is necessary to lower your stress."

"Duct taping the little ones to a wall is a bad idea, right?" Lexi asked.

"Did you have trouble with them this morning?" Polly hadn't heard anything and none of the girls had seemed upset when they came down for breakfast.

"Just a small discussion on treating other's rooms with respect. All four were much too comfortable in the apartment. Since it's my space, they thought I'd clean it up. You know, since they have to keep their own rooms clean."

Polly's eyes grew wide in surprise. "Are you kidding me? I didn't expect that to ever be a thing."

"It was this morning. Maybe it's a new idea." Lexi chuckled. "It did come from Delia, but Teresa and Kestra were more than willing to go along with it."

"That little girl is going to be a problem," Polly said. "Her little brain tells her that she's always right. I'm going to have to spend time reminding her heart to think about what other people need."

"Since that's the way this family lives, at least it comes naturally," Lexi said. "You just have to get past the stubborn independence. I don't know how to do that. I want Gillian to be independent, but I want her empathy to be stronger than her need for independence."

Polly shook her head. "I'm avoiding whatever is coming at us in the office. Poor Andrew could be close to wetting his pants."

"Which would make it even worse." Lexi grinned. "Let me know if there's more cleanup ahead."

"Now you're being mean." Polly stood and headed out. "Let me know if you need me to handle attitudes from little girls." She was fortunate to have Lexi in her corner. It had taken time, but as the young woman grew into herself, she'd become a formidable ally in raising children in this household. Neither she nor Polly competed with each other. Along with Henry, the kids within these walls were safe, loved, and held to high standards. Sometimes it took extra work to ensure those standards were met. Sometimes failure happened on every side. Polly had lost count of the number of times she'd messed up. It didn't do any good to keep track, but the failures were always present, reminding her that she didn't need to make the same mistake twice.

Obiwan lay on the floor in front of Andrew, who was seated by the door leading to the porch.

Henry had set aside his tablet and looked up when she walked in. "Did you get lost?"

"Talking to Lexi about the little girls and some new attitudes that have cropped up."

That took him back. "Everything okay?"

"If she can't handle it, we'll step in. Let her try first. Apparently, Delia's influence on her older sisters is about to get them all into trouble."

He nodded and gestured to a dining room chair he'd brought into the office. He'd set it beside the desk, but she moved it around to the front.

"Well, Andrew," Polly said. "You have our attention. What is it you want to discuss?"

"Rebecca's birthday is on Wednesday," Andrew said.

Henry laughed. "And we're taking her out to dinner on Thursday. This is not new news."

Andrew looked at Polly. His fear was palpable.

"Maybe we should let him get through the whole spiel without interruption," she said.

"This better be good," Henry said.

Andrew's look went from fear to terror with that. "I was going to ask if you would consider hosting a birthday party. I'll organize it and pay for everything."

"But you want her to have a birthday party," Polly said.

"It's her twenty-first birthday."

"We're not providing alcohol."

"No, no, that's not it at all," Andrew said. "I'm screwing this all up." He took out his phone, made several swipes, then stood and walked over to set it on the desk between Henry and Polly. "I want to ask Rebecca to marry me."

Henry sat back in his chair. "You want to what? You're too young."

"They'll both be twenty-one," Polly said with a smile. She'd known this was coming. "You go ahead and sit for a minute. Think about it. You'll get there." Polly picked up the phone and looked at the photograph of a beautiful diamond ring set.

"I have a plan," Andrew said. "First of all, I want to propose with her family around. We've talked a lot about it."

"You've talked to her about getting married?" Henry spluttered.

"To be honest, she's the one talking about it," Andrew said. "We don't want to wait forever."

"When do you intend for this wedding to happen?"

"Rebecca thought it would take a year to plan," Andrew said. "She doesn't know that I'm here today. She doesn't know when to expect the proposal. That's why I wondered if you would do the whole birthday party thing. If it comes from you, she won't know that I'm behind it."

"A year?" Henry asked. "Right after you ..." He took in a long breath. It was as if his brain had finally caught up. "Right after you graduate from college." With a pitiful look, he turned to Polly. "How are they old enough to do this? What happened to the children who played video games in the apartment at Sycamore House? I'm having heart palpitations."

"You're finally there," Polly said. "Tell Andrew what he needs to hear from you."

"What's that?" Henry asked.

"Give him permission to ask Rebecca to marry him."

"He doesn't need my permission," Henry protested. "They are both smart young adults. They can make this decision without me."

"He's doing the right thing," Polly said. "Tell him that it's a good idea and that you'll support the two of them as they start their lives together."

"It is a good idea. There's no one else I'd want to be with Rebecca." Henry looked at Andrew. "I trust you with her heart. The rest of her is her business." He shook his head before dropping it into his hands. "Drinking age. An engagement. Marriage. This is a lot to handle."

"Dramatic much?" Polly asked with a laugh. "How did you not know this was coming?"

"You knew?" Andrew asked.

"Of course I knew. Lexi knew. Why else would you be so formal about setting up an appointment with us?"

"I didn't know," Henry said.

"Either that or you deliberately ignored the signs," Polly said. "Andrew, we will support you. If you want us to host a party, we'll set it up. How many people do you want us to invite?"

"I'm thinking just the family. That means everyone in the family, but ..." Andrew shook his head. "How will you not invite all your friends?"

"I will do whatever you want," Polly said. "If you want only family, then it's only family."

"I don't know what I want. I don't know what she'd want. Rebecca is as crazy about friends as you are," he said.

"Cathy," Polly said. "I'll need to invite her."

"This is going to be a problem." Andrew shook his head. "Nothing with your family is easy. I don't know how we're going to have a wedding. Your house is big, but if you invite everyone in town, no building will hold them all."

"It will have to be a summer wedding so we can be inside and outside," Henry said. "I could work with Dad, Jack, and Heath to build a shelter if there's a threat of rain."

"Let's make plans when the engagement is in place," Polly said. "One step at a time."

Henry scoffed. "Like you aren't going to lie awake tonight thinking of all the things that need to be in place for Rebecca's wedding."

"That's on me," she said with a laugh. "Andrew, have you talked to your mother?"

"No. She's still confused about why I came home this weekend. I want to keep it a secret for as long as possible. Rebecca is a master at finding out my secrets. In fact, I have none."

"When will the ring be in your hands?"

"I'm picking it up on Monday."

"Did Rebecca have any say in it?"

"Of course she did," Andrew said with a pained laugh. "I'm not dumb. We've been looking at rings for months." He held up a hand. "Rebecca has been looking at rings for months. I didn't bring it up. She did. All I did was pay attention. She fell in love with this one right off. I wasn't sure how I was going to afford it. That's one of the reasons I've been working so hard. But after the accident last fall and me getting some money, things got a lot easier. At least this debt won't hang over our heads when we get married."

"Speaking of debt and future plans, what are yours?" Henry asked. "Where do you plan to live?"

"Iowa City for a couple of years," Andrew replied. "I'm going to get my master's degree. Rebecca is planning to talk to you about doing the same thing."

"She already has," Polly said. "Rebecca is calling this afternoon because she wants to make plans for the future. Now that I know what's happening next summer, it may kill me to keep it a secret."

"Rebecca will tell you that we plan to get married next summer," Andrew said. "My luck, she already has a date in mind. That girl doesn't let much get past her. I'm never going to keep up."

"Trust me," Henry said. "Stop trying. The best thing you can do is nod and smile."

"Your life is so hard," Polly said with a mocking tone.

"I didn't say that it was. In fact, my life is great. The main reason it works so well is that I am smart enough to pay attention when you tell me to."

"I didn't know what I was going to do if you didn't approve," Andrew said. "Rebecca would have my head if I didn't propose early enough to give you time to plan the wedding."

"How much planning has she put in?" Polly asked. "Does she already have a wedding dress in mind?"

"I'm not saying a word about any of her plans."

"We haven't seen any bridal magazines around the house."

"You haven't been to her dorm room. She kept them all there."

Polly huffed. "Making plans without me. That hurts."

Poor Andrew dropped to a crouch in front of her. "She'd hate that. We just wanted to have some thoughts in place before we brought it up."

"I'm kidding," Polly said, though now that she thought about it, she felt a little left out. It wasn't about her, but dreaming about a wedding is something that girls did with their moms. Nope. It wasn't about her. Even if it felt like it was.

"We couldn't wait to tell you. To tell everyone," Andrew said. "We were worried that you would think we were too young or something."

"That's on me," Henry said. "I still think you're too young."

"Really?"

"Not really, but in my head I do. You'll have four or five children and I'll still think you're too young." Henry chuckled. "You need to tell Rebecca that Polly wants to be involved as soon as possible. If all the decisions are made already, that's going to be a problem."

"No decisions are made," Andrew said. "The only one we're certain of is that we want the wedding to be here at the Bell House."

CHAPTER SEVEN

Every time Polly planned a family get-together, she was reminded how simple it was. Her family was used to her random parties. Rebecca had begged that she not create a twenty-first birthday party extravaganza. If they wanted to do anything, it would have to be after her actual birthday. Having Polly and Henry take her out to dinner would be enough.

Rebecca's friends had made a big deal of their very first drink as an adult and that was the last thing she wanted to celebrate. Had she been allowed to create a celebration around freely having her first coffee with Polly, she'd have been all over that. Rebecca saw signs of alcoholism in some of her college friends, and besides, it wasn't like she hadn't already had her first drink.

It had taken nearly four years for her to admit to Polly that she'd tried beer at a friend's house while in high school. That night, she'd walked around with a red solo cup, half full of warm beer because she hated the taste so much she didn't want anyone to insist on a refill. A year later, she'd been at another friend's house and tried a Screwdriver. She'd liked that, but felt so guilty that she didn't try anything again until she was in college.

Polly had listened as Rebecca confessed to her sins. There was no judgment. Polly was mostly thankful that Rebecca's youthful alcohol trysts were few and far between. She was also thankful that Rebecca was pragmatic about the entire thing. That would lead to fewer problems in the future. She was under no illusions that Rebecca and Andrew wouldn't experience several ridiculous drunken episodes. Polly remembered some of her own – she remembered them with a smile. The last one at Sylvie's house had been unexpected, something she hadn't done since she was much younger.

Andrew's presence in the house caused no small amount of excitement. He'd grown up well. Over the last few months, he'd made sure to spend time getting to know the new members of the Sturtz family. That meant that Kestra and Teresa had someone new to adore. Watching little girls flirt with him was a riot.

Polly had a flash of memory … a story that her father had loved to tell on her. When she was barely a toddler, he'd invited boys from the high school's Future Farmers of America group to visit his farm. Her mother prepared food and drinks for them when they were finished so Everett could tell them more about what he did. Her parents watched as Polly flat-out flirted with each of the boys, begging for their attention as she circulated around the living room. Even when her mother put her in the playpen, Polly continued. The boys loved it, and her parents thought it was adorable.

Now, she watched the young girls in her home do their best to get Andrew's attention whenever he was in the house. Even Delia and Gillian, who had known him for as long as they'd been around, were entranced by his presence. After he'd finished with Henry and Polly, Delia came downstairs to drag him away. Polly heard someone mention that they needed a prince. Andrew was going to have to step up.

Polly was in her bedroom, waiting to move more laundry through her washer and dryer when her phone rang. She closed the bedroom door so Rebecca wouldn't hear Andrew's voice in the next room where he was entertaining the girls.

"Finally," Polly said. "I didn't think you were ever going to get out of bed. How was the rest of your night?"

"We had fun," Rebecca said. "Can you believe I only have a year left of school?"

"No. I'm having trouble with all that. Next thing I know, you'll be married and raising a family on your own. I'm not ready." Polly let her words hang, hoping Rebecca would finally say something. When she didn't respond, Polly continued. "Henry and I talked about you this morning."

"Oh no. What did I do this time?"

"We aren't going to let you get away with no party for your twenty-first."

"Noooo," Rebecca moaned. "I didn't want you to do that."

"How about just family? Marie and Bill would be heartbroken if they couldn't celebrate with you."

"But I don't want presents. People don't need to bring me stuff." Rebecca chuckled. "They could give me cash, though. I still want to travel."

"How about you let me deal with that. Would you be okay with a family party two weeks after you get home for the summer? We'll grill steaks and burgers. Henry and the boys will make ice cream. Maybe we could talk Lexi into a chocolate cake. You know this family will take any opportunity to get together."

"I know that you will take any opportunity to get the family together," Rebecca replied. "Fine."

"You're grumpy about it. Why?"

"I don't know. It feels like a lot of attention."

"You like attention."

"Not so much. Last night was big."

"It was a big deal."

"Can I admit something?"

Polly had no idea what was coming, but said, "Sure. What's up?"

"I hate attention like that. This is me being selfish, but I get tired of having to smile and say thank you all the time."

"You do it well."

"Because it's the right thing, but sometimes I want to hide. Not all the time, but it's hard work when all the attention is on me."

"And here I thought you were an extrovert," Polly said with a laugh.

"Not as much as you. I like people and I like …" Rebecca paused. "I'm not like you at all. I prefer being with one or two people at a time."

"You're getting this party," Polly said.

"With no gifts."

"I didn't say that."

"You don't make it easy, do you?"

"Not for your twenty-first birthday. What are you going to do at your wedding, elope?"

"It's an idea."

"It's a very bad idea. Don't even think about it. I will have your head on a platter."

Rebecca laughed. "Got it, though I'm only having a wedding for everyone else. You didn't have a big production."

"I was old and had no one around to tell me that I couldn't."

"Okay," Rebecca said, "can I admit one more thing to you?"

"More? You're on a roll," Polly replied. "What else do you have?"

"I've been thinking a lot about my wedding. Andrew and I want to get married next summer."

"Next year or this summer?" Polly asked, doing her best to play dumb.

"Not this year," Rebecca said. "We want to finish college, but we don't want to wait forever. What would you think about that?"

"Where do you want to get married?"

"Since I can't elope, can we get married at home?"

"Here? I get to decorate the foyer for your wedding?"

Rebecca laughed this time. "Don't tell me you haven't already thought about me coming down those steps on Henry's arm."

"Honey, I had that in my mind the first time I saw those steps. I'd hoped it would be Andrew waiting for your hand."

"It will be. Polly, I have, like, a million bridal magazines and catalogs and websites bookmarked and ..."

"You've already started making plans."

"Not really. It's more like I've started looking for the plans to make."

"You're giving me a year."

"And a couple of months. Is that enough?"

"It's more than enough. Should we look for a dress this summer?"

"You're not freaking out enough. Did you know already?"

"I'm not freaking out because once you and Andrew figured it out, you were always going to be married here at the house. I assumed you wouldn't wait long after college. It makes sense to get married so you can start your lives together. You've been pushing for that for a long time. When Andrew was hurt in that accident, I watched you fall apart because you weren't his emergency contact. You had to wait to be near him and that nearly broke you."

"That was hard. I didn't handle it very well either. What will Henry think?"

"Henry will be proud to walk you down those steps. You know how much he loves you."

"But sometimes he picks on Andrew."

"Only because he wants Andrew to know how important you are to us. That boy better never mess with you."

"I can handle him if he messes with me," Rebecca said. "We both know he wouldn't."

"About your dress."

"I have ideas. I haven't looked at bridal shops, but I found pictures online of dresses that would look good on me."

"You're going to have a long train," Polly said. "It has to flow down the steps behind you."

"I know."

"Have you thought about bridesmaids? You have a big family that will want to be included."

"See, more attention. What will I do with everyone?"

"You haven't given it any thought?"

"I have, but the last thing we want is to have fifteen attendants on each side. Andrew doesn't have that many people in his life."

"He does if he wants them."

"Do you have any idea how expensive it will be to buy matching dresses for all the girls and tuxedos for the boys? I don't want you to spend that kind of money."

"We can discuss it. But what about the friends you want to stand up with you? What are you thinking?"

"Cathy," Rebecca said. "She's my maid of honor for sure. Then Kayla and Cilla and Amalee and Cassidy."

"Five. What about Andrew?"

"Jason for sure will be his best man. Then his roommate and he has two other friends from college that could do it, but he isn't sure they'll be around after graduation. That's where I run into trouble. We don't want to just insert people into spots because we want things to match."

"Then don't. Be innovative. Do your own thing. If Andrew only has two groomsmen, who cares?"

"Really? What about the pictures? They'll be out of balance."

"You're worried about the photographs being out of balance? Priorities, honey. This is one day. It's a special day, but it's your day. You get to do what you want. If balanced photographs are important, we'll figure it out, but that would be low on my list."

"It really is," Rebecca said. "My head spins with everything I have to think about. Catering, flowers, photography, dresses, colors. Polly, I don't have any idea about what color scheme I want to use. Nothing feels right."

"Then blow it up," Polly said.

"What does that mean?"

"I looked at the paintings you chose for the show. Do you know what the common theme was?"

"There was a theme? I didn't choose it."

"Your family is important. I saw that. Landscapes. You've adopted Beryl's love of nature. Now, what does that tell you about color choices?"

"Greens."

"And?"

"Flowers. Every color is important."

"There you go. We'll keep talking about it, but think of nature as a wild explosion of colors and shapes. What if you let the girls choose their own dresses? Give them a general idea of what you want and allow them to be creative. Each of your friends will talk about it with you, right?"

"Why didn't I think of this? I'm the artist."

"You are looking at bridal magazines and websites. Those are geared to brides with traditional ideas."

"Some things are pretty crazy."

"But still with the tuxedos and matching bridesmaid's dresses, right?"

"I'm breaking tradition. That feels different ..." Rebecca hesitated. "It feels good, though. I don't have to do what everyone else does."

"Except the beautiful dress with a long train. You have to do that."

"White dress?"

"I don't care," Polly said. "That's up to you."

"What if I wore a green dress?"

"If you find a long train that works with a green dress, that's fine."

"I'm kidding."

"I know. Maybe I'll wear a green dress."

"That would be cool. You always wear blue."

"You know, by choosing to use all the colors, you've opened up a world of possibilities for your flowers. Agnes, Eliseo, and Judy Greene all have gardens filled with colorful flowers. Agnes would plant her garden next year with your choices. Unless you want carnations and roses."

"I don't know what I want," Rebecca said. "You made my brain 'splode."

"Then you shouldn't discuss it with Beryl. She'll make it worse."

"No kidding." Rebecca drew in a loud breath. "You have to invite her to my birthday party. She'd never understand it if you didn't. And that means you have to invite Lydia and Andy. And Sylvie and Eliseo. Then, Jason and Charlie, because they're family, too. And then Elva and her family. We should invite Kayla. That means Stephanie and Skyler. If we're doing that, then Cilla should be there, too. Her whole family. Sal and Mark and their family. Good grief, Polly, you have to tell them no presents. I can't handle all of that."

"You can handle all the people, but not gifts."

"Please, no gifts. I get it that Bill and Marie might do something. She can't help herself, but no one else. Please."

"I make no guarantees. That's all you will get from me."

"The whole house and back yard will be full of people, won't it?"

"Maybe. Speaking of people and attention," Polly said, "did you talk to Beryl this week?"

"She called to apologize for not coming to the opening, but she's coming down before the show closes. Then she asked if I would work for her this summer. Is she serious about that?"

"Yes," Polly said. "She needs you."

"Beryl told me she talked to you about it. I can do so much to help her, but I hate having her pay me to do it."

"She has the money. Don't worry about that."

"It's funny. It's like everything I learn in college is background for learning the real life of being an artist. Beryl teaches me that. I'm going to learn how to interview galleries that want to hang my work. Like I'm the one in charge. I always just thought that I'd be lucky to have my stuff hanging in a gallery. Beryl says that they're lucky to have her because she's just that good."

"I love that woman," Polly said with a laugh. "She will teach you how to be confident in your own artist's skin if nothing else."

"I'm going to help her be more organized with her calendar and stuff on the computer. She wants me to help her go all the way back and track her sales. She has all these pictures and invoices and dates. She wants a database of everything."

"From the beginning?" Polly asked. Beryl had been doing this long enough, that was going to be quite the task.

"She said we'll go backwards year by year until we get to the end of her paperwork. I'm going to help her buy a scanner so we can get it all on the computer and she can throw out excess papers. I've seen the closet where it's stored. I could work for her for ten years and never finish."

"That would put a crimp in your own work."

"Beryl won't let that happen. She already told me that part of the time I spend with her will be in the studio."

"Sounds like you have long days ahead this summer."

"Isn't it great?"

A knock sounded on Polly's door, and she jumped to her feet. "I need to go."

"Right now?"

"Right now. Something's going on. I'll talk to you later."

"Okay. Before Thursday?"

"Of course. I love you."

"I love you, too." Rebecca sounded confused, but the call ended before Polly got to the door.

Andrew stood there. "I need to take off," he said. "Mom called and asked me to help her at the bakery."

"Good enough," Polly said. "Thanks for hanging out with the girls. They all love you, you know."

"We had fun. They're downstairs now. Elijah is home and the dogs went crazy."

Polly nodded. "I just got off the phone with Rebecca. She's prepared for a birthday party. We're inviting everyone, not just family. Three weeks. Tell your mother that I'm sending out invitations to anyone who is part of our extended family. If I'm not thinking of someone you want to invite, tell me."

"Rebecca's okay with that?" He shook his head in disbelief.

"Not really. She doesn't want gifts, but I'm ignoring that."

"Did she tell you about wedding planning?"

"Finally," Polly said. "This will be a fun summer."

"You're excited?"

"What mother of the bride isn't?"

"You aren't going to be one of those, are you?"

She frowned at him, disdain in her eyes. "How well do you know me?"

"Got it." He laughed and pursed his lips before saying, "Will you and Henry let me help pay for the food at Rebecca's birthday party?"

"How well do you know me?" she asked again, then turned the look of scorn into a smile. "I'll ask people to bring a side dish. We'll grill meat and make a ton of ice cream. Maybe your mother could bake some cakes. I was going to ask Lexi to do it, but Sylvie has that big ole bakery."

"What kind of cake?" he asked.

"Chocolate." Polly shook her head. "I don't care. We need at least one chocolate cake for Rebecca, but your mother could bring anything. I'll let her know a better count after I send out the invitations. Will she be okay with that?"

"If I tell her now, she will. She wants to help with everything. She's worried that Jason and Charlie will never get married."

"They'll decide to do it someday and surprise us."

"That's what I tell her. Mom knows Charlie has trouble with her parents and since it's usually the bride's family who hosts the wedding ..."

"Your mother doesn't want to push. Let her know that she can be as involved with your wedding as she wants to be. If Sylvie wants to be in on all the planning and listen to Rebecca dream about the day, we'll make sure she is part of it."

"Thanks." Andrew looked down the hallway. "I really need to go. Thank you for making this easy. I was nervous."

"Henry made you nervous?"

"Not really. He picks on me, but I know he doesn't really mean it. Except that I have to treat Rebecca like a queen, or he'll make me pay. I was more nervous about you."

"Me? Why do I make you nervous?"

"Because you're like a second mom and I want you to be okay with what I do, especially when it comes to Rebecca."

Polly took his arm and then drew him into a hug. "I love you more than you'll ever know. I trust you with everyone in my family. I especially trust you with Rebecca."

"When I screwed up that year in high school, I didn't know if any of you would ever let me come back."

"You're going to find ways to screw up again," Polly said. "Not like that and probably not that severe, but no one is perfect. The one thing I want you to remember above all else is that love should never be based on a person's actions. I don't stop loving someone because they don't do what I think they should do or because they mess up. I might dislike a behavior, and I might not spend time with someone who hurts me intentionally, but that doesn't mean I stop loving them. Love is bigger than you and me."

CHAPTER EIGHT

Polly silently cursed herself as she helped Lexi prepare dinner. After all that had happened today, she could have used a quiet night. Not that nights in this household were ever truly quiet, but entertaining guests was more than she wanted to handle.

Eve had called before leaving Ames. They were on their way to Bellingwood. That had been twenty minutes ago, so things would get busy any minute.

"We're missing spoons."

Polly was surprised to hear Agnes' voice behind her. "Why are you setting the table? Teresa and Cassidy are responsible."

"Because I'm a helpful-Hannah. We need spoons."

Polly emptied the drawer of spoons and set them on the island.

"You're a grumpy-gus," Agnes said. "What bit you in the tushie?"

"At least it wasn't you." Polly shook her head. "I don't know what's up. It's been a long day."

"Worried about the girl from this morning?"

"I suppose. A lot is happening during the next few weeks, and I don't feel prepared."

"Grumpy won't make it better."

Lexi's shoulder shook as she laughed. She didn't turn around, and she didn't say a word.

"You've been picking on sweet Lexi, haven't you?" Agnes asked Polly.

"Did you get spoons?" Teresa asked. When she realized she'd interrupted, she shrank back into the dining room. "Sorry."

"It's okay, Teresa," Polly said. "Mrs. Agnes is only giving me trouble. She does it all the time and I love her all the same. I'm used to it."

"Then I'd best up my game if you're used to it. By the way, I didn't tell you that I invited a friend to join us for dinner."

Polly's eyebrows nearly lifted off the top of her head. "What? You're telling me now? We need an extra place setting?"

"I planned for it and spoke with your top chef. She knows how many people will be here. We've set enough places for everyone."

"Who in the world did you invite?" Polly had no idea how many people Agnes knew in town, and the woman had never done anything like this before.

"I thought I was family," Agnes said. She stuck her lower lip out. "You told me that I was to treat this place like home. Did you lie to me?"

Polly breathed and then let it out, trying not to lose her cool. "Who did you invite?" she asked as sweetly as she could manage.

"I should have told you," Lexi said under her breath.

"Will someone tell me who it is?"

The doorbell rang. It wasn't Eve and Bergie because they had Elijah with them. Dogs barked and ran toward the door. Even that got on Polly's nerves tonight. She wished she could pin down her stress. It was overwhelming her good nature.

Cassidy had run from the dining room, through the kitchen, and to the back door. "He's here!"

Ray Renaldi walked in carrying a bouquet of crazy daisies and a tote from Secret Woods. "I'm here and I brought presents." He handed the daisies to Polly. "These are for you. I heard about your morning."

Polly's stress left her body. If there was anyone Agnes could have invited to dinner without fear of recrimination, it was Ray.

She gave him a hug. "Thank you for the flowers. They're my favorite."

"And I brought wine. Dani, the sweet girl who runs the gift shop at the winery, told me which ones to buy for you. Now I know." Ray held onto her for a few moments. "How are you?"

"She's grumpy," Agnes said. "She's been kind of a pain in the hind end, if you know what I mean."

"Not my girl," he said.

"You wouldn't think so, but she is."

Ray kissed the top of Polly's head. "Did you do something to her, Mrs. Agnes?"

"You mean other than work hard to make things easier? What would I do?"

Polly chuckled. "I do love this woman, even when she makes me crazy."

The dogs barked and headed for the porch again. They hadn't received nearly enough attention from Ray.

Elijah came inside and said, "Ray! You're here, too?"

"I'm here, too. How are you?"

"I'm good, but we need to bring Bergie inside. I was going to find Dad."

"I'm right here," Henry said, coming in from the hallway. "Ray. I didn't know you'd be here tonight. Welcome to the party."

The two men shook hands and Ray said, "Let me help."

"Were you the one who brought flowers and wine?" Henry laughed. "You're a better husband to Polly than I am."

"Flowers and wine don't a husband make," Ray said.

The two men headed out with Elijah following.

"Difficult life," Agnes muttered.

"What was that?" Polly asked.

"Two beautiful men vying for your attention. It's pitiful."

"Why did you invite Ray to dinner? I'm glad you did, but what made you do it?" Polly asked. It was better to ignore some of Agnes's noise.

"The girls and I saw him at Sweet Beans this morning. He was sitting by himself while working on his laptop. I thought that was a shame, so we joined him." Agnes picked up a large pan of cheesy potatoes and headed for the dining room.

Polly picked up the other and followed her in. "And?"

"And I invited him to dinner. Since you'd already invited Eve and Bergie, I figured your table could handle one more person."

"Thank you," Polly said.

"Now, that's the response I was looking for."

Polly shook her head.

"Kind of a pain in your tushie, ain't I?" Agnes asked.

"I'd never say that."

"Don't worry, I'll say it for you. I get away with it because you love me so much."

"I do love you," Polly replied. She patted Agnes on her shoulder. "And that's all I'm going to say."

"Such a smart woman."

Eve Mansfield opened the doors from the foyer into the kitchen. "It sounds like you're having a party."

"What do you mean?"

"All of us."

Polly chuckled. "No, this is what my family looks like. You never know who will show up for dinner. You've met Ray, haven't you?"

Eve allowed a shudder to pass through her body. "Yes." She stepped in and whispered. "When God creates a masterpiece, he gives it everything, doesn't he?"

"He is a gorgeous man," Polly agreed. "I still have a crush on him."

"That would be easy to do. I might join the gym over here." Eve clapped a hand on her face. "Why didn't I think to invite him to build his gym near the community center? What was I thinking?"

"Eye candy all day long," Polly said. "Where are the boys?"

"In your living room. Elijah just got some new music he wanted to show Bergie."

"And how was my boy?"

"He's a good kid," Eve said. "Easy to have around. He'd do anything for Bergie. When he's in the house, I get a break. Both of us trust Elijah, and if there's a problem with anything, he isn't afraid to let me know. It's nice. Is he playing baseball this summer?"

Polly nodded. "Already signed up, but it's not every day. We'll find a way for them to be together. It isn't as if you're hundreds of miles away any longer."

Henry and Ray came in next and Henry glanced around. "Where is everyone?"

"The kids?" Polly asked. "I have no idea. Family room, library, bedrooms, living room. I haven't rounded them up yet. Lexi?"

"We're ready now," Lexi said. She handed a large platter filled with ham balls to Henry.

He took it from her and blinked. "Heavy food."

"A lot of ham balls. I have hot dogs for kids who won't eat them. Everything else is on the table," she said.

Polly tapped the intercom. "Dinner is on the table. Wash your hands. We're ready for you now."

"I only have one kid," Eve said. "Thank goodness he has a phone, and I can text him. We lose each other in that house sometimes. I can't imagine living here."

"The intercom was the best thing we ever put in," Polly said. "If I had to chase everyone through the house, I'd lose my mind."

The sound of feet on the stairs coming down from the top floor and more in the main hallway was deafening. Polly wanted to yell at them to walk, but the additional noise wouldn't stop anything. When the kids rushed into the dining room, Ray's presence stopped nearly every one of them. In different ways, he'd managed to connect with her children. Delia was enamored by the tall man who smiled when he saw her. Caleb was impressed with Ray's physical strength. He often walked up town to the gym after school. Ray or one of the other trainers took time to show Caleb how to use the different machines and helped him set up a workout routine.

While JaRon and Zachary weren't interested in spending time at the gym, Ray always made sure to ask them about their interests. Kestra, Cassidy, and Teresa were simply in awe of him. And the first time Amalee met him, she'd reacted the same way that Eve did.

It didn't take long for the conversation at dinner to turn to the people Polly had stumbled upon early that morning.

"Have you ever thought about offering a program for women?" Eve asked Ray.

He tipped his head. "We're planning to host classes for women only. I have two excellent trainers moving to the Midwest." Ray smiled at Polly. "You know one of them."

"I do?"

"Tonya Adkins. She was here after Joey and that Marcus Allendar kidnapped you. How long ago was that?"

Many of their kids hadn't known about that episode in Polly's life. The looks on their faces ranged from shock to concern.

"At least nine years," Polly said. She smiled at her family. "It was a long time ago. If you haven't heard the story, I'm willing to tell you about it, but the two men who were responsible are long gone."

Her words didn't stop the responses from nearly everyone. It was strange to realize that so many things had happened before she knew the people at this table. Noah and Elijah had been part of their family the longest, but they hadn't arrived in Bellingwood until a year after the serial killer prompted Joey to focus on Polly again.

"Those were dark days," Agnes said quietly. "I remember hearing the stories in town. Everyone was nervous."

Polly shot her a look.

"I know, I know," Agnes said. "Not post-dinner conversation. But I knew more about you and your family than you realized that day you and Cassidy plucked me from the brambles."

That brought more looks of confusion and concern from the kids.

"Cassidy, haven't you told your brothers and sisters the story?"

Cassidy shrugged. "I thought everyone knew."

Agnes stood and began collecting empty dishes around her into a stack. "You all recognize that I'm an old lady, don't you?"

Giggles erupted.

"I knew it," she declared. "You all think I'm old and feeble. Well, I'm in better shape now than I was five years ago." Agnes looked at Polly. "Has it really been five years? It feels like a lifetime. Look how much you've changed since we became friends. And look at how much my girl has changed. She was just a little thing back then."

"What happened?" Kestra blurted out.

"Young Cassidy begged her new mother to stop in the middle of the road because she saw something. Saw something, indeed. There I was, struggling to lift my old body with all its aches and pains out of a hedge that I'd fallen into. Polly lifted me out and the rest is history. I fell in love with the whole family. How could she help but fall in love with me?"

Attention turned to Agnes and her escapades. The woman could tell a tall tale. When she implied that she had known of Ray and his security group, that drew even more attention.

Eve chuckled as she listened, then asked Polly, "How much of what she says is true?"

"I have no idea," Polly said. "I assume she's completely truthful and telling grand fabrications all at the same time. It's the only way I keep my sanity." Polly looked at Ray. "Tell me more about Tonya coming to Bellingwood. She wants to live in the Midwest?"

"She'll probably live in Ames or Des Moines and commute," Ray said. "The quiet of a small town like Bellingwood is hard to get used to."

"It's very quiet here," Eve said. "I like Ames. It's more small-town than Des Moines, but still has all the benefits of living in the city. Would your friend teach a women's self-defense class?"

"She's been through it," Ray acknowledged. "It's her story to tell, but she'd be great at working with women. She understands more than most what women need to know to protect themselves.

Not only physically, but Tonya's background goes deeper than security. Before I hired her, she was finishing a master's degree in counseling."

"After all these years, why would she want to move out here?" Polly asked.

"Part of her story. It's time for her to move beyond her past." He shrugged. "Her words, not mine. When I decided to open a location here, she was one of the first people who asked if I'd consider bringing her with me." Ray smiled at Polly. "It's because of you. And that horse she fell off when you all went riding."

Polly frowned. "She fell off a horse?"

"You don't remember? Tonya certainly does. She still talks about trying to get off that big Percheron and landing on her backside."

"I remember now," Polly said with a laugh. "She was embarrassed, but it didn't last long. She's one tough cookie."

"Tonya has had to be tough. What do you think about having her nearby?"

"I hope she's happy here," Polly said. "You know, it's so strange. I spent a lot of time with her, and who was the other gal?"

"Gerry," Ray said. "She doesn't work for me any longer. Started a family and decided this life was too much. We're friends, but she has other things to do."

"That's right. I was thinking about how close I got to them while they were here. We kept in touch for a month or two after they left, but it all faded away. I thought of them as friends. We talked about the craziest things when we were together. How could we not? They were protecting me from Joey. Because it was a professional relationship, when it ended, so did our friendship."

"Or so you thought," Eve said. "She remembers it. Otherwise, she wouldn't have requested to be part of Ray's team in Bellingwood."

"That makes me happy," Polly said. "I can reclaim a friendship."

"And you didn't have to do any work," Agnes said with a wry smile.

Polly pointed at the woman. "We have a large hedge out front, you crazy woman, you."

"Are you going to let her speak to me that way?" Agnes asked. When no one responded, she aimed her bony finger at Henry. "You. I'm talking to you."

"If I let you speak to her however you want, the right thing is to allow my wife to respond without any reaction from me," he said. "Polly Giller doesn't need me to control what she does."

"That's what I'm talking about," Eve said. She ducked her head in embarrassment when everyone turned to her. "Sorry. I was thinking about the woman whose husband was killed this morning. From everything that's been said about her, it sounds as if he was abusive. I grew up with a father like that. Abuse can look like a lot of different things. Physical, mental, emotional, and it's so destructive. Once I escaped, I never looked back, but too many people don't know how to get away. I don't know if women who are in the middle of that would even be able to attend a self-defense class at your gym, but having someone who understood that a person needs to be strong not only physically, but mentally and emotionally would be amazing."

Ray nodded. "You and I should have a longer conversation."

"Okay?" Eve stared at him.

"You have resources. My company has helped women escape from terrible situations. We've never followed up after they found new lives, though. Did they need more help? Could we have done more?"

"What do you mean I have resources? I'm not involved in anything like that," Eve said.

"Maybe you should be. What will you do once the community center and elementary school are completed?" Polly asked. "You're crazy-involved right now, but when it's over, what is next for you?"

"Bergie ..." Eve started. "I understand. Now's the time to begin planning for a future beyond these projects. I never considered advocacy for wounded women."

"What do you think about it now?" Agnes asked.

Eve shook her head. "I don't know. It never occurred to me. Until we moved down here, my life revolved around Bergie. But he's growing up." She smiled at her son. "And he's getting independent. I look forward to the day he doesn't need me, but it scares me."

"Why, Mom?" Bergie asked.

"Not for you, but for me. What will I do with myself?"

"I'll always need you."

"No, honey, you won't. And that's the way it should be. It's what we've worked for all these years." Eve looked at Polly, then Agnes, then Ray. "This is a lot to think about. And it's another big conversation for the dinner table."

Ray handed her a business card. "Call me any time you want to discuss it. I'd also be interested in talking to you about how we can help at the community center."

"That would be a conversation to have with Sal Ogden," Eve said.

Henry stood up. "Lexi. Help me."

Lexi nodded. "With what?"

"Dessert. We're changing the subject."

She laughed and stood with him. "Since Mrs. Agnes already started clearing dishes, the adults will take care of that tonight. Fair?"

"Yay!" Elijah said. "It was my turn."

"You're on dessert duty. You and JaRon and Zachary. Teresa and Cassidy, would you like to help?" Lexi asked.

The kids pushed back their chairs.

"At least take your own dishes to the kitchen," Agnes said. "Don't expect us old folks to do all your work. We take care of you all week long. The least you can do is this."

Lexi grinned. She put a hand on Eve's shoulder as she walked past. "I'm interested in what you and Ray are talking about."

Eve nodded. "What interests you?"

"Being part of something bigger than myself. Especially when it comes to helping women understand how strong they truly are. Polly taught me things that my own mother never understood.

Things that would have stopped me from walking into a situation I should have ignored. This is important."

Polly gathered the empty platters and bowls. Her family could put away a meal.

When Henry walked past, he bumped her with his shoulder and said quietly, "You have impacted the lives of many young women."

She shrugged. "I loved them."

He leaned in and kissed her cheek. "You have no idea, do you?"

"What do you mean?"

"How easy it is for you. I don't think you, or anyone else, truly understands that you are different. Most people don't share love like you do. They hoard it and protect it, thinking that it makes them weak. You know the truth. Showing love makes a person strong."

CHAPTER NINE

Easing the phone back in its cradle so she didn't bang it and break something, Polly closed her eyes, muttering, "Patience. Patience." She'd just finished a call with a woman who insisted she had great ideas for how they could make things better at Sycamore House. The woman had attended a wedding reception Saturday night and made a list, then sent the list to Jeff via email. Since he hadn't responded yet, she called the office to speak with the owner.

Thinking she could end the call, Polly explained that they'd tested different ways to do the things the woman wanted to fix, but nothing she said mattered. When Polly explained that Monday was Jeff's day off, that didn't matter either. It hit Polly. The woman needed to be seen and heard, so she sat back and listened. When she described how they should use a different vacuum cleaning system to better pick up things dropped on the floor during the reception, Polly had to hold back laughter.

This wasn't an unusual conversation for either her or Jeff. Three or four of these conversations happened every month, usually from someone who felt comfortable enough to cross boundaries after attending only one event.

Polly was still taking in long, stress-relieving breaths when the sound of a hand slapping down on her desktop brought her fully alert.

"I need you to listen to me. I need someone to listen to me." Beryl stood in front of Polly, her face red and fury in her eyes.

"What in the world?" Polly asked.

"That woman won't listen to me. She's going to get herself in trouble and then what will I do? She's one of my best friends and this is going to do nothing but hurt her."

"What are you talking about? Who are you talking about? Lydia? Andy?"

"That one." Beryl pointed at Polly. "Andy Specek. What am I going to do with her?"

"Dump her in the creek?"

"You're not helpful. I need your help."

"What can I do?"

"I don't know."

"Now you aren't being helpful." Polly gestured toward a chair. "Sit and tell me what's going on. If I can help, you know I will."

Beryl dropped into the chair, then leaned forward. "She is taking on too much. That woman always does it. I think she believes she is the backup Polly Giller. The only problem is that she doesn't have a Henry Sturtz in her life to ensure she stays safe."

"Henry doesn't get to do that as often as he'd like. He trusts me," Polly said.

"But when someone dangerous is around, he's capable and strong enough to handle anything that comes your way. Len Specek is a wonderful man and he's perfect for Andy, but he's a lover not a fighter."

Polly chuckled. "Henry would love to hear that he's a fighter, not a lover."

"That's not what I mean. Len is more comfortable in an office or seated at a piano. He doesn't use those big muscles very often."

"He moves pianos."

"They're on rollers," Beryl said. "Don't try to calm me down."

"I thought that's why you were here. Why are you here? Don't you usually talk to Lydia about these things?"

"Lydia is as bad as Andy. Those women don't give enough thought to their own protection. Sticking their noses into everyone's business, thinking they're being helpful. They don't know what's going on behind that closed front door. It could be murder."

"No murder unless I'm there," Polly said.

"Unless someone is there to murder them."

"What did Andy do?"

"She spent the weekend at the hospital with her new neighbor."

"The entire weekend?"

Beryl scoffed. "Don't try to make sense of my fury. Just listen to me. No, she didn't spend the entire weekend. She went to the hospital Saturday evening, but the girl's family was there. She was just out of surgery. Why did Andy have to go so soon? She went back after church yesterday. Left Len at home and took off."

"She didn't tell him where she was going?"

Beryl rolled her eyes. "Of course she told him."

"Did they have lunch together?"

"Of course."

"So, Andy made a plan to visit her neighbor in the hospital and then followed through."

"She's getting involved in something she knows nothing about. She doesn't know who the shooter was."

"Right."

"What if he comes back to finish the job and Andy is there? Collateral damage. That's what they call it. Collateral damage. I don't want my friend in the path of a danged bullet. So there."

"How old are you?" Polly asked.

Beryl sat back. She looked a bit offended. "You know better than to ask a woman that question."

"Old enough to know how to handle yourself. You've lived this long and can take care of yourself, right? You know that sleep is good for you. Most of the time, you eat well."

"Only because Lydia and Andy make sure I have food in the house."

"Maybe you don't have that one down perfectly. What I'm trying to say is that you're a grown woman. An adult. One who makes big decisions every day. You are a successful artist. You know which paints to buy and what size canvases you want to work on. You know how to get yourself out of bed in the morning. You take care of your cats and your house and your car and your business. You're an intelligent woman."

"What does that have to do with my age? What does that have to do with Andy?"

"Is Andy dumber than you? Has she made so many dumb mistakes in her life that she needs a keeper to ensure she doesn't drool when she eats?"

"You're being ridiculous."

"Because you want to tell Andy that she's dumb for taking care of people when it's something she has done her entire life. She's a smart woman. She makes good decisions. For pity's sake, she chose to be your friend. She trusts you when you travel. She believes in your talent and supports you without question. She knows you are a grownup, and you don't need her to second guess every decision you make."

"But she won't listen to my concerns." Beryl's voice was softer and less abrasive. "What will I do if something happens to her?"

"The same thing all of us will do. We'll rally and take care of whatever needs to be done. What would you do if she was in a car accident or run over by a deer when she's walking through the cemetery?"

"A what?"

Polly chuckled. "Ridiculous things happen to everyone. We can't control any of it. If we spend time worrying about the frightening things our imagination creates, we miss a lot of joy. It's like the monster under the bed."

"Do your children fear that monster?"

"Not with all the dogs in the house," Polly said. "They root out monsters and alleviate any fears. Obiwan senses which kid needs him. Most of the time it's Noah or Elijah. They still have nightmares left over from their previous lives. Both of them know that none of it is real, but late at night ..." She paused. "This worry started in the middle of the night, didn't it."

"I don't know what you're talking about," Beryl said. "I sleep very well."

"Until you don't. You woke up in the middle of the night, went to the bathroom, curled up under your blankets with the cats snuggled all around, and started thinking. One of the thoughts that took up residence was Andy's concern for Bailey Jenkins. Dark shadows haunt us during late-night hours."

"I know better," Beryl said. "I have a notebook beside my bed to write down lists of things I don't want to forget."

"Do you write down ideas for paintings?"

"All the time."

"But you don't write down your fears."

"Because that would make them real."

"Or it would help you see how insubstantial they are. Those things are as important to release from your mind as the lists and ideas that you have. If I don't write them down, they grow bigger and bigger until I have to get up and wander through the house."

"What does Henry think when you do that?"

"He understands. If I'm really out of control, I'll read. Reading usually calms me down."

"It takes you to a different world," Beryl said. "I should do more reading. Andy would appreciate it."

"What time did you talk to her this morning?"

"I didn't wake up until nine o'clock, so, nine-fifteen. Had to go to the bathroom and make sure the cats were taken care of first."

"Coffee?"

"I haven't had any yet."

"You haven't what?" Polly laughed out loud. "This is my third cup."

"That's why you make sense and I make trouble."

"Do you want to call Andy and invite her to have coffee with us at Sweet Beans?"

"She'll think I want to holler at her some more."

"Tell her that you're with me and all we want to do is have coffee. I'll call Lydia."

"She has something going on this afternoon, but if you ask, she'll make time."

~~~

"When is the girl able to come home?" Lydia asked Andy.

"I didn't get to that," Andy responded. "I don't know if she wants to live in that house any longer."

"They just moved in."

"And her husband was murdered there. It sounds like he paid for the house up front, but there will be financial responsibilities. How will she pay for any of it?"

"Life insurance?" Beryl asked.

"I don't know," Andy said. "Her family was in the hospital room the entire time. I like her mother. She's quiet, but a nice person. However, since I'm a stranger, no one said much. I only wanted Bailey to know that if she needed anything, I was glad to help."

Polly picked at the cinnamon apple muffin in front of her. "It will be hard for her to live alone with that wound in her leg."

"The bullet shattered her femur," Andy said. "It's going to take a long time for that to heal."

"Where did the other bullet hit her?" Lydia asked.

"I always expect that you know these things," Beryl said. "What with being married to the sheriff and all."

"The sheriff and I don't talk about sheriffy stuff," Lydia said with a leer. "We have more interesting things to discuss ... or not discuss."

"Don't," Beryl said, clutching her head with both hands. "Don't make me see those things in my mind. You're hurting me. You're hurting me."

"Why do you think Len and I got married?" Andy asked. "We can't keep our hands off each other."

"Make it stop," Beryl said. "Please. Make it stop."

"You're just jealous."

"That's it, exactly," Beryl said. "You are being mean to me by continuing this conversation. Let's talk about pretty things." She turned to Polly, her hands still wrapped around her head. "Like Rebecca's art show. How was it?"

"Very nice," Polly said. "I hope you're prepared for all the angst she will bring into your house this summer."

"Angst?" Beryl dropped her hands. "About what?"

"Her future. She's beginning to worry about what to do after graduation."

"What about grad school?" Andy asked. "Is that a possibility?"

"Andrew is already accepted into a program at the university." Polly wanted to tell her friends about his plan to propose so that they could be married next summer, but it wasn't her story to tell. "Speaking of Rebecca, this is late notice, but we're throwing her a twenty-first birthday party at the house. I thought about only inviting family, but you all are family and it's an important celebration. How could I not invite you?"

"Her birthday is this week, right?" Beryl asked.

"Henry and I are taking her to dinner. Then she dives back into cramming for finals. It will be two weeks from Saturday. Don't tell me now. Check your calendars. Rebecca insists on no gifts."

"That's horse doo-doo," Beryl said. "I can't watch my favorite girl turn twenty-one without a present."

"You can deal with her," Polly said. "She asked and I promised to let people know."

"I don't like it," Lydia said.

Polly grinned. "Rebecca hates the idea of people doing too much for her."

"Your twenty-first birthday is a big deal these days," Andy said. "Are you going to do the whole first drink on her birthday thing?"

"Rebecca thinks it's ridiculous."

"Really," Lydia said. "Most kids can't wait to have their first legal drink."

"Sometimes I worry that my pragmatism has worn off on her," Polly said. "She knows people in college who are already alcoholics. That bothers her."

"Hello, ladies." Sylvie stood beside Beryl, drying her hands on a towel. "What bothers Rebecca?"

"Alcoholism in college. We're talking about her birthday party." Polly gave Sylvie a look, praying the woman wouldn't say anything about Andrew's proposal.

"Rebecca and Andrew have talked about it," Sylvie said. She pulled a chair over from another table. "I don't remember thinking about it at all. But then, I had alcoholism in my family. I'm thankful that wasn't one of my problems. Raising the boys with Anthony in the house was enough work. I didn't need to be drunk. When we took Andrew out for his birthday, he wanted nothing to do with it. Come to think of it, Jason wasn't interested in drinking with me either."

"We spend their entire lives keeping them away from alcohol, and when they turn twenty-one, suddenly it's appropriate for parents to change the rules."

"No one changed the rules," Andy said quietly.

"I know," Polly said. "It feels strange, though. Who knew I was so old-fashioned?"

"But you won't be upset if she drinks, will you?" Lydia asked.

"As long as she's smart and safe, it's her business."

"Did Andrew talk to you about Rebecca's birthday?" Sylvie asked Polly.

"What part?"

"That boy," Sylvie said. "He spends too much time in fictional worlds. He took his car back to school yesterday. It's only two weeks. He can afford a parking pass. He wants to meet you all in Des Moines on Thursday to celebrate her birthday."

Polly shrugged. "That sounds great. It would make Rebecca happy. Is he prepared for finals?"

"When he wasn't working this weekend, he was studying," Sylvie said.

"I remember those days," Beryl said with a shudder. "College finals were enough to make this girl want to become an alcoholic. Some of my courses were nearly impossible. How was I supposed to keep all that knowledge in my brain?"

"Luckily it was only for a week," Andy said. "I remember talking to you on the phone one year. You were stressed out." She laughed. "Do you remember when we had to wait until after seven o'clock to get the cheaper nighttime rates to make a phone call?"

"My phone bills with Dad were awful," Polly said. "He'd let me call and talk for a minute, then call me back so they were on his bill, but my own bills were still out of control. In the early days of cell phones, you watched every minute tick by, knowing that each one cost more than you wanted to spend."

"We're old," Sylvie said.

"Wise," Beryl said.

Polly's phone buzzed with a text. Since it was sitting beside her on the table, she glanced and saw it was from Tab. "Excuse me. I want to check this," she said.

"Are you at Sweet Beans again?" Tab asked. *"Do you mind if I join you?"*

"Come in. I'm here with the gang," Polly responded.

"I don't want to interrupt."

"We're having coffee and muffins. Get'cher butt in here." Polly looked up. "Sorry. It's Tab. She's coming in."

"We need another chair." Lydia stood and walked to a table where two young women were having coffee. After a short conversation, she brought one of the extra chairs back to the table.

"Do you know them?" Andy asked.

"Who?"

"The two you spoke to at that table?"

"That's Emily Gant and her sister, Devin Forester. They're Morrie Sorenson's girls."

Andy glanced over at them again. "No way. They went to school with my kids. How has everyone grown up so fast?"

Tab slid into the seat that Lydia had placed next to Polly. "I want coffee and a muffin."

"It's Muffin Monday," Polly said. "You have choices. Would you like me to get your coffee and choose which one you'd like?"

"I would," Tab said. She stood again. "But that would be rude. Hello, all. I'll be right back."

"She looks tired," Lydia said. "Aaron worries about her."

"Aaron worries about all of us," Polly replied. "You're right. Tab does look tired. I wonder what's up?"

Sylvie laughed. "Other than you finding a dead body along with a woman who has two bullet wounds in her body?"

"We talk about this stuff like it's commonplace," Andy said. "Doesn't that seem strange?"

Beryl shot her a look. "Strange became commonplace when Polly Giller moved to Bellingwood. If we didn't talk about the dead bodies that she finds, that would be strange. It's better to have it all out on the table than to act like the strange doesn't exist."

"You're right," Lydia said. "If we acted like Polly's talent ..." She used air quotes around the word *talent*. "... was nonexistent, we'd be hypocrites. Phonies. Polly would have to hide what she does from us. That would make for a lousy friendship."

Tab returned with a variety of muffins and a thermal pitcher. "I brought more coffee."

"And more goodies," Polly said. "Thank you."

"I couldn't choose which one, so I bought one of each. Please help yourselves so I don't have to think about it."

"We all noticed," Polly said. "You look tired."

"A lot is going on. I drove by Sycamore House first. If you hadn't been here, I was headed straight to your home. It's been a long weekend." Tab smiled at Andy. "Bailey Jenkins' mother told me that you visited her yesterday. That was very nice. She has a long difficult road ahead. Not only healing her body, but her heart and soul."

The news about Bailey's abusive husband hadn't taken long to get around Bellingwood. Not that anything did. Whenever someone was surprised to hear about a bit of gossip days after it had happened, Polly was in disbelief. People talked about everything in the small town. If they didn't talk about it in person, stories were shared on social media.

"Ray Renaldi and Eve Mansfield discussed ways to help women who live with abuse," she said.

Tab's head turned her way. "Really? I'd like to be part of that conversation."

"I'll tell them."

"Self-defense training?" Lydia asked.

"Eve wants to make it bigger than that. Not only physical self-defense, but teaching ways to protect yourself from emotional abuse."

"Sometimes you wait for them to die. Like Bailey," Andy said.

Beryl put her hand on top of Andy's and gave it a squeeze. "You're okay."

"Bill was a good husband," Andy said in way of explanation. "His mother was nasty. Sometimes he couldn't help himself and said awful things to me. I didn't think of it as abuse because that's not how we dealt with it. I learned to walk away until he was ready to speak to me in a normal tone of voice. Staying calm in the face of it was never easy, but it was all I could do."

"No one should have to put up with another person's issues," Tab said. "My heart aches with all that I see every day. There have been times I wanted to punch a guy in the face." She chuckled. "Luckily, I know better. But the worst of them won't bother to even fake it when we arrive at a domestic call. There's nothing more satisfying than to park them in the back of the car and haul them off to jail. The only problem is that they go back home. I'd like there to be a way the wife or girlfriend could get help right away. Give her options beyond lying down on the sofa and weeping until he returns to start the abuse all over again.

CHAPTER TEN

Once their friends started leaving, Tab had put her hand on Polly's knee, asking her to stay. "I know we just ate muffins, but would you have lunch with me?"

"Here?"

"I don't care where," Tab said. "I'd like a few more minutes with you. Do you have time?"

Polly chuckled. "I have time. I could be working, but I'd rather have lunch with you. What's up?"

Tab said nothing and stared off in space. "I need to talk to someone about this case."

"What do you mean?"

"I could talk to the sheriff or one of the guys, but they have their own cases. You're part of the job." She grinned at Polly.

"I am the job," Polly said. "Talk to me."

Tab looked around, as if to make sure no one could overhear their conversation. "There were two guns."

"How do you know that already?"

"The wounds were different in Bailey Jenkins' body from those in her husband's body."

"You've found neither of the guns," Polly said.

"That's where I was this morning. At the house, doing another search. When I was told about it, I came back to Bellingwood to look for anything that might point the way. I found nothing."

'Which means the gunman picked them up. I have a question for you, then."

"Shoot."

"Bang," Polly said. "That's twisted. Anyway, how did no one hear the gun shots?"

"We don't know yet, but a pillow from the sofa is also missing."

"How exactly do you know that?"

"Believe it or not, social media posts. Bailey was excited about decorating her house. Anita dug through her pages and pulled pictures of the house. We couldn't figure out how the Specek's didn't hear anything either. But muffling the shot through a small throw pillow would take care of the sharpest sounds."

"What are you thinking?"

"Ethan Jenkins shot his wife as she ran out the back. The other gunman shot Jenkins, picked up the guns and the pillow, and left. I assume the shooter had a silencer. The whole thing is strange."

"Bailey told me that the gunman shot her."

"She was running and had her back to the others. She might not have known." Tab shook her head. "That doesn't track with me. Here's what I think."

Polly nodded.

"She's not telling us who the shooter is, but she knows."

"I was afraid of that," Polly said. "Go on."

"He … or she was at the house for some reason or other. Maybe she called the person because she was afraid. Her husband got himself worked up and decided he was done with her, so as she ran away, he shot her."

"Luckily, he's a lousy shot," Polly said.

"And in retaliation, the shooter killed him. How Ethan figured he could shoot at his wife through two rooms and from the staircase, I have no idea."

"Again, lucky for her. How do you propose to get the name of the shooter from her?"

"I don't know," Tab said. "I don't dare press her too hard right now. Her family won't let her out of their sight, and she's filled with so many painkillers that she isn't reliable. I don't want to drag her through a harsh interrogation. If her husband shot her, that's a terrible place for a woman to be."

"Can I help you?"

"No," Tab said, shaking her head. "I just needed to get it all out. My interpretation of what I see could be off. I'll rework my theories a thousand times before the end of this."

"Should I get involved?"

Tab smiled. "You will whether I think you should or not, but it's not imperative today. We can enjoy lunch and you can go back to work."

Polly picked up her phone. "I need to tell Kristen that I won't be back."

"You aren't going back?"

"I can do everything I need to do from home. Sitting in the office when my mind is circling other things frustrates me. Let's order something to eat."

They walked to the front of the shop where Josie Riddle was wiping down the counter. "You're staying for lunch?"

"Me too."

Polly and Tab turned to find Sal Ogden standing behind them.

"You didn't come back to the office," Sal said. "I assumed you would be here."

"I'm always here," Polly replied. "How are you?"

"Good. I saw you drive away. Sorry I wasn't in earlier. Little Miss Betsy-Kate decided to throw a tantrum this morning."

"That's the worst," Josie said.

"It was a bad one. I finally had to draw a warm bath for her. That helped. I don't know what her problem was, but she was in meltdown mode."

"I hate it when they can't tell you what's going on in their little minds," Josie said.

"I hate it when my entire being wants to throw down with the child," Sal said. "I'm the adult, but this morning I wanted to lie down on the floor and scream at her to shut the heck up."

"Instead, you ..." Polly started.

"Instead, I told her I loved her, walked out of the room, and took a deep breath. I thought about calling Mark so he could hear her and commiserate with me, but I didn't do that either. Now I'm here, asking for your sympathy."

Polly put an arm around Sal's waist. "I sympathize. The thing is, as they get older, sulking and pouting replace tantrums. It's quieter, but no less annoying."

"And this is why I'm never having children," Tab said. "I experience those nasty emotions from the fine citizens of Boone County. There is nothing like watching a grown woman screech at the top of her lungs because she's drunk and out of control."

"The benefits outweigh the trouble when it comes to babies," Josie said. "Right?"

Sal laughed. "Ask me tomorrow."

After they placed their order, Sal followed Tab and Polly to their table. She looked at the number of chairs. "Was there a party?"

"A big one," Polly said. "You missed it."

"I always do. How are you?"

"Okay. Why do you ask?"

"You found a body on Saturday, and you found a second victim of a gunshot. News gets around, you know."

"Where were you that you heard about it?"

"Not me. Mark. He gets all the best gossip. When it's about you, he lets me know. So, how are you? And Tab, are you investigating this one?"

"I'm hers," Polly said. "If I'm involved, Tab is in charge of me."

"I hadn't had a chance to meet them. Too new to the neighborhood," Sal said. "Mark heard that she was abused, which brings me to my next topic of conversation. I got an email from Eve Mansfield this morning. She said you told her to contact me."

"I did not," Polly said. "She brought up your name, not me."

"I know," Sal said with a smile. "I was only teasing. Her idea sounds promising. We need more resources for women. Do you think Grey would agree to be involved?"

"Alistair Greyson?" Tab asked. She glanced at Polly. "He'd be great. Everything I've heard about him is good."

Polly wasn't certain whether either of her friends knew about the rape that Nan had endured before she came to Bellingwood. Polly had encouraged many of the young women who had faced trauma to spend time with Grey. He was wonderful with all of them.

"He is good," she said.

"Lexi and Shelly both talked to him, didn't they?" Tab asked.

Shelly Foster was still seeing Grey. She had grown since Polly and Henry found her cold and shivering in a parking lot in Boone after escaping a sex trafficker, but she might never be finished dealing with that trauma. Her life was good now. She lived with Marta, who worked with Sylvie in the bakery. Shelly worked at the nursing home, and because Marta was involved with the community theater in Boone, she found herself working on sets, props, and costumes. She refused to be on stage, but had fun with Marta's friends.

"They did," she said. "He's helped so many friends. My kids love him. If he'd consent to giving his time, he'd be perfect."

"No way," Sal said.

"What?"

"Ray Renaldi just walked in with the most gorgeous woman I've ever seen."

Polly turned in her chair. She waved at Ray and laughed, then stood and walked over to them. "Tonya, you're here. In Bellingwood. And you aren't here to keep me safe from crazy kidnappers. It's good to see you."

"Ray called Saturday night and said it was time. I packed a bag and flew out this morning. He told me you would be here, so we thought we'd surprise you."

"Come meet my friend, Tab," Polly said. "She's in charge of me."

Tonya laughed. "No one can truly claim to be in charge of you. I've never met anyone who is so nice about it, but still insists on doing things her own way."

"I know," Tab said. "But she wouldn't be our Polly Giller if she suddenly allowed the rest of the world to be in charge. Polly told me about you long ago. Are you really leaving the east coast to live in Iowa?"

"Ray talks about Bellingwood to everyone who will listen," Tonya said. "About how peaceful it is." She laughed again. "Unless Polly is involved in something. I've never lived in anything but a city. I'm used to the sounds of helicopters flying over and sirens screaming past no matter what hour of the day. Don't forget the noisy neighbors."

"We have those," Tab said. "The other noises are unfamiliar. If we can avoid using sirens in the middle of the night, we do our best. Some of the bigger cities have helicopters that disrupt peace and quiet, but those are generally medical, and we understand their importance."

"I don't know if I could live in Bellingwood," Tonya said. "Too much peace and quiet all at once might disrupt me. Though you have a coffee shop. It was barely a structure when I was here the last time. Is the coffee any good?"

Polly scowled. "It's better than anything you've ever had."

"I don't know. There are a few coffee shops that hold my heart."

"Black?" Polly asked. "Let me get you a mug. Then you can judge. Have you eaten anything yet?"

"Not since breakfast. What is good here?"

"Name it and it's good. Walk with me." Polly led Tonya to the counter and grinned when Ray was right behind them.

"I haven't eaten either," he said.

~~~

Polly was still at Sweet Beans with Tonya and Ray after Tab and Sal left to return to their work.

"What are your immediate plans?" she asked Tonya.

"I'm here for three or four weeks," Tonya responded. "I have a dim memory of the area, but I want to reintroduce myself to it." She laughed and put up a hand. "And no, I don't want you to take me on a field trip. My understanding is that those are dangerous to the local populace."

Polly glared at Ray. "What have you been telling people about me?"

"Only the truth, little sister. Only the truth."

"It isn't every time," Polly protested. "I regularly travel throughout the county with friends and never find a dead body."

"Not tempting fate," Tonya said. "Especially since you've already found one body and a living victim. Anything can happen now. Do you have any idea who the murderer is?"

"No," Polly said, shaking her head. "I don't know anything. Things are still up in the air."

"And you haven't gotten down into it yet?" Ray asked.

She shot him another glare. "Rotten man." She glanced at Tonya and then at Ray again. "What are you two plotting?"

"Nothing," Ray said, a little too quickly.

"I don't believe you. Is there something about this murder that I don't know? Something that's a threat to me and mine?"

"We don't have any answers," Tonya said.

"But you've asked questions?"

She shrugged. "Ray always asks questions when it comes to murder and you. We might spend a little extra time digging down in the victims you find."

"And you never told me?" Polly huffed out a breath. "You drive me nuts, Ray Renaldi."

"It's not like you would do anything with the information I find," he replied. "What about the background checks I did on all your employees?"

"Don't want to know. Don't need to know. Was there something I should have known before hiring them?"

Ray smiled at her. "Not in the least. You have a good head for people. There were youthful indiscretions, but nothing criminal and nothing scary. Eliseo's time in the service was harsh. He has more than enough reasons to fight PTSD, but he was always honorable. Your catering head, Rachel Endicott, got herself in trouble once while she was in high school, but that one time scared her. She straightened up."

"See. Not knowing everything is right for me," Polly said. "I don't want to know things about people that they don't want to tell me. It's not fair to them or to our relationship."

Tonya nodded in agreement.

"But you both know way too much about me," Polly said.

"Nothing that you wouldn't share," Ray replied. "You're an open book."

"To people who know me. Otherwise, I like to keep my private life, private. There are too many people out there who think they are entitled to know things. Even people in Bellingwood who see me every day. They want to know the minutest details and are offended if they don't."

"About you?" Tonya asked.

"About the kids, me, Henry, relationships with our friends, the house, the business. Would you believe that I get questions about how much money we make and how we can afford to do all the things we do? Puh-leeze. If I wanted you to know those things, I'd publish a newsletter telling you."

"You're getting worked up," Ray said with a laugh.

Polly took a deep breath. "When I think about how easily people cross boundaries because of their danged curiosity, I become incensed. Imagine how much fun Henry has when I get like this. I need to calm down."

"Right."

She shrugged. "This morning, a random customer who had never been at Sycamore House before thought it was important to tell me how we should run things. Because after eleven years, we haven't tried everything and discovered the best process? She had no idea, just had to stick her nose in my business. They don't understand how much I don't like people telling me what to do when they have limited information. Even when someone has all the information and tries to push me, I rebel. The response is usually a nope, not gonna."

"You're funny," Tonya said. "Everything I know about you is that you are gracious and kind."

"And strong-willed," Ray supplied. "Polly will do everything in her power to make the world a better place until someone pushes back. She lets them do their thing, screw it up on their own, and then returns to pick up the pieces. She won't be pushed into doing anything."

"Danged right," Polly said, smacking her fist on the table. "I'm all that. Back to my question. What's the real reason you're in town, Tonya? You didn't decide to visit on a whim."

"I do plan to move to Iowa," Tonya said. "Things in my life need to change. When Ray offered me the opportunity, I said yes without hesitation. That means I need to find a place to live."

"And you want to live in Ames."

"Bellingwood is a little small for all this." Tonya gestured at herself.

Just then, Camille walked in the front door, carrying four bags of books. She set the bags in front of the shelves, then straightened and stretched.

"Wait," Tonya whispered. "Who's that?"

"Camille Specht," Polly said. "She's the manager here."

"No way."

"Polly has also managed to integrate Bellingwood. She does it quietly and forcefully," Ray said. "Between her family, her friends, and her employees, a little white rural community has found itself all mixed up."

"Does she live in town?" Tonya asked.

"With a friend. They live just past the hotel." Polly waved Camille over to their table.

"Hi there," Camille said. She nodded at Ray. "Good to see you again."

"Camille, this is Tonya Adkins. She's planning to move to the Midwest to work with Ray. I'm convincing her that Bellingwood is a good place to live, but she's a city girl."

"You won't miss the city much if you move to Bellingwood," Camille said. "I don't know where you're from, but I grew up in Omaha. This is nice. People are kind and helpful. Sometimes they get a little too nosy, but I ignore that. Will you work at the gym Ray is putting together?"

Tonya nodded.

"Then people will get to know you there. It helps for them to see you regularly. Small towns get a little insular and outsiders freak them out. It didn't take long, though, for me to be recognized." She winked and smiled. "For every negative person in town, there are ten who will welcome you with open arms and open minds. I remind myself of that every day."

"That's true in the rest of the world," Ray said.

"We're only a microcosm," Camille agreed. "Bellingwood has everything you need and it's only a short drive to a city. You should think about living here. If you're leaving behind a city because you want peace, you'll find it in a small town. Very few sirens ..." She looked at Polly. "... unless Polly has found someone who needs help." She pointed at the coffee cup in front of Tonya. "How do you like our coffee? We're proud of it."

"It's good," Tonya said. "Polly told me it would be better than anything I'd had. I didn't believe her, but it's right up there at the top of my list."

Camille put her hand on Polly's shoulder. "Gotta keep checking. Don't want to fall behind the rest of the world when it comes to an excellent brew. I should relieve Josie."

"Where did the books come from?" Polly asked.

"Used bookstore was getting rid of some overstock. Since ours is often depleted, I thought it was time to fill the shelves. It's nice to meet you, Tonya. I hope to see you again." Camille walked toward the front counter, stopping to chat with customers along the way.

"She's comfortable here," Tonya said. "I had a picture in my mind of two or three hundred little old white ladies in their housedresses, all keeping an eye on the comings and goings of everyone in town."

"Trust me," Polly said. "They're out there. The number you have in your head is close to reality. But there are more than fifteen hundred residents who are too busy to spy on their neighbors."

"This is a lot to think about," Tonya said.

"While you're thinking, you could tell me exactly why you're here this week. Why did you decide Saturday evening to travel to Iowa?" Polly sent her trademark glare to Tonya this time. "You have managed to avoid that question long enough."

"You don't want to know," Ray said practically under his breath.

"Remember me?" Polly asked. "The girl who doesn't like to be told what to do? I do want to know."

"Ethan Jenkins got himself into trouble, which is why he left the Quad Cities and moved back home. I don't know why he thought that the trouble wouldn't follow him, but if this is something other than just a domestic dispute, I wanted someone with more training to nearby," Ray said. "Because you get yourself into trouble. I'm going to avoid that if I can."

"Do Tab and Aaron know what you know?" Polly frowned. "Tab didn't say anything."

"I have a meeting with them tomorrow morning," Ray said. "I've spoken with Aaron. The thing is, if it was a professional hit ..."

Polly gasped. "In Bellingwood?"

"By professional, I mean a hired hit. Not a big-time professional hitman," Ray said. "Anyway, if it was a hired hit, the murderer has likely left town. No reason for him ..."

"Or her," Tonya interjected.

"Right. Or her, though the victim's wife identified the murderer as a male. Anyway ..."

"Sorry," Tonya said.

He shook his head. "There is no reason for him to stick around, unless something else is going on. Since the location of the house is close enough to yours, Polly, I want someone to keep an eye on you."

"What about my family?"

"They're safe enough. It's probably nothing. He's probably long gone."

"You know better than that," Polly said. "We all know better than that."

"Then Tonya is here until you figure out who he is and why he came to Bellingwood."

CHAPTER ELEVEN

Polly had just sat through three meetings in a row at Sweet Beans. She was worn out. Fortunately, there had been food and coffee. She drove home, and as she flipped on her blinker to turn into the driveway, saw Andrea Waters wave while pushing a stroller. Interesting.

Polly stopped before turning and rolled down the window. She and Andrea hadn't talked much in the last couple of months. Only short conversations as they both went about their business. That was already changing as temperatures warmed up and spring rainstorms gave way to summer weather. Neighbors spent more time outside, and with Memorial Day only a few weeks away, plans were already in motion for a block party.

"Hello!" Polly said.

Andrea walked toward her. "Do you have a minute? I miss you."

"Sure," Polly said, though what she really wanted to do was hide in her office until the kids got home from school. "Let me park this beast and I'll meet you. Do you want to come my way or should I come to your house?"

"I don't want to be in my house today," Andrea said. "Is it okay if we hang out in your kitchen?"

"Of course. Meet you at the door." Polly drove into the driveway, waited for the garage door to open, and pulled in. She closed her eyes, wondering what Andrea wanted. Their conversations were rarely easy. Andrea was a strong-willed, bull-headed woman who, though she loved her family, was judgmental about their behavior. She had notions and they weren't easily swayed. "You've got this," Polly said to herself and opened the door.

Since Cilla's baby was sound asleep in the carrier, Polly and Andrea gently lifted it up the steps and into the house.

Lexi started to ooh and ahh when Andrea pushed it into the kitchen, but with one look, Polly stopped additional noises.

"Sleeping baby," Lexi said. "I know how important that is, though it's been a few years."

"It had been a few years for me, too," Andrea said.

"Never for me," Polly retorted with a grin. "I like my chilluns to be a couple of years older so I can put them down for a nap and expect them to stay there."

"Uh huh," Lexi said. "Because that's how it works."

"In my dreams," Polly said. "Andrea, would you like something to drink?"

"I made strawberry lemonade," Lexi said. "It's amazing."

Andrea nodded. "That would be nice."

"What are you doing out with Fiona?" Polly asked. "Cilla's home today."

"Cilla's sound asleep. I told her that I had time this afternoon and would watch the baby while she slept."

"It's good that she has your support," Lexi said. "I couldn't have made it through Gillian's early years if Polly hadn't been around."

"We all need Polly in our lives."

"What about the rest of the kids? They're old enough to watch the baby," Polly said.

"They're busy with school. Nat and Lara have things going on nearly every night and Abby tries, but she's young and is easily distracted."

Polly had thoughts about kids helping with household responsibilities, but kept them to herself. Andrea wasn't asking for that type of response. So instead, Polly said, "You know, this summer, Cassidy and Teresa would be great babysitters. Agnes would love to teach them everything she knows about watching over little girls."

"Agnes Hill?"

Polly nodded, a bit perplexed. "You know the girls are at her house nearly every day. They'd love to play mama and get paid for it."

"I don't know if Cilla can afford it."

"Cassidy is too young to have her certification. The only way I'd allow it to happen would be if Agnes was there to keep an eye on all of them. It would be affordable. I happen to know Cilla's salary. Unless she's paying you an extravagant amount for rent, she could afford them."

"She's not paying rent. Everything is going into a savings account for her return to school."

"When does she want to go back?" Lexi asked.

"I want her to go back this fall, but there are a lot of hoops to jump through. She tells me she isn't ready." Andrea shook her head. "I don't know what she thinks she's going to do with her life."

"Live it," Polly said. "With her little girl beside her."

"That's not what I wanted for her."

"Things change."

"But to be saddled with a child at this age. What ..." Andrea looked at Lexi. "I'm sorry."

"That's okay. Choices I make aren't what others would make. You should be proud of Cilla, though."

"Proud? Why do you say that?"

"Because she's taken on a huge responsibility. Raising a child isn't all sunshine and roses."

"Oh, she's figuring that out," Andrea said. "Sometimes I wish she's made a different decision, but she informed her father and me that it was her choice."

Polly nodded. "She's twenty-one and an adult."

"Then she should act like one."

"How is she not acting like an adult?" Polly asked.

"Living at home, for one thing. Playing at being a mother for another."

"She's playing at it? From what I've seen, she's working hard. Not only to be a good mother, but she works hard at Sycamore House, too."

"You see her in a different light." Andrea took a drink of the strawberry lemonade and smiled at Lexi. "That's good. Thank you."

"I probably do see her differently than you," Polly said. "She's not my daughter."

"I had such high hopes for her. I can't say anything because it would sound like I'm disappointed."

"It sounds like you *are* disappointed in her. That's too bad. Have you asked her what her goals are for her future? What she wants to do?"

Andrea frowned. "What do you mean?"

"Lexi's goals have changed since she left college. Right?"

Lexi nodded. "I was big-time into neuroscience. Thought I'd be a researcher and an academic. Now that I'm away from that life, I've discovered how much more there is than a college or medical campus. I don't want to be stuck in a lab all day. I love my life, and I still take classes, and learn what I want to learn. But now I choose what I want. I don't have to answer to a curriculum that's been laid out for me to learn."

"That's interesting," Polly said. "Are you glad that you had those first four years?"

"Absolutely. Those gave me a structure. But after living within that structure, I realized I didn't want to spend the rest of my life constrained by it."

"Cilla never learned to live within the college structure," Andrea admitted. "I always hoped she'd figure it out, but from day one, she fought against going to college. We were just lucky to get her admitted somewhere since she'd put off applying for so long."

"You worked hard to help her start, but she rebelled the entire time," Polly said. "Maybe college isn't her thing."

"I don't know what to think about that," Andrea said. "Education has always been a large part of our family life. It's my career. Cilla did so well in high school. She excelled in everything."

"High school and college are two very different entities," Polly replied.

"How else is she supposed to learn the ins and outs of her craft?"

"By working at it." Polly grinned. "What if she were to teach instead of attend classes?"

"She doesn't know anything to teach."

"Come on," Polly said. "She knows a lot. I'll bet anything she could direct a group of people with no problem."

"But she's not a director. She's an actor, a dancer, a performer."

"You're limiting her."

"That's why I pushed her to go to college. I wanted her to expand her horizons."

"You wanted to control her expansion," Polly said.

Andrea grimaced. "That's not true." She took a breath. "It's maybe true. I am a control freak. It's one of the things Kirk always tells me. He acts like he's teasing me, but we both know it's true. Am I supposed to allow her to do whatever she wants? How is that raising my child?"

Lexi had her back to them, and Polly watched her shoulders go up.

"Cilla isn't a child; she's an adult," Polly said, hoping Lexi would relax.

"Where would she teach? She doesn't have an education degree so she can't teach in the school system. She doesn't have any degree at all," Andrea spat.

"You need to let that go."

"I'm not going to. I believe in the power of education."

"Education isn't about a degree. It's about learning. I believe in college. I believe in advanced degrees. But those are for people who want those things. Insisting that every person fit into the same round hole is ridiculous. Did Justin go to college?"

"Trade school."

"And ..."

"And he went to trade school."

"But he didn't live on campus. He didn't participate in college activities. He worked and learned a trade. Why is Cilla different?"

"Because she has so much more to offer." Andrea heard her own words. "Wow, that's awful of me to say."

"She has different things to offer. Justin loves working with his dad at the garage. Why wouldn't you want Cilla to love doing something as much as her brother does?"

"She loves performing."

"Do you think she'll give it up because she has Fiona now?"

"She has so far."

"You really just want to argue, don't you," Polly said with a smile.

"I've been trying to work it all out. Kirk is no help. Cilla argues with me all the time. Who else do I have to talk about it with? You're the only person in my life who won't let me get away with anything."

"Polly does that to all of us," Lexi said. "Somehow, we still love her."

"I don't like her very much sometimes," Andrea said.

Polly laughed. "I can live with that. Answer my question. Do you believe Cilla will give up performing because Fiona is here?"

"I don't know. She hasn't expressed interest in anything outside of work and the baby."

"Let's see," Polly said, holding up her fist. She lifted her index finger. "She got pregnant and had to tell you and Kirk about it." The middle finger went up. "She put on baby weight and hormones ripped through her body, so she felt fat and ugly." Then she lifted her ring finger. "It's been less than three months since Fiona was born. Not only is Cilla nursing her baby, but she's trying to regain some of her pre-pregnancy strength and agility. Do I need to continue? Oh yes ..." Polly lifted her little finger. "And her mother insists that Cilla is a failure because she isn't doing what her mother thinks she should be doing."

"Wow," Andrea said. "Harsh."

"All you heard was the final point. What I'm trying to say is that your daughter has had a lot going on this last year. She's only twenty-one. Why in the world should she have her entire life laid out today? Let her live a little. Let her explore her options. Let her grow up and find her way. Give her the space to do those things. It won't take anything away from you, will it?"

Lexi quietly spoke. "She needs to move out of the house."

Both women looked at Lexi.

"What?" Andrea demanded.

"She needs to move into her own apartment with the baby."

"Why in the world would I let her do that?" Andrea asked. "I can't keep an eye on ..." She trailed off. "That's why. If Cilla is going to grow up, I need to encourage her to do just that."

"She's ready," Polly said. "There are apartments all over town. She has a good job and can afford it."

"Especially if I stop forcing her to put everything into a savings account for college." Andrea shook her head. "This will be a very long conversation between the two of us when I get home."

Fiona chose that moment to let out a small noise, catching everyone's attention.

"Well, that was adorable," Lexi said.

"Hold on." Andrea pushed her glass back. "Fiona and I need to go home before she comes fully awake. It's time for food and she will tell us in no uncertain terms that she's hungry. I hope Cilla's awake."

"Tell me you left her a note."

Andrea shook her head and chuckled. "Nope. I intended to be out of the house for a short walk. I did not intend to find you and withstand a lecture."

"You asked for it," Polly said.

Lexi had to turn away before her giggles burst out.

"I did. You always come through for me."

Fiona opened her eyes and sounds of frustration erupted.

"There it is," Andrea said. "I need to hurry. Thank you for the lemonade, Lexi. Polly, thank you for helping me to remember that it isn't about me. This is about Cilla." She pushed the stroller onto the porch.

"Let me help," Polly said, hurrying to catch up.

Fiona's cries continued to grow as Andrea and Polly carried the stroller down the steps. All Polly could think as Andrea rushed across the street to her own house was how grateful she was not to have an infant in the house.

When she got back inside, Lexi was lifting containers of baked ziti out of the oven. "What do you think is going to happen over there this afternoon?"

"If the roof doesn't blow off the top of the house, they'll come to an agreement. I wouldn't be surprised to find that Cilla moves into an apartment by the end of the month. Andrea will buy furniture and decorations for her, and then be over there all the time."

"Do you think Cilla made the right decision?"

"Which one?" Polly asked.

"Keeping Fiona."

Polly smiled and shrugged. "I don't know. Don't tell anyone I said this, but if Andrea hadn't pushed, Cilla would have given Fiona up for adoption and re-started her life. That girl will always do exactly the opposite of what her mother wants. She's as stubborn as anyone, so that ensures Fiona will have a good life with her. Cilla will never admit that she chose to keep her baby because of rebellion. She will love that little girl with everything she has, and someday, Fiona will be exactly like her mother."

"Stubborn?"

"Yep. Andrea did things her own way. Cilla does things her own way. Fiona will be another in a long line of strong, independent women. Can I help you get anything ready for your customers?"

"I'm close," Lexi said. She sliced a long loaf of Italian bread that she'd baked earlier in the day. "You have no idea how much of a relief it was when you recommended that I stick with our friends and not try to grow too fast. The holidays were nuts and I never want to go through that again. Someday, I might open a shop, but right now, I like the intimacy of cooking for a few people who appreciate what I do."

"Whenever you're ready for more, you know I'll support you. Is Will coming for dinner tonight?"

Lexi looked at Polly in surprise. "How did you know?"

"That." Polly pointed at her.

"What?"

"You're dressed up under that apron. Not only that, you're wearing the full-cover apron. You don't plan to have time between preparation and dinner to change your clothes."

"I'm so obvious. Is it okay?"

"That Will joins us? You know better than to ask. He's always welcome. In fact, he's becoming part of the family. Good grief, Agnes invites Ray to dinner without telling me."

"She told me."

"Uh huh. That old bat did so just to mess with me. I wish I had the courage to mess with her, but I have two problems with that. First, I don't want to hurt her in any way, and second, I don't want her to hurt me back."

"Were you serious about Teresa and Cassidy babysitting this summer?"

"I need to talk to Agnes about it. Why?"

"I don't know. I'd love for Gillian to spend more time with your old bat, and if the girls are willing to play with her once a week, I'd pay them. I don't want to take anything away from Marie, but Agnes is a different kettle of beans."

"And everyone needs to experience those beans," Polly said.

"It would also be great if Gillian could experience being around a baby."

That set Polly back. "Why?"

Lexi had been spreading butter across the sliced bread. She

stopped what she was doing, looked at Polly and then gasped. "No. Not that. I've seen her with Sal's little ones and she's afraid of them. She isn't afraid of Delia, but that's because they're together all the time. Little Patrick is something to be ignored, not enjoyed. If babies are going to be part of our neighborhood, I want her to be comfortable with them."

"Just so babies aren't showing up in our house," Polly said.

"You know," Lexi said, "I never intended to have children. I planned to live a solitary life in the ivory towers of academia. I didn't grow up around little ones either, and my mother was not what you'd call a nurturing soul. Before I showed up in your life, I had no idea how I was going to take care of a baby, much less a toddler and whatever else comes next."

"You figured it out."

"Because you told me I could," Lexi replied with a laugh.

"I know you told Andrea that you changed your mind about your career path, but do you ever regret not continuing with your education?"

"I am continuing my education. That's the thing. I really am grateful to independently learn the way that I want to learn. As for regrets, no. I have none. How can I regret anything that brought me to where I am now? That would be foolish." Lexi stared at Polly. "You taught me that, too."

Dogs rushed to the outside door, barking and yipping.

"Kids are home," Polly said. She laughed. "Duh."

JaRon and Zachary were the first into the house, laughing as they were slobbered over by four happy dogs.

"Let them outside, would you?" Polly asked.

JaRon stopped to put his things into his cubby. "Ask me what we did today."

"What did you do today?" Polly responded.

"We worked on a newspaper. We had to choose someone in the school to interview. I did that last week."

"You didn't tell me. Who did you interview?"

"Mrs. Jones in the office. She told me lots of secrets about how she does things."

"Secrets?" Polly pointed at the glass doors. "Dogs, please."

He nodded and walked backward. "Like the way she talks to teachers when she needs a student to come to the office. And she has a candy dish hidden in a drawer for when students are upset. But not if they're really upset and need to see the counselor. Just a little upset. And she has a secret buzzer for Mr. Gordon when there's a problem he needs to deal with. Because sometimes the problem in the hallway is bigger than the problem in his office."

"I didn't know that schools had problems," Polly said. "How is that possible? Aren't you all perfect children?"

"Mom," JaRon said with disgust. "You know better than that. We aren't even perfect when we're home. Georgia, go outside!"

Noah's little dog wandered toward him, looking back toward the door. Though Georgia knew that Noah came home later than the others, she was always hopeful.

"He'll be here later. Go outside, please," JaRon said. When she sat down in front of him, he picked her up and walked down the steps, then put her on the patio. Before she could race him back inside, he closed the patio doors and came back to the island.

"Will I be able to see a copy of the newspaper?" Polly asked.

"They're going to post it online for our parents. But guess what?"

"What?"

"They put my article on the front page."

"Congratulations!" Polly lifted her right hand and JaRon high-fived her. "I think we should celebrate that tonight."

"How?"

"I don't know. What would you like?"

"Ice cream?" He looked at her with hope in his eyes.

"Ice cream it is." Polly glanced at Lexi. "Tell me we have plenty of ingredients."

"Someone needs to bring milk from the refrigerator in the storage room, but we have plenty of everything." Lexi smiled at JaRon. "Congratulations to you. That's awesome."

CHAPTER TWELVE

Leaving early had been Polly's idea. Henry hadn't been thrilled, but he didn't argue. However, he did give her a bit of trouble. "We're going to be early," he said.

"That's okay," Polly said. "We can drive around campus. You can show me all the places you used to take girls to make out."

He burst out laughing. "That's so me. Reckless and thoughtless."

"What? We've done some crazy things."

"Not like the Ogdens."

"They aren't so crazy now with four kids in the house. Sal is a respected member of the community. It wouldn't do for them to climb all over each other in public. Wouldn't it be embarrassing to be caught?"

"It's hard for me to believe they ..." He shook his head. "Don't want to think about it. No one needs those images in their mind. Horrifying."

"You're funny." Polly's phone buzzed with a call. "It's Rebecca. Wonder what's up?"

"Polly, I can't find Beryl," Rebecca said.

"What does that mean?"

"She was coming down this afternoon. I planned to take her to see my show. She hasn't shown up and it's, like an hour after we were supposed to meet."

"Have you called her?"

"Duh. Over and over. No answer. What should I do?"

"That's weird."

"I'm scared. She never drives to Des Moines by herself. I told her to come down with you guys, but she wanted to run in and run out and not bother anyone. I just knew this would happen. Beryl's the worst when it comes to driving in a city. She's either lost or was in a wreck or … maybe someone kidnapped her."

"Don't let your imagination lose control," Polly said. "Beryl might not be good at directions, but she's excellent at finding her way out of problems. She'll stop somewhere and ask for help."

"Unless she's dead in a ditch."

"It didn't happen on her trip down here. We'd have seen signs. And if she was dead, who would be the person to find her?"

"I'm being ridiculous, but this woman needs a keeper."

"And that's exactly what she's hiring you to do this summer."

"Two weeks, Polly. Two weeks and I'd have been there to take her anywhere she wants to go, but I had to insist that she come see my work. I thought she'd bring Andy or Lydia or even you. What was she thinking?"

"That she's a grownup and can do grownup things."

"She can't do this."

Henry nodded in agreement.

"We're on the north side of Grimes," Polly said. "We'll be to you shortly. Is Andrew there?"

"Yes. At least he showed up when he said he would. I'm really worried."

"So am I. When we get to you, we'll try to figure this out. She's only lost, not dead in a ditch."

"I hate it when I have to worry about people," Rebecca said.

"Get used to it. That's life as an adult."

"Then I'm turning in my adulting card. When I didn't hear

from Andrew last fall, I thought I was going to lose my mind. I can't keep doing this."

"It's not easy caring about people. The more people you love, the more people you care about. This is why I appreciate your texts when you travel."

"Got it," Rebecca said. "I'm going to hang up and try calling her again. Let me know when you're close. Maybe we can drive around and find her car. She knew right where to go, so …" Rebecca trailed off. "Oh, who knows. That woman is going to be the death of me."

"And Lydia, and Andy, and me, and everyone else who loves her. I won't tell you to stop worrying, but you need to believe that she's okay."

"I'll try. See you later." Rebecca ended the call.

Henry tapped his fingers on the steering wheel. "Now what?"

"I don't know," Polly said. "Beryl would be embarrassed about getting lost. Admitting it to Lydia or Andy would only get her into trouble. They'd never allow her to leave town alone again. Who else would she ask for help?"

"You."

"I hope so."

"Maybe her car broke down."

Polly shook her head. "That doesn't sound like Beryl. She makes sure that it's in good running order."

"Anything could happen. Maybe she was hit by another car. Maybe she was arrested for something."

"Maybe, shmaybe," Polly said. "Beryl is lost and doesn't know how to find her way out of the situation she's gotten herself into. Let's not make trouble where there is no trouble."

"I wouldn't even know where to begin to look," Henry said. "We could drive for days and never find her."

"Twenty-four hours and we call the Des Moines police. They can help us."

"Aaron can call the police down here," Henry said. "He'd have more pull. By then, you'd have to tell Lydia something."

Polly's phone buzzed with another call. "Rebecca is in panic mode," she said. But the number wasn't one she recognized, so she picked it up and tentatively said, "Hello?"

"Help me," Beryl said.

"Where are you?"

"I'm lost. I'm at a gas station and the nice girl here let me make a couple of calls. My phone isn't in my bag. I don't know where it is. I don't remember anyone's phone number, so I asked for help."

"Rebecca is worried sick. Let me talk to the girl who is helping you and find out where you are. We'll come get you."

"She hasn't called Lydia, has she?"

"Only me. We're here to help."

"Then here's my new best friend, Allie," Beryl said.

"Hello?" a young voice said.

"Allie? Hi. Thank you for helping our friend. Can you tell me where you're located?"

"Fifty-eighth, well, Merle Hay Road and Hickman. Do you know where that is?"

Henry rolled his eyes and nodded. Even Polly knew enough about the streets in Des Moines, she could find it without trouble. "I do. Tell Beryl to buy herself a coffee and donut. We should be there within ten or fifteen minutes. Thank you so much."

"No problem. She's a nice lady."

"She's amazing."

"Here she is."

Beryl came back on the phone. "You can find me?"

"We know exactly where you are. We'll be there soon."

"I'm sorry to be such a problem."

"You know what? You are an amazing woman. We all have things that trip us up. If your worst thing is that you get lost, then Henry, Rebecca, Andrew, and I will always be there to find you."

"I should have made sure I had my phone."

"I'm not judging you," Polly said. "Stop beating yourself up. Things happen and we make the best of them. I'm glad you found someone who could help. Buy yourself a drink and a treat. I want to call Rebecca to assure her that you aren't dead in a ditch. Before you know it, you'll be on your way to see her."

"I've messed up the gallery tour she was going to give me. I only wanted to spend time with her around her birthday."

"Stop it," Polly said. "Everything will work out. You're fine. I love you and Rebecca will hug you until your stuffing comes out. We'll be there soon."

"Thank you," Beryl replied, her voice choked with emotion. "Thank you."

When Polly put her phone back down, she breathed a sigh of relief. "I told you. Just lost."

"At Hickman and Merle Hay," Henry said. "A rather large intersection."

"I'm glad she stopped somewhere and asked for help. That's all that matters. Now I need to call Rebecca and calm her down."

"Why would Beryl try to drive to the Drake campus on her own?" Henry asked.

Polly put her finger up to stop him from talking as she made the phone call.

"What do you know?" Rebecca asked.

"One of these days you'll say hello first," Polly said. "I just heard from Beryl. She left her phone somewhere and she's lost in Des Moines."

"Where is she?"

"At a convenience store on Hickman. Henry and I are headed there now. Trust me. I'll either ride with her or drive her to you. She's done driving for the day. And that's not me telling her what to do. That woman scared herself."

"At least she's safe. I'm going to sit beside Andrew and cry for a minute before you get here."

"Wash your face when you're done with the tears. We're not beating Beryl up or making her feel guilty. She feels bad enough. I told her that you would hug her when you saw her."

"So hard she might pop," Rebecca said. "I need to cry now. I don't know how you do it with so many friends and family, Polly."

"Go cry. We'll let you know when we are in front of your building."

Polly took another breath. What could have been a terrible evening would work out well. Hopefully, Beryl intended to celebrate Rebecca's birthday with them at dinner tonight. Much as Polly insisted on not judging Beryl, she wasn't letting her drive home alone.

Henry turned off the interstate onto Hickman Road and headed east. In only a few miles, they were at the convenience store. Beryl's little car was parked near the front of the store, but Henry pulled in at the end of the row. "Do you need me to go in?" he asked.

"No. I'm not letting her drive."

"I figured. Go find your friend." He chuckled. "It's always a story with you people."

"This one you can't tell until Beryl gets past her embarrassment."

That caused him to lift a nostril in disgust. "Doggone it. I never get to have any fun."

Polly smiled, took her phone, and dropped it in the tote bag. "Brat." She walked toward Beryl's car and waved when she saw the woman sitting in the passenger seat.

Beryl opened the door, got out of the car, and rushed toward her. "I've never been so happy to see you. Thank you for rescuing me."

"Any time. Have you done everything you need to do here?"

"My baby could use some gas. I should have filled up before I left Bellingwood, but I didn't expect to drive all over Des Moines looking for Rebecca."

"We'll fill it up and follow Henry to Drake. You'll go out to dinner with us, won't you?"

"I'm such a bother."

"You are no bother. You're one of my closest friends and I'd do anything for you. Just like you'd do anything for me."

"I wouldn't drive to Des Moines to find you if you were lost."

Polly laughed. "That's one thing. Do you want to drive?"

"Hell, no," Beryl handed Polly a set of keys. "I've done enough damage today."

"Then let's do this." Polly took the keys and sat in the driver's seat. She had to adjust things. Skinny little Beryl sat close to the steering wheel. When she pulled up beside a gas pump, Henry pulled in on the other side.

"I've got it," he said. "Might as well fill your tank, too." He swiped a credit card and walked around as Polly opened the filler door. "This should only take a minute. Little cars. Bah." He chuckled and nodded toward the passenger side. "How is she?"

"Good enough. We'll follow you to Drake, then pile everyone into the Suburban. Not so early any longer, are we?"

"You're amazing."

"What does that mean?"

"You pushed to get out of Bellingwood, and we were here in time to rescue a friend. Sometimes I just sit back and am amazed."

"Uh huh."

Henry pulled out the nozzle and walked over to insert it into the Suburban. "This will take longer."

"It's okay," Polly said. She made sure the little door was latched closed. "Beryl needs time to feel safe. You take off and I'll follow." She walked back to the driver's door and got in. "There," she said to Beryl. "The gas tank is full."

"If I rode back to Bellingwood with you, would Rebecca like to keep my car for the next week? It might make moving out much easier for her."

"Except your car is awfully small to pack her things. Have you seen her room?"

"Maybe you and Henry could bring some of her things home tonight. You have that big Suburban. Did he just pay for my gas?"

"He's rescuing you. You have to let him do what he can when he can."

"Silly man."

"That's why I love him," Polly said. "I'm curious. How did you find my cell phone number?"

"Allie called Sycamore House after I cried all over her shoulder. We had to come up with someone who would know your number. With these crazy cell phones, I don't memorize phone numbers any longer. That was my worst panic. I don't even remember Lydia's."

"Smart thinking to call Sycamore House." Polly pulled out as Henry drove in front of her.

"Do you know where you're going if you're separated from him?" Beryl asked.

"Absolutely. He's in rescue mode right now, so I'll stick close. That will make him feel better about everything."

"You know that man pretty well."

"Sometimes I don't know him at all, but there are things I've learned over the years. Have you ever been to campus?"

Beryl shook her head. "Can you believe it? Rebecca's been here all this time and I've never visited."

"She'll be home in two weeks."

With a deep sigh, Beryl sat back. "I'm looking forward to it. You know, I'm busier than I've ever been. Too many of my out-of-the-studio activities have taken a back seat. I need her more than ever. I was thinking about it. If I hire Rebecca as my assistant, I can pay for the trips she takes with me. It would be much better if I had her along when I met with gallery owners. She'd get great exposure to the business end of it all, and I'd feel safer."

"That's interesting," Polly said. "It won't be easy when she goes back to school this fall."

"And if she marries that boy and moves to Iowa City while he's getting an advanced degree, it will be even more difficult, but I'm willing to work with her schedule. Right now, I'm looking at a couple of trips this summer. One back to Boston and another to a gallery in Florida."

"Florida? That would be a new experience."

"Florida in the middle of the summer. Hot and humid, but we'd make the best of it. Are you okay with her traveling more often?"

"With you? I think it would be great. The person you have to worry about is Andrew. He'll either complain or ask to travel with you. Rebecca is an adult now. I don't need to approve her travel choices."

"He's not a bad sort, but Rebecca is sleeping in my room."

"They're twenty-one," Polly said.

"So?"

"So, okay. That's a conversation you have with her." Polly pulled into a parking space next to the Suburban and took out her phone. She didn't need to call Rebecca; the girl rushed out of the door and ran toward Beryl's side of the car.

"You should lock the door on her," Polly said.

"Or get out before she breaks a window. I'll do that first." Beryl got out and was wrapped in Rebecca's arms.

Polly waved at Andrew, who came toward them. "She was a wreck," he said.

"She was a wreck when you were hit by that car," Polly said. "Looks like you're going to spend a lifetime taking care of her emotions."

"It's not that hard," Henry said. "You give them a little wine and a dog or cat, and they relax."

"I had neither. Is Beryl going to dinner with us?"

Henry nodded. "Would you let her drive home alone?"

"Nope. Rebecca would throw a fit."

Rebecca had Beryl's hand in hers as the two walked toward them. "Beryl said I could keep her car this week. I'll need a parking pass."

"Get a parking pass," Polly said. "We talked about it. Do you have things we can take home tonight, so you don't have to try to fit everything into her car?"

"I haven't packed anything, but after dinner, we could throw a bunch of unnecessary stuff together. Cathy's coming to dinner, too. I just need to text her and tell her that you're here."

"I'm always okay with it," Polly said. "The more the merrier."

Rebecca took out her phone and sent off the text. "Tonight will be fun. Thanks for coming down."

"We wouldn't miss your birthday," Henry said. He gave Rebecca a quick hug.

"Beryl, you take the front seat," Polly said.

"Because I'm old and decrepit?"

"Exactly. The kids can climb into the back rows. Rebecca and Andrew, no snogging in the back seat."

"Been watching too much British television?" Andrew asked.

Polly laughed. "It just sounded right. And here's Cathy."

By the time they got to the steak house, everyone had relaxed enough that laughter filled the Suburban. Before they were seated, though, Rebecca made everyone promise to say nothing about it being her birthday.

Until the server, a young man named Monty, asked if they were celebrating something. Beryl, with a sideways glance at her young friend, said, "A birthday. We're celebrating a birthday."

"Oh? Whose?"

"We can't tell you," Beryl said. "We've been sworn to secrecy."

He chuckled. "That's a new one. I hope the celebration goes well, then."

"It's a twenty-first birthday," she continued.

"So, a drink for the birthday girl?"

Beryl winced and scowled down at her leg. "I was kicked. By the birthday person. It seems we aren't celebrating with drinks. Except I would like something fun. How good is your bartender?"

Monty nodded. "Pretty good. What are you thinking?"

"Ask if he's ever made a Humble Pie." When her companions stared at her, Beryl said, "What? I'm twenty-one and I'm not driving tonight."

"You're the birthday girl?" Monty asked.

"Sure."

He took the rest of the drink orders. Henry ordered appetizers for the table and Monty took off.

"Birthday girl, bah!" Beryl said. "Nothing to drink for you, Rebecca?"

"Not if I have to pack tonight. I have a final tomorrow. No reason to fog my brain."

"One drink won't do that."

Rebecca looked at Polly for help.

"She gets to do what she wants," Polly said. "I'm not going to push her."

129

"And I won't either. This Humble Pie drink has been on my mind. It's been a while since I tortured one of Davey's bartenders. They miss me when I don't visit them regularly."

"What's in it?" Cathy asked.

"Depends on the recipe. One has applejack and whisky. Another has blood orange vodka, lemon juice, and Aperol. Either will entertain me."

"Did she do this to bartenders when you were in Europe?" Andrew asked Rebecca.

"I don't remember. We didn't drink much over there because mornings were early and evenings were late."

"We?" Henry asked.

"Drinking age is eighteen," Rebecca said. "You knew that."

He smiled. "Just checking."

"It's no big deal. I'm not really a fan of alcohol anyway. It bites going down and hurts later."

"How do you know this?" Polly asked. "I remember my first terrible binge. I was in college and whoo-eee, did my head hurt the next day. That didn't stop me from trying it again and again, but the hangovers were always there to remind me that I'd been a fool." She grinned at Beryl. "And I'll do it again someday, just because I've lost my mind."

After Monty delivered their drinks and went away, Andrew scooted his chair back. "I want to say something tonight." Once he had everyone's attention, he took a small box from his pocket, opened it, and slid to a knee in front of Rebecca. "I'm going to do this again in front of everyone at your birthday party, but tonight is special. It's your night. It's your birthday. Rebecca Heater, I love you more than you will ever know. It feels like I've loved you for a lifetime already. Will you marry me?"

Polly's eyes filled with tears and hers weren't the only ones. Rebecca had already been emotional, so this display nearly pushed her over the edge.

She leaned forward and put her forehead against his. "Andrew Donovan, I love you, too." They stayed that way long enough that Polly wondered if she was going to respond to his question.

"Of course I will marry you. It feels like *I've* waited my entire life to say yes to you." She kissed him.

Beryl blew her nose. "That was unexpected. What are we planning for an encore?"

Andrew laughed, sat back in his chair, keeping Rebecca's hand in his. "I could ask you the same question. That would raise a few eyebrows."

"I like this boy," Beryl said. "Now, let's see the ring he chose."

CHAPTER THIRTEEN

Each Friday brought something different since Polly rarely spent the day at Sycamore House. Today, she was back in her Suburban on the way to Boone. She'd received a call from Bailey Jenkins' mother. Bailey wanted to meet Polly and say thank you.

Last night's surprise proposal from Andrew had made for an emotional meal. Rebecca couldn't stop looking at the ring on her hand. Every time she did, she got teary-eyed and scooted her chair closer to Andrew. He put his arm around her and the rest of them made fun of the two for their googley-eyed love.

At the end of the meal, Rebecca returned the ring so Andrew could propose again at her birthday party in front of all their family and friends. Andrew begged the others to tell no one what he'd done. His mother would be broken-hearted to find that she had missed this moment. Rebecca was as uncomfortable with surprises and attention as Polly. Something small and intimate made more sense for her. Now, she would be able to prepare for a big proposal at their party.

They'd gone back to Rebecca's room and packed up a large amount of her belongings. Polly laughed as she glanced in the rear-view mirror. Most of it was still in the Suburban. She and Henry had gotten in late and didn't have it in them to empty the vehicle. The kids would help tonight. She smiled to herself as she thought about dumping it all in Rebecca's bedroom for the girl to sort through when she got home next week.

Polly's mind moved to other things. Seeing Bailey again. There were so many questions about the shooting. She didn't know how much information Tab had gotten from the girl. Polly was also curious about the conversation between Ray and Aaron regarding a possible hit on either Ethan or Bailey Jenkins. The whole thing was strange. Dragging that type of craziness into Bellingwood? Then she laughed at herself again. This wasn't the first time that craziness erupted in her little town.

Aaron Merritt was laid-back, yet he was the sheriff in a county that had more than its share of odd murders. He wasn't one to draw attention to himself or his department. In fact, he avoided publicity as much as possible. Aaron refused to be competitive with other law enforcement agencies. When everyone worked together, investigations went much more smoothly. That attitude had rubbed off on his deputies and staff. Polly was often amazed at how cooperative they were with each other. The few deputies who had joined the force and attempted to stir up trouble found that they didn't get very far and were soon gone.

"Call Tab Hudson," Polly said to her vehicle's system.

Tab answered on the first ring. "You're calling me, not Aaron. No body?"

"Not yet," Polly said.

"Don't even. What's up?"

"I'm heading to the hospital to see Bailey Jenkins. What has she told you? Anything important?"

"Are you asking for details of an ongoing investigation?" Tab asked.

"Bad Polly. I'm so ashamed."

"Good. At least that conversation is out of the way. Bailey insists that she didn't know the other shooter. But she has yet to give me a clear picture of what happened that morning. She says that she was running from her husband, who was furious at her for not having breakfast ready when he got up. She thought he was going to beat her, so she took off. The next thing she knew, she felt pain in her leg and then in her shoulder."

"How did the other shooter get into the house?"

"That's where she has trouble with her story. She either won't say or she truly doesn't remember."

"That's helpful. What about Ray Renaldi's conversation with Aaron? Were you there for that?"

"I was. Aaron likes the idea of a security company's executive living in Bellingwood. We could dig for information, but Ray looks at the world differently than we do in law enforcement."

"Interesting."

"Ray looks at the world differently because he worries about you."

"Stop it."

"He thinks outside the box, then."

"Not because of me."

"Polly, you're wonderfully naïve. Ray would turn the world upside down if he thought it would keep you safe. This time, it was because of a conversation with Tonya. They dug into Ethan Jenkins' background and, though he doesn't have an arrest record that would point to a hired hit, they uncovered friends and associates who live outside the law."

"And one of those people might have hired someone to kill Ethan?"

"We're investigating all possibilities."

"Do you think Bailey hired someone to kill her husband?"

Tab laughed. "That's one possibility. She didn't have control of their finances, so it would have been difficult for her to pay someone."

"She has control now," Polly said. "If she convinced the killer that it would be worthwhile to wait, that would work."

"Except she hasn't touched any of their accounts."

"What about the possibility of Ethan hiring someone to kill her and having everything all go to heck?"

"Another possibility. There have been three large withdrawals from their accounts in the last three months. It could be the cost of moving. It could be something else."

"We know nothing."

"We know nothing," Tab responded.

"I'm at the hospital," Polly said. "If I get more information, I'll let you know."

"The best part? Most people don't know that we're friends. She has no idea that you're the source of my insider information."

"I hope Bailey is as innocent in all this as she claims," Polly said. "She seems like a nice person who has been through a lot in her life."

"And you talked to her when she was in terrible pain. We count on the fact that you're a good judge of character, you know."

"That's so weird. Ray said the same thing to me. After allowing myself to get caught up in Joey Delancy's world, I quit trusting my senses about people. That boy really messed with me."

"That was more than ten years ago. Are you still the same person?" Tab asked.

"No. You're right. That worry just won't go away, no matter how different my life has become."

"I get it. There are things from my past that blow up my state of mind with no warning. Okay, you go inside. I am about to knock on the door of a woman who accused her employer of sexual assault. I have all the fun."

"Did he do it?"

"Probably. Why men think they have the power to do whatever they want with a woman, I'll never understand. Makes me insane. My first instinct is to punch those men in their nether regions."

"I'm glad you restrain yourself."

"So is everyone else around me. Trust me, though, the thoughts are always up there."

"I've managed a couple of those punches."

"And you have no idea how satisfying it is to know that about you." Tab laughed. "I need to go now, and quit thinking of corporal punishment for idiot men."

Polly made sure she had everything in the tote bag that she carried all the time now. Gone were the days of tucking cash in her phone case and rushing off without a care in the world. Having multiple children in her life required an entirely new style of travel. She carried everything ... just in case.

Once inside, she smiled at the volunteer who greeted her by name. Yes, this was still small-town Iowa, but it felt strange to be recognized at the hospital.

When she got to Bailey's room, the door was open, and the television was on. Bailey looked up, fumbled for the remote wrapped around a bed rail, and turned it off.

"You came," she said.

Polly walked into the room filled with flowers and balloons. "I did. How are you feeling today?"

"Better than yesterday. I'm not going anywhere in a hurry, but the doctors tell me I will heal."

"When do you go home?"

"I'm not going home to Bellingwood. At least not for a while. Mom and Dad are putting together a room for me at their house. It will take a long time for this leg to allow me enough movement to live alone."

Polly nodded. "Will you keep the house in Bellingwood?"

"I haven't figured that out yet. It's a lot of house for one person. Come on in and sit down." Bailey pointed at the single chair in the room. "I wanted to thank you for helping me."

"Of course," Polly said. She set her tote bag on the floor and sat, realizing she should have brought a gift.

"Your dog is amazing."

"Obiwan?" Polly smiled. "He really is."

"You named him Obiwan? That's cool. Almost like the force is with him."

Explaining her relationship with Doug and Billy when they gave her the dog was a story that didn't need to be told to a stranger, so Polly just smiled and nodded.

"I don't know what I said to you when you found me and Ethan. Did I say anything crazy?"

"Other than saying *good* when I told you Ethan was dead, you didn't say anything strange. Do you still feel that way?"

Bailey released the breath she'd been holding. She closed her eyes and nodded. "I was happy when he chose to move back to central Iowa, thinking I'd find a way to escape, but it hadn't worked out yet. My parents weren't certain what was going on with me and him. They would have helped, but he threatened to hurt them." She snarled. "He also threatened to kill their dog. That wouldn't have been the first time he hurt an animal. I had to bide my time and watch closely for my chance."

"What about during the day when he was at work?"

"Ethan set cameras up all over the house so he could spy on me. If I wasn't doing what he thought I should be doing, he'd call and yell at me. Every morning, there was a list of tasks I needed to complete before he got home."

"Wow," Polly said.

"It's unbelievable when I say the words out loud, but that was my life."

"I'm sorry."

Bailey shrugged. "It's over. I quit feeling anything a few years ago. I quit feeling sorry for myself because nothing was ever going to change. I quit feeling anything at all for Ethan. But I had to put on a show for him because if he thought I didn't care about him, he'd beat the heck out of me. So, I became someone else." She shook her head. "I didn't ask you to come down so I could use you as a therapist. I really just wanted to meet you again and tell you how grateful I was."

"Do you know who shot you?"

"Ethan did, I guess. That's what the deputy told me. I was running to get away from him. I can't believe he finally followed through and used that gun. He threatened to all the time." She shuddered. "Once he was so mad, he jammed it in my mouth. I gagged and gagged until he pulled it out. He kept yelling at me to tell him that I'd never do it again, but I couldn't say anything. Not with that in there." She pointed at her lips. "Why am I telling you this? I haven't even told my mother any of it."

"I have that effect on people," Polly said with a smile. "No judgment. I can listen and stay calm. I have a multitude of children in my house and if I were to react to everything that happened, I'd be emotional every minute of the day."

"Do your kids walk through the cemetery sometimes? I see one boy every once in a while. Walking with a dog."

"That's Elijah. He and the groundskeeper are great friends. Walking a dog gives him an excuse to visit Charlie. Did you meet him yet?"

"The groundskeeper?" Bailey shook her head. "I wasn't allowed to leave the house without Ethan. That's why I didn't know any of our neighbors. The woman to the west of us stopped in to see me. What was her name? Andy something?"

"Andy Specek. She's a wonderful person," Polly said. "One of my close friends. She's been worried about you. I wouldn't be surprised if you saw her more often. Especially if she knows you're willing to make a new friend."

"I don't know what that's like. I didn't have many friends in high school. Ethan was really possessive. I thought it was love. Mom tried to tell me that men didn't act like that if they were confident in themselves. I assumed that I wasn't showing him enough love, so he thought that he needed to keep me close to assure himself that I would always be there. Little did I know."

Flashes of memories hit Polly hard. She flinched and then shook her head. The man's behavior reminded her of Joey's insecurities. She had always thought she could make it better, not realizing that nothing would change his behavior. "I understand."

"How could you?"

"I lived a life before moving to Bellingwood," Polly said. "That's one of the reasons I'm here. A man much like your husband decided that I would make the perfect wife. He desperately needed me to be exactly the person he wanted. When I couldn't do that, he grew controlling and mean."

"How did you escape?"

"I tried to run away. I broke up with him, moved to Bellingwood from Boston, and started my life. The man showed up and kidnapped me, taking me back to Boston."

"No way."

Polly nodded. "I had friends who helped me, but he returned a few years later."

"He wasn't in jail for kidnapping?"

"A mental institution. And he escaped with a serial killer. The two of them came to Bellingwood, murdered women who looked like me, kidnapped me again, and well, all hell broke loose. It was a bad time in my life. No," Polly said, "that's not true. It was a hard time in my life. What I discovered was that my friends never stopped loving me. They never stopped helping me."

"I don't have friends."

"That would be hard. If Joey had a chance to change anything, he would have isolated me from my friends."

"Why do people have to be like that?"

"They're broken, Bailey. If you were anything like me, you recognized that in the beginning and thought you could fix it. That you were strong enough to handle anything. You were attracted to Ethan because he needed you."

"You're right. He did need me."

"We grew up in loving families and knew we could handle anything. But we can't handle mental instability. We can't handle sociopaths either."

"How does someone identify a sociopath? I honestly thought the whole mess was my fault."

"Because he told you over and over that you were a screw-up. The only person who could ever love you the way you needed to be loved was him. He'd buy you wildly inappropriate gifts for no reason at all and the next thing you knew, he told you that he was the most important person in your life. No one else could compare."

Bailey nodded. "Ethan bought expensive household items for me, expecting me to be ecstatic. I learned to be ecstatic because he'd break them if I wasn't appreciative enough. We had a perfectly acceptable vacuum cleaner and one day he came home with some expensive thing that would change the world. I hadn't asked for a new vacuum cleaner and didn't particularly want to deal with learning about all the bells and whistles, but when I didn't throw my arms up in the air and jump up and down with joy, he took it to the garage and destroyed it with a maul. Then he threatened to beat me with the business end of that maul if I didn't make sure the floors were perfectly cleaned every day."

"You have a lot of history and stories that you need to get off your chest," Polly said. "Would you consider seeing a counselor?"

"Mom told me I need to find someone to help me get through this." Bailey gestured to her arm and her leg. "By this, she means the fact that my husband shot me. She doesn't know the full extent of what I have bottled up inside."

"I know a couple of wonderful people who have helped friends and family. Would you like me to reach out and ask if they'd see you?" Polly wasn't certain that Grey would take on something this big, but the woman who had helped Jessie Locke deal with all she had built up was a possibility. She'd need to find that contact information. It was buried in her computer contacts. Polly could also ask Jessie. That girl was organized enough that it would be right there at the tip of her fingers.

"I should let you," Bailey said. "I've talked your ear off, and you shouldn't have to take responsibility for my past. I was the one who made all the mistakes."

"Not mistakes," Polly said. "Don't blame Ethan's behaviors on yourself. You survived. That's strength. That's amazing."

"There were days I wanted to let him beat me to death," Bailey said. "It seemed easier than putting up with another day of his crap. He always stopped just short of anything devastating. It was like he knew how far he could go. I was surprised when he shot me. He told me that he'd never let me die."

"He shot you to wound you," Polly said. "Not to kill you."

Bailey stared at her, then down at her leg. "I didn't think about it that way. You're right. And he'd have punished me for not doing housework while I recovered."

"You're lucky that someone else was there. Do you have any idea who that person was?"

"I think Ethan let him in, not knowing what was about to happen. It all happened so fast."

"No one heard anything."

"He always talked about a poor man's silencer. He told me the pillows on the couch would ensure gunshots would only be heard in our house. He thought the whole thing through, telling me all about how he could take me down and no one would ever know."

"And the other shooter?"

"I heard loud, like puffs of air, and I heard Ethan's scream and a big thump. By that time, I had dragged myself through the patio door. All I could think was that I wanted to get out of the house."

"You didn't get a good look at the shooter?"

"I didn't look at all," Bailey said. "I didn't want to see him. I didn't want him to focus on me. The only thing on my mind was getting out of the house."

"Good for you. If you'd seen the shooter, he might have come after you as well."

"Is it strange that the same morning Ethan decides to punish me by shooting me, someone kills him with a gun?"

"It's a coincidence, that's for sure."

"The deputy doesn't believe me."

"About what?"

"About any of it. Why would that man shoot Ethan?"

"That's a question that needs to be answered," Polly said. "Was it because he hurt you? Did he do something that angered someone with money and power?"

"He would definitely have done that. He was always making people mad. That's one of the reasons we left Davenport."

"What happened there?"

"I don't know," Bailey said. "All I know is that two months ago, he told me to pack the house. I couldn't believe it when he said we were coming back to the Boone area. I thought that he finally gave a hoot about my family. No, he came back so he could hook up with his former friends."

"Who were they?"

"People he knew from high school and from work. They were all losers, and he was like, their leader. Whatever he wanted them to do, they did. That's how he found the house so fast. And that's how he got a job right away. His old buddies made it happen."

"Do you have names?"

"I'd have to think about it. Ethan's contact list would have all their information. Does the sheriff have that?"

"Good question. If Deputy Hudson came by with a list, could you tell her if they were Ethan's friends?"

"Do you think they had something to do with his death?"

"There are too many unanswered questions. The more information you can give the deputy, the faster this whole thing will be over. When do you leave the hospital?"

"They're talking about Monday. If I call you, will you visit me at my parents' house?"

"If you want me to come, I'll be there."

"We'll have to be careful what we talk about."

"The conversation will be whatever you want it to be," Polly said. She put her hand on Bailey's elbow. "If you need help selling your house in Bellingwood, I know realtors. If you want to move back to Bellingwood, but live somewhere else, we can discuss that. If you would like to meet with a counselor, I will get information for you. If you just need an ear, I can be there."

For the first time since she'd walked in, Polly saw a glimmer of emotion in Bailey's face. "I can't believe you are real. I haven't had a friend in forever. Thank you for coming. I'll quit talking so you can go back to your life. I'm sorry I dumped all this on you."

"Don't be sorry," Polly said. She squeezed the elbow gently. "You've been through a lot and your life is changing now. You have an opportunity in front of you. It will take time to get through the morass of baggage you've held inside, but today is the first day. And if tomorrow is too much to handle, then the next day will be the first day. Your choice. Your timing. Your life. Don't let anyone take that away ever again."

CHAPTER FOURTEEN

Saturday morning. Thank goodness. Though Polly spent time overnight processing her conversation with Bailey Jenkins, she wasn't finished. She'd called Tab as soon as she was in the Suburban, and though they knew nothing more than before the conversation, Polly was unsure if she had gotten a good read on the girl. She had no doubt that Bailey suffered at the hands of her husband. Anita had contacted hospitals in the Davenport area and every one of them had records of her in their emergency rooms. She spread her injuries out across the Quad Cities hospitals, hoping no one would notice a pattern. The problem with attempting to avoid a pattern is that it becomes a pattern in and of itself. Several hospitals had recognized obvious signs of abuse, but there was nothing they could do if Bailey wouldn't willingly admit it and point a finger at the man who was beating her.

Polly couldn't imagine shutting herself down for so many years. Because it was unimaginable to her, she understood that she might not recognize that behavior in someone else. Bailey related her abuse with no emotions at all. It was as if she was telling someone else's story.

After all the women who had come into Polly's life during the last ten years, she should be more accustomed to a variety of responses. She took another long drink of coffee and shook her head. All the women ... so much abuse. Her heart ached. Though she'd had to work through all that Joey did to her, Polly didn't compare herself to girls like Stephanie, Shelly Foster, or Lexi. Maybe it was because she had a support system in place. None of them did until they found her.

Being that support for people in need was more important than owning businesses in Bellingwood. She'd like to think that she'd give her companies up in a heartbeat if necessary, but they were one of the foundational supports she relied on. A place for someone to work, if necessary. The income she took in gave her the freedom to do whatever was necessary to help others. From paying late electric and heating bills for families in need, to supporting someone as they tried to pull themselves out of a hole, Polly wanted to be there.

When her phone rang, she looked at the face of it and saw Rebecca's name. It was eight o'clock on a Saturday. What was her daughter doing up and awake at this hour?

"Rebecca, what are you doing up?"

"Drinking coffee as fast as I can," Rebecca said. "You'll never believe who just called me."

"At this hour? You bet your sweet bippie, I won't believe it. Who called you?"

"Kayla."

Polly laughed. Kayla knew about Rebecca's late-night habits. "Why would she wake you up? She knows better."

"She works all day and knows that I'm studying, so she woke me up because she was so excited. Polly, I hardly talked to her this semester. She ignored my calls and then texted me to tell me that she was busy. She wasn't busy. I've been worried about her, but I can't do anything from Des Moines. I hoped that I could talk to her this summer and find out what's going on."

"What's going on? Is it her boyfriend? I worry about that girl."

"No, it isn't Quentin. He's a really good guy. And he's been putting up with her ... " Rebecca paused. "... her stuff without complaint. She loves him. That's not it. It sounds like she hates her job. She doesn't fit in with her co-workers and they treat her like crap. She applied for different positions within the company and someone else was always chosen over Kayla. So, she took it all on herself and decided that she was worthless."

"That's not a good place for anyone to land."

"I knew something was up, but I have so much going on that I could never get to her face to face."

"Don't beat yourself up," Polly said. "Life moves too fast to regret every decision. Why did she call you this morning?"

"Because she's quitting today."

"Oh my. Does she have another job? If she already feels worthless, being without a job won't make her feel any better."

"She has two new jobs!"

"Really. Two? Where is she going to work?"

"In Bellingwood. Stephanie read her the riot act at lunch one day. That's how Kayla interpreted their conversation. I think Stephanie was worried. She was right to be worried. She told Kayla she was worth more than a job at a grocery store. Lucy at the diner was in on the conversation, too. She had a whole list of places in Bellingwood that might hire Kayla. One of them was the Antique Shoppe."

"Simon Gardner's?" Polly had no idea he was hiring.

"Yes. After they had lunch at the diner, Stephanie dragged Kayla down the street to talk to him. He hired her on the spot. She's going to learn all about antiques and she's really excited."

"That is exciting. Having a strong young person in the shop will help Simon, too."

"Kayla said as much. She is strong, so she can help with some of the bigger pieces of furniture. The guys at the hardware store always come over if things are too heavy. She'll get to know them, too. It never hurts to get to know more people, right?"

"A support system," Polly said with a smile. "I was just thinking about how important that is. Stephanie built hers, but Kayla slid out from under it."

"She thought she could do it all alone. Just her and Quentin, but that's not enough. Even I know that."

"What's the second job?"

"She applied at a bunch of places in town. She applied at the grocery store and at Pizzazz."

"Kayla would be a good waitress."

"But she also talked to Nan Stallings."

"No way."

"Total way," Rebecca said. "She's going to work for Nan in the mornings during the week and Mr. Gardner in the afternoons. I'm surprised Nan hadn't hired anyone. She needs someone else to help her organize her meetings."

"Be an administrative assistant. You did that for her."

"And I was always busy. When I wasn't around, Nan just took it back on herself."

"That was the job she did for Grey before she branched out on her own."

"I think she's been killing herself trying to keep up. Kayla has a lot to learn about computers and technology, but she's smart, and Nan is a great teacher. Polly, Kayla sounded more like herself today than she has in forever."

"Having two people tell you that you are good enough to work for them is a big deal," Polly said.

"We talked until she had to get dressed to go to work. Nan called her this morning and offered her the job. Kayla couldn't wait to tell me. I love that!"

"It was worth the wakeup call."

"Only because Cathy brought me coffee. Otherwise, I'd be grumpy."

"Not with good news like that. Does this mean that you'll start on your studies early?"

"Probably. I'm going to call Cilla later."

"That's good. She needs to hear from you."

"Yeah. I have a voicemail from her. It sounds like she and her mom had a long and loud discussion about Cilla's future. Like she isn't an adult and can make her own decisions."

"You still talk to me about your decisions," Polly said.

"But you don't tell me what to do. By the way, did Andrew really ask your permission to marry me?"

"It wasn't really asking permission."

"But he talked to you about it before he asked me."

"Does that upset you?"

"A little bit. Why do we need your permission?"

"You don't. But you understand how intimidated Andrew is by Henry, don't you?"

That made Rebecca laugh. "Oh yes. He's totally freaked out about us being married and coming to visit you guys. He's certain Henry will make him sleep in the office."

"Henry thinks the world of Andrew."

"You'd never know it."

"The fact that he allows Andrew to be part of our family in such an intimate relationship with the girl that stole his heart all those years ago should tell you something."

Rebecca paused. "I never thought about it that way."

"If Henry didn't love Andrew, the boy wouldn't be part of your life."

"Yes he would. I'd have some say in that."

"Uh huh. What's next on your agenda for today?"

"You mean, now that I have the whole day in front of me? I don't think I've ever been up this early on a Saturday. I don't even know. I do need to find some breakfast." Rebecca laughed. "I've never eaten breakfast on a Saturday here. They won't recognize me in the cafeteria. I usually show up at the end of lunch."

"That might have to change this summer."

"You mean with Beryl? Yeah, no. She's not an early bird either. If I'm at her house at ten o'clock, she'll be just out of bed. Sometimes she paints until the deepest darkest hours of the night. It's a good thing I have a key to her house."

"Are you starting the day you come home?"

"No. I'll be home on Thursday. Beryl said I could start on Monday. That will give me three days to put everything away. I don't want to get in trouble for having a messy room."

"It's messy right now. The kids helped haul your stuff inside and we didn't organize it."

"That's fine. If Kayla is around, she'll help me."

"Rebecca Heater," Polly scolded.

"Just kidding. I'm going to call Cilla when we're done talking. If Kayla doesn't work next Saturday, the three of us, and even Fiona if Cilla wants to take her, are going shopping for new clothes."

"For who?"

"Kayla mostly. She's all worried about being fat."

"She's not fat."

"You know that. Stephanie knows that. I know that. Kayla doesn't know that yet. We're going to build her up and help her find clothes that fit her well. We'll start at some of the thrift stores, just because things are so expensive these days. That way, Cilla can also buy new things for Fiona."

"And maybe a new apartment," Polly said.

"Really? Was that part of the conversation with her mom? That she needs to move out?"

"I don't know that Andrea wants her to move out, but if Cilla is going to ever ..." Polly stopped. "Not my business. You could take the Suburban. Maybe Amalee would want to go, too."

"That would be awesome," Rebecca said. "All my sisters hanging out with me. Okay, not all of them. The littles aren't there. Good grief, Polly. How am I ever going to fit everyone into my wedding party?"

"There's a lot of planning ahead for you."

"For us. We have a whole year. Are you ready to be wedding crazy this summer?"

"At least we don't have to look for a venue."

"Best home ever," Rebecca said. "We'll decorate the back yard and the foyer. It still might not be enough room for everyone to mingle."

"Then we'll talk to Sal and Mark. Their yard is available. Unless you want to move it into the cemetery. We can go that way, too."

"You are weird."

"At least you're awake enough to recognize it."

"One more question before I go. Has anyone said anything to you about Mother's Day tomorrow?"

"Nope. And that's fine with me."

"No, it's not. The least they could do is take you out for a nice lunch."

"Stop worrying. Henry isn't an idiot. He'll do something."

"He'd better."

"He knows you don't have time to come to Bellingwood, and we can't haul everyone to Des Moines."

"I know, but still."

"Stop worrying. These things aren't as important to me as they are to other people. I won't feel unloved because we don't celebrate."

"I get it. I need to take a shower and start this long day. Wouldn't it be weird if I was in bed by, like ten o'clock tonight?"

"On a Saturday?" Polly asked. "Be still my heart."

"Hang up now, Polly."

"It's Mother's Day weekend. Aren't you supposed to be extra nice to me?"

"I am being nice. I didn't end the call without saying good-bye."

"I love you too," Polly said. "And I can't wait to see you on Thursday."

"Bye, crazy mama person," Rebecca said, and ended the call.

Polly took another drink of coffee and glared at the refrigerator. She really didn't want to make breakfast for the kids who were still in the house. Elijah, Noah, and Caleb had left with Henry this morning. Her kids weren't old enough to have regular jobs, but they all loved doing what they did and were out of bed and moving on Saturday mornings so they didn't miss anything.

"Good morning," Amalee said. She was dressed in shorts and a sweatshirt, her eyes were still sleepy, and her hair was a mess.

"You look like you've been up for hours," Polly said. "No work today?"

"I didn't sleep very well last night, and no, I'm not on the schedule this week."

"What's up?"

Amalee sat on one of the stools and looked toward the refrigerator. "I don't know. Maybe I'm worried about finals and then I'm worried about graduation and all that."

"I know you said you didn't want a graduation party ..." Polly stopped when Amalee put her hand up.

"I got a text last night from one of Grandma's friends from church. She hadn't received an invitation to a graduation party, and assumed you weren't treating me well. I told her that it was my choice. I don't want one. She didn't believe me."

"What do you want to do?"

"Hide."

Polly chuckled. She finished the last of her coffee and headed for the refrigerator. "Breakfast sandwiches, eggs and sausage, or pancakes?"

"Toast and jam is enough," Amalee said. "What am I going to do? I really hate the idea of having a party. I mean, I really hate it."

"Why do you hate the idea so much?" Polly took out a dozen eggs, two types of jam, another stick of butter, and opened the freezer to look for sausage links. All of that would be easy to fix. "How do you want your eggs?"

"My what?"

"How many eggs do you want for breakfast and how do you want me to cook them?"

"Over-easy. Two. Really? I could help you."

"Okay. Get dishes down for seven of us. The older boys left early with Henry. I think he bribed them with breakfast at the diner."

"When I work at the grocery store, I eat at Joe's Diner sometimes. I love their French fries."

"I love their pork tenderloin and onion rings. I'll eat anything, though. Now, why is it you hate the idea of a party to celebrate your graduation?"

"It's been a weird year. Grandma died. We moved in here. I don't have a grand plan to go to college or start my career. I don't want people to make a big deal out of me being done with high school. I just want to spend the next few months figuring out my life."

Polly nodded. "I'm not sure how I managed to have so many people in my life who don't like parties. I love hosting parties. Rebecca doesn't want one. You don't want one. When Noah graduates, he won't want one."

"Elijah will, though. He'll be all over a big party. How do I get out of this? She was really upset with me."

"Honey, I know it's hard to put your foot down around your elders. You weren't raised that way."

"That's for sure. Can I help with anything else?"

"Four slices of bread into the toaster," Polly said. "You and me? We're having breakfast without everyone. Once the rest of the family gets here, we'll feed them."

"You should make them all get up at once."

"I could, but I like the peace and quiet and I enjoy chatting with the kiddos as they make their way into the kitchen. A big rush and I don't get to spend individual time with them."

"You're so good to us. I hope I remember all of this for when I have kids." Amalee shook her head. "I don't know how I'm going to tell Grandma's friend that this is my decision."

"Is there someone else in the church you can tell? Someone who would understand and help you deal with this woman?"

Amalee tipped her head back. "That didn't occur to me. Miz Marion is tough and won't let people railroad me. I'll call her this afternoon. I just want this to stop before it gets rolling."

"You know they want to give you gifts to help you get your life started."

"I don't need anything," Amalee protested.

"I love you, sweetheart," Polly said. "You have spent too many years sacrificing yourself so that your sisters and brother have what they need. People notice that. For once, they want you to allow them to take care of you."

The toast popped up and Amalee accepted the butter dish from Polly. "I can't do it. Sorry."

"You know that we'll have a family dinner to celebrate."

"The whole big family?" Amalee's eyes nearly popped out of her head.

"I wouldn't do that to you. No, it will just be us. But there will be cake and there will be presents. The kids are already working on those."

"Homemade presents? That would be cool. I like cake, too. See, that's the kind of celebration that I like. My family." She chuckled. "My new big family."

"If that's what you want," Polly said, "that's what you'll have. We'll make homemade ice cream and cook whatever you want. I'll have Lexi talk to you about the meal."

"You make it so easy. I don't know how you do it."

"Life doesn't need to always be a challenge. We have enough of those. When you're home, I want you to feel safe. This is your haven. Even when it gets noisy." Polly pointed to the upstairs. The sounds of children clattering around had begun. "We'd better eat fast. We're about to be busy serving food to the hordes."

"Only half the hordes," Amalee said. She spread jam on a piece of toast and took a bite. "That's what I'm talking about."

CHAPTER FIFTEEN

Having a big family meant that Mother's Day wasn't going to slip past without someone noticing. Polly lay in bed early Sunday morning, listening to the sounds of whispers and footsteps outside her bedroom door. Henry had left the room at least an hour and a half ago, making sure no dogs were left with her. The cats would sleep, tucked in close, as long as she allowed them to be there. That was the beauty of her feline friends. They were always there, ready for snuggles ... and sleep.

She turned to her side and thought about getting up. It was still early; they had plenty of time before heading for church. What Polly didn't know was the plan for the morning. If she got into the shower now and the kids were ready to do something to celebrate Mother's Day, would she upset their plan?

No. She was overthinking it. Get into the shower, get out and dressed, and act like it was a normal morning. Any surprises they had in store were predicated on that information. But lying here with Leia tucked in by her head and Luke tucked in front of her tummy felt wonderful. She didn't want to move.

Showers were running, more excessive attempts at silent

movement happened, whispers and giggles occurred. Polly couldn't stand it. She had to get up. She also had to go to the bathroom. That sensation wasn't going to go away because she wanted to lie in bed.

"I'm sorry about this," she said, rubbing Luke's back. "You have no idea how much I want to stay here with you, but not today. Today, I have things to do, people to see, places to go."

Polly rolled away from the cats and got out on Henry's side of the bed. She readjusted the sheet and comforter in an attempt to straighten it. The cats weren't moving. "Fine, then. My fault. I'm the one leaving you. When I come back, you'll have no choice. I will move you. Sleep well for the next ten minutes, my friends."

Luke turned over on his back and stretched. He curled back in on himself, tucking his head between his front paws. Stinking cute cats. They didn't make it easy to walk away.

At least she felt more awake after a shower. Polly snicked the lock on her door so no one could walk in while she was naked. It was going to take a minute to decide what to wear today. Mother's Day. She was as bad as her daughters about focused celebrations. Only the celebrations that focused on her. Polly was much more comfortable celebrating anyone else. She'd put together a party for them with no problem, joyful at doing it. She did have a house full of children, though. It wouldn't do to ignore their celebration of her. She smiled at the number of kids she'd loved throughout the last ten years. For someone who made it into her thirties without bearing children, she'd more than made up for it. Every one of them was unique and important. How could she have lived without knowing these wonderful people?

She took a blue dress with white and yellow flowers from the closet. She'd gotten it in town from the dress shop. It had nearly jumped off the rack at her one day when she'd gone in to help Amalee find something to wear for graduation. The dress wasn't one Polly would normally choose, but when she tried it on, she felt young and fresh. Like spring. And spring was definitely here.

Lush green grass, the buds in trees bursting with new life. Eliseo was close to planting his gardens at Sycamore House, and two weeks ago, when Polly went out to the bed and breakfast, Judy's greenhouse was exploding with life.

"Okay, kitten-cats," Polly said. "Your sloth-filled morning has come to an end. I've given you as much time as I dare."

The sounds outside her door had died down while she was in the shower. Polly unlocked the door, opened it, and laughed out loud. Her family had been busy. Folded note sheets were taped to the door. Multitudes of crazy daisies, her favorite flowers, lined the hallway leading to the back steps. They'd placed an empty vase next to the first flower. She took the notes off the door, picked up the vase, then one by one, gathered the flowers. There were too many, but she stuffed them in all the same. Her heart filled so much that Polly couldn't help herself. She cried, the tears making it difficult to see.

She passed Lexi's door, wondering if the young woman and her daughter were already up. They went to church nearly every Sunday with the family, but this was still a little early.

"Happy Mother's Day," Henry said. No one else was in the kitchen.

"Thank you."

"Breakfast is in the foyer today," Henry said. "We have guests."

"Err, what?" Polly was surprised that he'd organized something for this early in the morning.

"We weren't going to fit in the dining room. Your kids want to tell you how much they love you. Let me take the flowers. You keep the notes." He took the vase from her, split the flowers up, and filled another vase.

Polly was surprised to see three vases with pink roses. "What are those?"

"You didn't want roses, did you?" he asked, concern in his eyes.

"You know how much I love these flowers." She brushed her hand across the top of one of the vases filled with daisies.

"Those are for Lexi, Cat, and Jessie. Go on, we're ready for you."

"How did you know what time I'd be down here?"

"You're ten minutes later than I expected, but we have plenty of time. Go ahead." He nodded toward the foyer door.

Polly wasn't ready. "I hate surprises."

"Too bad. Your family loves to do things like this for you. Suck it up, smile, and go forth, milady."

She pushed the foyer door open, took a look around the room, and pulled it closed. "What did you do?" Polly asked Henry.

"Not my circus," he said. "You can thank your daughter."

"Which one? The one who hates surprises as much as I do? The one who asked me yesterday if I had heard anything about a Mother's Day celebration? That daughter?"

"If by all that you mean Rebecca, yes. She organized the whole thing and swore us to secrecy."

"This isn't the first time she's done this," Polly said. "You'd think I'd know better."

"They all know you're up. It's time you face the firing squad."

"You go first." Polly chuckled. She was just making it up now.

"I have a couple of things to take out of the oven. I'll be right in. Please, stop stalling."

Polly nodded and opened the door again, this time to applause. Every single young person she had mothered over the last years was here. Stephanie and Kayla with Skylar and Quentin. Shelly Foster, still in her scrubs, sat with Marta, the woman who had continued caring for Shelly even when she wanted her independence. Jessie and Molly Locke. Heath and Ella. Hayden, Cat, and their little family. Rebecca and Andrew, Jason and Charlie. Will Kellar had come early to be with Lexi and Gillian. Jack Archer and his sister, Jill sat at the farthest table, but Agnes sat with them, beaming at Polly's discomfort. And then there were the kids who filled the Bell House with noise and laughter every day. Noah, Elijah, Caleb, JaRon, and Cassidy. Amalee, Teresa, Zachary, and Kestra. Delia bounced out of the chair beside Noah and ran over to hug Polly's legs.

"Did you see the flowers?" she asked.

Polly nodded and crouched down. "Did you help?"

Delia beamed. "We all brought two flowers and put them in a row so you would have a ..." She looked at Noah. "A what did you call it?"

"A royal red carpet." He smiled. "Or a multi-colored floral carpet."

"Thank you," Polly said. She looked around and spoke louder. "Thank you all for coming to breakfast. At this hour! I want to express everything that I'm feeling right now, but words seem to be misplaced. I am so in love with everyone in this room. Thank you."

Rebecca stood. "We did this to thank you. When Andrew and I started talking about how many lives you've touched, simply by being open to whatever came your way, the list grew exponentially. We could have added many more names." She smiled. "We decided that the easiest line to draw was to invite those who had lived with you at some point. And Stephanie and Kayla, because they are such a big part of your life. Do you see this? Polly, you are amazing. The thing is, we all know that we aren't the last of those you will take into your heart. And that's not scary to any of us because you've taught us that love is limitless."

"I don't have words," Polly said. "Other than thank you and I love you all. Those of you who have extended my family by adding to yours? I love that for you. You've given me that many more people to love. Now, I'm going to sit and look for a tissue or several."

She sat down in the first empty chair. Lexi took Polly's hand. "Your girl is pretty special. Those notes in your hand? I had a pile of them taped to my door, too. They left a vase with pink roses for me. Rebecca put it all together. When I talked to her, it was all about you, which was perfectly fine with me. Will planned to take Gillian and me out to lunch after church. But she surprised me."

"She's good at that," Polly said. "Happy Mother's Day. I'm proud of the mom you've become. Gillian is a lucky girl."

"One of the notes on my door was from her. It was a drawing of the two of us. Your family figures out how to get things done."

"Did you make all the food?" Polly asked.

"No," Lexi said with a laugh. "That was all Henry. He set it up with Rachel weeks ago. When I asked him last week if I should be planning breakfast, he told me that I was a mother and should take the day off."

"He's wonderful," Polly said.

Henry walked into the foyer with two large aluminum pans. "The cinnamon rolls are ready. I'm sorry that I didn't separate them, but y'all can do that. More will be out in a minute."

"Let me help," Heath said.

Henry gestured with his head toward the kitchen. "Thank you."

Scrambled eggs, sausage links and patties, bacon, potatoes, a large bowl of fruit, carafes of coffee, juice, milk, and water. And now cinnamon rolls. Polly was in heaven.

"You two go first," Rebecca said, coming up behind her. "That way everyone will feel okay about stuffing themselves with all this food."

"Cat? Jessie?"

"I've already told them to follow you. Move it, move it, move it." Rebecca smiled.

"You and I are going to have a conversation."

"I'm ready for you." Rebecca took Polly's arm and gestured for Cat and Jessie to join them.

"I didn't expect anything like this," Jessie said across the buffet table from Polly. "When Rebecca called me, I thought it was all about you."

"She's sneaky that way," Polly said. "How are you?"

"Good. It's strange being out in the country all the time, but I love my job. Molly's doing well in school."

The little girl perked up at the mention of her name. "I was in the play."

"I know," Polly said. "I saw you. You were wonderful."

"I know," Molly said.

Jessie blinked and touched her daughter's shoulder. "The proper response is *thank you* when you receive a compliment."

"But ..."

"No buts. Say thank you."

Molly shrugged and rolled her eyes at her mother, then sweetly turned back to Polly. "Thank you."

"I didn't know about today either," Cat said as she helped James with a plate of food. Hayden had Lissa in hand.

"I'm telling ya," Polly said. "Rebecca is a force to be reckoned with. That girl's mind is always churning. I'm constantly surprised, and then I'm surprised that I was surprised."

Molly laughed at Polly's turn of phrase. "You're funny."

"I try," Polly said.

She had just set her plate and coffee cup on the table when Shelly Foster stopped her. "I can't believe I'm here today. When Rebecca called me, I was surprised."

"You're part of my family," Polly said. "You'll always be part of my family."

"And mine, too," Marta said. "How lucky are you?"

Shelly hugged Polly. "I'm the luckiest girl in the world. Sometimes I look back at those dark, awful years and it feels as if that was a different person. I never thought I'd have any other kind of life. And now, that life is what feels strange. I can't believe I was ever in that place."

Polly held on to the girl until Shelly stepped away. "I'm thankful you had the courage to get in our truck that day. That was a huge step for you."

"I still have nightmares sometimes," Shelly said. "But if I make too much noise in my sleep, Marta shows up and holds me until I settle down. I don't know what I'd do without her."

Marta's eyes filled with tears. "And I don't know what I'd do without you, my dear. I'm so proud of you. We should let Polly eat her breakfast while it's still warm. The feast looks amazing."

Shelly gave Polly another quick hug. "Thank you for saving me," she whispered.

"Thank you for trusting me," Polly said.

She had just taken her seat when Elijah showed up, his plate heaped with food. That boy could eat. "Happy Mother's Day," he said, and sat down beside her. He leaned in and whispered. "Noah and I went together and got you something, but we didn't want everyone to feel like we were trying to outdo them, so we'll give it to you later."

"What did you do?" she asked.

"Just something. No big deal."

"Are you going to sit here and eat breakfast with me?" Polly asked.

He harumphed. "You all are boring. I'm going back where it's fun."

"Is that any way to treat your favorite mother?"

"She'll understand. It's what she does."

Polly gave him a hug and he wrapped his arms around her. It was awkward in the chairs, but they made do. Elijah would always take whatever affection he could get from her. He broke away and hopped to his feet. "See ya." And he was off.

"I know you're trying to eat," Stephanie said, "but I wanted to stop by and say thank you for everything. I've learned so much from you about how to ... well, everything. Mostly how to talk to Kayla when things aren't going well. Did you hear that she will be working in Bellingwood?"

"Rebecca called yesterday morning to tell me. Both of those jobs will be fantastic for her. Which one do you think she'll enjoy more?"

"I don't know. Working with Nan will be challenging. And Nan has already asked if Kayla would consider taking classes at the community college. Simon Gardner was very excited to have her work for him. You know, I think he'd planned to hand his shop to a child or grandchild. When that didn't work out, he decided to live forever."

"The idea of Simon living forever is a good one," Polly said.

"We're all planning to live forever," Agnes said. She put an arm around Stephanie's shoulders. "I don't see enough of you. You're much too busy being an important part of Sycamore House."

"I don't know about important, but I am busy," Stephanie said.

"If you ever walk our way, stop in. Other than Sweet Beans, we have the best coffee."

"Because you carry Sweet Beans' coffee," Agnes said.

"Yes, we do. You should stop in on one of your excursions through town."

"One of these days," Agnes said. "One of these days. Then you'll never invite me to visit again."

"I can't imagine that's true." Stephanie smiled at Polly and led Agnes to the buffet tables.

Polly looked at her plate and then at Lexi. "I should have known better."

"Than to put food on your plate? I could ask Rebecca to tell everyone to leave you alone so you can eat your breakfast."

"She'd do it. I should have taken only a bit of everything. I'd rather talk to my family. They'll settle down to eat pretty soon."

"Did you count the number of people here?" Lexi asked.

Polly shook her head. "It's a lot."

"I don't know how you've done it. I couldn't help this many people no matter how hard I tried."

"That isn't your thing," Polly said. "Your thing is taking care of me so that I can."

"I tell her that all the time," Will said, leaning across Gillian. "She's wonderful at what she does."

Lexi just shook her head. She wasn't any better than Polly at accepting compliments.

Rebecca sat down with her plate on Polly's other side. "Andrew and I are leaving after breakfast."

"Not staying for church?"

"We're both swamped. This has been a crazy couple of weeks. Every time I turn around, I have something else going on."

"Only a few more days."

"I know."

Polly put her fork down and peered at Rebecca. "Don't tell me you got up early to be here for breakfast."

"I'm smarter than that," Rebecca said. "Although this is day two of me not getting to sleep in. Luckily, my first exam tomorrow

is at one o'clock. No, we spent the night at Sylvie and Eliseo's."
She leaned in and whispered in Polly's ear. "She knows."

"Sylvie?"

Rebecca nodded. "We told her last night. Andrew didn't want
to wait."

Polly smiled. "Thank goodness. Of all the people, I didn't want
to hide it from her. What about his brother?"

"No." Rebecca shook her head. "The more people we tell, the
more chances of it spreading all over before we're ready. That
makes five people we can blame if rumors start."

"You gotta keep an eye on Henry. That man's a sieve."

Rebecca let loose a laugh. "Funny. He's known about today for
a month. Have you heard anything from him?"

"Not a hint. Your threats must be strong."

"When I added up all the people we had to invite this morning,
I was kind of blown away, Polly."

Lexi leaned over. "Me too. We keep talking about it. What a
crowd."

"Every one of them is important to me," Polly said.

Jack Archer stood behind Rebecca. "I know we weren't
supposed to give you presents, but I made this at the shop." He
handed Polly a wrapped gift.

Rebecca took his hand and smiled at him. "You make the most
beautiful things."

He blinked in surprise at her response. "Thank you."

"Grandpa Sturtz told me that he's still trying to figure out how
to set up a shop for you to sell your pieces."

"We have ideas and then they fall through. Maybe someday,"
Jack said. "And it would be cool if Jill could show some of her
photography."

"The two of you make art. Have you thought about showing it
at Greene Space? Reuben is easy to talk to."

Jack shrugged. "I'm not so good at that."

"I'll be back in a week. I'll talk to him. Would you have some
pieces ..." Rebecca stopped talking when she saw what Polly held
in her hands. "Wow. That's beautiful."

Jack had cut a heart from a piece of gorgeous striped wood. The center of it read, "She loves." But the frame of the heart was a channel filled with colored marbles.

"This is gorgeous, Jack."

"I talked to Henry and Mrs. Sturtz," he said. "Those are all the colors of the birthstones of everyone here."

"They're what?" Rebecca took the heart from Polly. "You found out everyone's birth month?"

"It took a little doing. Marie did most of the work. And you know, there are only twelve months, so I added extra for, you know, those months with multiple birthdates. I had to measure a lot so there was the perfect amount of space."

Polly stood and pulled him into a hug. Jack wasn't fond of physical affection, but he'd learned to take it from her. "Thank you. This is amazing. I don't know yet where I'll hang it. Here or at Sycamore House, but I'll find the perfect spot." She hugged him again. "Thank you so much."

"Thank you," he said.

CHAPTER SIXTEEN

"Are you available to help me, Polly?" Kristen walked into Polly's office, a worried look on her face.

"Hey there, what's up?"

"No hot water on the main level."

"Who do we normally call?"

"Eliseo." Kristen chuckled. "Then he figures out whether we have to call someone else."

"And Eliseo is ..."

"I don't know. I tried calling the barn and he didn't answer. I tried calling his cell phone and nothing."

"How long ago did you call him?"

"Just a few minutes."

"So he hasn't had time to call back. How necessary is hot water this afternoon?"

Kristen looked at Polly as if she were nuts.

Polly smiled. "Is Rachel in the middle of something?"

"No."

"Are there any groups on site today who need baths or showers?"

"We never have those," Kristen said. "So, no. I guess not."

"Do you need hot water?"

"Not really."

"Then we have a little time to bring someone in. If necessary, I'll call Henry."

"I could go to the barn and see if Eliseo is there," Kristen said.

"No, you stay here. I'll go down. This isn't a big deal," Polly said. "We'll fix it."

"Usually, Jeff or Stephanie will take care of something like this."

"I believe that I can handle it. Don't worry."

"They make a much bigger deal."

"Probably because they aren't here on a Monday when the place is quiet. Don't worry. I can handle it." Polly was already out of her chair. She glanced behind her through the windows to the barn. The horses and donkeys were in the pasture.

She walked out of the office with Kristen, but before she headed out the door, Eliseo walked in.

"Good morning, Polly," he said. "I hear you had a party at your house yesterday."

"It was a beautiful morning," she replied. "I'm not sure how everyone managed to keep the secret, but I was surprised."

"Rebecca hoped you would be. That girl is great at organizing things." He was about to say something else, but stopped himself. "Kristen. Hot water?"

"Nothing on the main level. Bathrooms, kitchen, nothing."

He nodded. "I'll check. Might be easy. Might need Hoffman. Sorry I missed your call. I have it now."

"Thank you. I didn't know what else to do," Kristen said.

Eliseo eyes twinkled. "When in doubt, call me. I'll fix it."

"Should I have called someone else? Jeff always makes you look at things first."

"I wasn't joking. Call me. It's my job."

Cilla came down the hall. She waved to get Kristen's attention.

"Cilla needs me. Thank you, Eliseo." Kristen went through the double doors and disappeared into the main office.

Eliseo shook his head. "Poor girl. She worries too much about little things."

"She was pretty concerned when she couldn't reach you."

"Man's gotta go to the bathroom every once in a while. That's one time I won't answer the phone," he said with a laugh. "I hear we're going to be related in a year or so."

Polly loved that he considered himself part of Sylvie's family. "I've always thought you should be related to me," she said. "I'm glad they told you. I didn't know how I was going to keep it a secret."

"It wasn't much of a surprise. Everyone in Bellingwood knew those two would end up married to each other. Only a matter of when."

"And for them, the sooner the better. To feel comfortable, Rebecca needs to know where her life is going."

"Poor Andrew," he said with a huff that sounded like a laugh. It was so hard to tell because his face never showed his emotions.

"Poor Andrew?"

"That boy is all about the moment. Rebecca keeps him on task, looking forward to future moments. I worry about what he'll do when he's finished with school. His schedule will no longer be laid out for him. He's relied on that his entire life."

"Rebecca will do the scheduling," Polly said. "For someone as creative as she is, Rebecca's left brain controls much of her life."

"That will be good for Andrew." Eliseo glanced at the door to the main building. "I should take care of this."

Polly nodded and headed back to her office.

"Hello!" Sal called out just as Polly made the turn into her office.

She stepped back into the hall. "About time you got here."

"I know!" Sal did a quick dance step. "I'm a slug. I should be fired."

"You're in a good mood."

"I'm always in a good mood."

"You never dance into work. That's an exceptionally good mood."

"Yesterday was a wonderful day, the baby slept through most of the night. I'm feeling alert and alive."

"Sleep will do that for you. What did you all do yesterday?"

"Mark was home the entire day. No calls, no people, no nothing. Just his family. He made breakfast and then mid-afternoon, he grilled steaks for us and hot dogs for the kids. My babies all wished me Happy Mother's Day, and I did nothing. I didn't even open my laptop. I did nothing."

"That sounds like a fabulous day."

"Let me drop my stuff in the office and get a cup of coffee," Sal said. "I'll be right in."

Mondays were a great day for the two of them to catch up. With summer drawing closer, they'd be outside more often. Sal and Mark's boys were old enough that they enjoyed being in the swimming pool they'd installed last year. Polly's kids enjoyed it as well. She smiled at the thought of Kestra, Teresa, and Zachary discovering there was a pool next door. Lessons at the community pool would start soon. If nothing else, her kids should know enough to be unafraid around bodies of water.

Mary Shore, Polly's second mother while growing up, was terrified of the water. She couldn't come up with any good reason other than the fact that she'd never learned how to swim. That meant that she insisted Polly learn.

Polly met Sal in the hallway and held out a mug. "Refill?"

"Lazy bum?" Sal said with a laugh. "Is there anything interesting to eat? Leftovers from the weekend?"

"Do we need to go to Sweet Beans?"

"No," Sal declared. "No, no, and no. If I go up there, I will never get to work. Don't worry, I'll forage. Do you want anything other than coffee?"

"I'm good." Polly went back into her office and sat in front of the computer. She'd gotten through most of the reports. They'd had a few great weeks at the hotel, which wasn't surprising given all that went on during the first two weekends in May.

Eliseo stopped at her door. "I fixed the hot water heater. We need a new one."

"Okay."

"It's been working to fulfill growing needs for eleven years," he said. "I want to purchase a bigger appliance."

Polly smiled. "Eliseo, I trust you. Order whatever you need. Hire whomever you need to install it."

"I can do the installation."

"No. Hire it done. That's the joy of management. You don't have to do everything. Other things need your attention."

He shook his head at her. "Now that I'm thinking about it, a conversation with Rachel and Jeff about other appliances in the facility might be in order. Rachel has had to call for repairs on the stoves a few times this last year. They take care of her, but maybe it's bigger than we realize."

"It's been eleven years of constant use," Polly agreed. "You should put together a replacement plan. I can't imagine not approving it, but I'd like Henry to have a look when it's finished."

"Good idea. That would make me feel better. You've owned this place for a long time, Polly." His eyes twinkled, a sure sign that he was smiling. "That's a big deal in Bellingwood."

"Businesses have been around longer."

"It's still a big deal. I've never said this to you, but I'm proud of you."

"Thank you," Polly said. "Now I feel awkward."

His eyes twinkled again. "I've done my job for the day. Kristen feels better and you feel awkward. It's a good day."

"Good morning, Eliseo," Sal said as she slipped past him into Polly's office. "Did you take Sylvie out for Mother's Day yesterday?"

"We went out to dinner with her kids Saturday evening."

"Andrew was in town?"

Polly smiled. "Andrew and Rebecca snuck into town to wish me Happy Mother's Day yesterday morning. They stayed with Sylvie and Eliseo Saturday night so it would be a surprise."

"And then yesterday, we took Elva and her kids to lunch. Sam had called earlier in the week and asked if I'd go with them. He's growing up into a good young man. The other kids are wonderful, too. I think he wants to stay on at the stables after he graduates from high school. He's good with the horses they board, and he's learning a lot about training them and their riders from his mother. It's a good life for a young man."

"Does he have a girlfriend?" Sal asked. She set Polly's coffee cup on the desk. "He's a good-looking boy."

"Gabby tells us that girls are interested in him, but he's so innocent that he doesn't realize what's going on."

"He'll figure it out when the right one comes along," Sal said.

"That's what I told him. Elva wants him to get some college. We'll see."

"A business degree would be helpful," Polly said. "That way he could help his mother with more than just the outside work."

"Elva would like that." Eliseo nodded. "Ladies, you are always a joy, but it's time for me to go back to work. Polly, I will work on the replacement report for you. Give me a couple of weeks?"

"No hurry," she said. "Thank you."

Sal sat down in a chair, leaned back and stretched out her legs. "I'm all about the relaxation these days."

"One day," Polly said. "You had one day."

"And I liked it." Sal sat up and blew across the top of her coffee cup. "There was nothing interesting in the kitchen. Sad days at Sycamore House. I don't want to work."

"What are you working on?"

"A proposal to take to the board about adding another wing with an indoor swimming pool."

"Wow."

"The pool across from Sycamore House desperately needs to be updated. Only the very basics of repairs and upkeep have happened in the last twenty years. It will cost more to bring it back into good shape than it would take to build new. We have the space for it." She smiled. "Or we will have as soon I sit down with Eve."

"She owns more land?"

"More than we'll ever need. Once the community center is finished, she's talking about building affordable housing."

"Eve Mansfield is completely transforming her father's legacy," Polly said. "It's exciting to see it happen. She is happier now than when I first met her."

"And she seems to like living in Ames. Her son likes his school and she's spending time with parents of the kids he knows."

"Really," Polly said. "That's wonderful."

"We're boring," Sal said.

"We're what?"

"Boring. I have nothing important to say."

"Neither do I," Polly said with a laugh. "We could talk about important books or philosophy."

"Or I could get my butt moving and go to work. Since it's Monday, I know you have things to do."

"I've been here since eight thirty."

"Well, lah-di-dah, Miss Top-of-the-class."

"You *are* relaxed," Polly said. "Go to work. Let me finish what I'm doing. If you want to go to Sweet Beans for lunch, I'll be ready and willing."

~~~

Tab walked into Polly's office. "It's good to know that you are where you should be on a Monday morning."

"What are you doing in Bellingwood? No ruffians to manage in Boone?"

"We have plenty of those. No, I was back at the Jenkins' house. Just walking through, trying to picture what happened. Why in the world was that killer there at the exact same time Ethan Jenkins shot his wife? Why did that person take Ethan's gun and the pillow? The wife's story is so filled with holes ..."

Polly interrupted. "As is her body."

"You're hilarious. The thing is, I don't have enough information to make sense of it all. I can't even make assumptions."

"Have you talked to Bailey again?"

"No. When I called, they told me she's being released today.

That's a big danged day for someone who's been shot. She'd be worthless."

"She was doing much better when I saw her on Saturday," Polly said. "Still on painkillers, but the heaviest of them are leaving her system."

"I'll stop at her parents' house tomorrow. I need more answers." Tab looked at Polly. "Do you want to go with me?"

Polly laughed. "The last time I went with you to visit a suspect, there was a shootout. Things got crazy." She was referring to visiting Frank Mansfield's home when his wife appeared to have lost her mind. Crazy family. All of them. The only reason Eve was normal was that she got out of that place before they destroyed her.

"I don't even know if Bailey Jenkins is a suspect. It's hard to pin a murder on her when she's recovering from being shot by her husband."

"But if she hired someone?"

"Weird timing," Tab replied. "Early in the morning before the world is awake, a stranger shows up at their front door carrying a gun and a silencer. He walks in just as Ethan is trying to kill his wife."

"I don't think he tried to kill her," Polly said. "I think wounding her was exactly what he wanted to do."

Tab frowned. "Why do you say that?"

"Thinking about our conversation on Saturday. He was fully in control, but bringing her back to central Iowa where her family lived made it more dangerous for him."

"How?"

"She had someplace to go with people who would protect her. By injuring her, he could assure himself that she was unable to negotiate the world without him. I'd bet anything that he would have taken her to a hospital in Des Moines or Ames and never told her family what happened."

"I see enough of this that I shouldn't be surprised," Tab said. "How broken do you have to be to think that hurting another human being is appropriate?" She nodded. "You know, that's one thing I haven't done yet. I need to talk to his family. Try to understand his motivation."

"What if they're just a normal family and don't understand his behavior?"

"Sociopaths aren't always created. Sometimes they're just broken inside."

Sal walked in. "Tab Hudson. What are you doing here?"

"Complaining about my job," Tab said. "Polly's a good listener."

"She is that. Even when it's silly stuff. Have either of you looked at the time? It's after twelve. We should be stuffing food in our mouths, and I'm starving."

"You are looking a little gaunt around the edges," Tab said.

"I told Mark that Patrick was our last child. It took much too long for me to get back to fighting weight this time."

"Like anyone noticed," Polly said. "You always look gorgeous."

"You think I should have more children?" Sal asked.

"I didn't say that. Do you want more?"

"I love being pregnant right up until the end when I want nothing more than to not be pregnant any longer. It doesn't matter, though. Mark has been snipped. We're finished."

Polly chuckled to herself. Sal usually told her everything, but this information was new.

"Don't look at me that way," Sal said. "The choice between me having major surgery or him having outpatient surgery was easy. And he didn't have a problem with it."

Tab shook her head. "I ended up at a domestic call because the wife wanted to neuter their dog and the husband thought that somehow it would destroy the dog's manhood. Are you freakin' kidding me? It wouldn't even destroy the guy's manhood."

"When fears and misinformation live in the same brain, it's a problem," Sal said. "Mark also didn't want me to deal with birth control. He's so good to me."

"We should all have a Mark Ogden," Polly said.

"You have your Henry, and Tab, you have your JJ. It works out well that way. Henry would make me crazy." She tipped her head. "I don't know JJ enough to know which of his attributes would get under my skin."

Tab laughed. "He has a few, but he's a good man and I love him."

"How would Henry make you crazy?" Polly asked.

"He's too nice. He thinks about other people all the stinking time," Sal said. "It's like he wants to make you happy or something."

"Sounds horrible," Tab said.

"You have no idea how awful it is working with that man," Sal said. "He listens politely, he never looks down on me because I don't understand something in a blueprint, he doesn't gossip about his workers, and when he thinks I'm making a mistake, he never says so in public. Instead, he waits until we have a private moment to ask if that's something I really want to do. The awful thing is, he's always right. But I don't feel embarrassed or anything. It's just his way."

"Horrible, horrible man," Polly said. "Tab, we're going to lunch. Will you join us?"

"Please do, Tab," Sal said. "We can come up with more heinous things that Henry Sturtz does to annoy us."

"I'm not involved in that conversation," Tab said, putting her hands up.

"You should be. Everyone should be. Imagine being married to Polly Giller. He does it and still takes care of others. She'd be a full-time job for most people, but not Henry. The man lets her live her life without trying to tell her whether she's right or wrong in what she does."

"The diner or Sweet Beans?" Polly asked. She needed to get Sal off this subject. Yes, Henry was amazing, but he'd be chagrined to know that people noticed and commented on what a nice person he was. If you asked him, he'd like to be thought of as a gentle tough guy. That was exactly who he was.

CHAPTER SEVENTEEN

Rebecca's text was all it took. Polly hadn't thought about Beryl's isolation since she had no vehicle. When Rebecca asked Polly to check on their friend, she felt awful. Beryl had too much pride to call anyone. Actually, it was worse than pride. She didn't want Lydia, Andy, or even Polly to think for a minute that she couldn't take care of herself. Somehow, Beryl was able to be honest with Rebecca.

"*Beryl needs attention,*" Rebecca had texted. "*She can't go get food and she can't make a trip to Sweet Beans to meet anyone, so she's hiding in her studio.*"

"*On it,*" Polly sent back.

Rebecca would be home in two days, but Beryl didn't need to wait any longer for someone to show up.

The first thing Polly did was send a message to Kristen that she was leaving. Not that anyone really minded if she took off. They were used to that. But it was good to let the office know that she wasn't here.

The next thing was to send a text to Beryl. "*Dress yourself. We're going to lunch. Do you want to invite Lydia and Andy to join us?*"

"*I'm grumpy,*" came an immediate response.

"*Get over it. I'm leaving the office and coming your way. It's either me or all of us. You choose.*"

"*What if I choose none of you?*"

"*Then you have to put up with me pounding on your door. Get yourself dressed up! And get over the grumpy. Or bring it along. Whatever you need to do. I'm out.*" Polly grinned and closed her laptop.

She headed to Sal's office. The woman had barely come up for air in the last few hours. "Hey there, you okay?"

Sal looked up, blinked and shook her head as if to refocus. "I've spent the morning going over numbers, more numbers, and then some extra numbers."

"Everything look good?" Polly was glad she didn't have Sal's job. The last thing in the world she needed in her life was to look for donors to fund all the projects that landed in Sal's lap. The woman was amazing. She was able to talk passionately about these projects to the right people. So far, things had gone well.

"Not good enough," Sal said.

"What are you missing?"

"About a million and a half."

"It's missing?"

"In that it hasn't shown up yet, yes. I need to get out and get busy again. The city has been setting aside funds to repair the swimming pool, and they're willing to discuss investing those monies in the community center. Of course, they want information that I'm only beginning to gather. And until they commit to it, getting other donors to commit anything will be difficult. It's the classic Catch-22."

"I don't want to sound flip," Polly said, "but you do know you're the best person for this job, right?"

"I'm the only person who will do this job."

"You're amazing."

Sal flung a piece of paper across her desk. "See that?"

"What is it?"

"An email informing me that a group of residents will be

attending the next city council meeting to protest any further expansion of the area north of Bellingwood."

"Because?"

"The town is growing too quickly and losing its identity." Sal shook her head. "It isn't enough that I'm doing the work, but I have to soothe change-resistant people at the same time."

"Hire someone."

Sal shook her head. "It has to be me. Anyone else would take it on the chin." She shot Polly an evil grin. "I grew up with Lila Kahane. My skin might be pasty-white, but it is thicker than armor. And besides, this isn't about me. It's about what's good for Bellingwood. I just need to ensure that people understand that every time I speak about the community center."

"I'm sorry you have to deal with it at all," Polly said.

"You have. You lived. And yours was personal."

"Not really. It was never about me. It was always about their fears. Once I figured that out, I didn't care so much. I do my thing. They do theirs. If they whine and complain, I just keep doing my thing. I still get some pushback and people still want to gossip about me, but all of that has grown quieter as time passes."

"That's because they have a new focus."

"And in ten years, they'll have something completely different to complain about while using the community center's facilities."

Sal laughed out loud. "You're right."

"Many of my complainers have ended up here at wedding receptions or meetings or other things. We make the experience pleasant, and it dulls their annoyance bit by bit. Okay, I'm heading out to lunch with Beryl."

"Are you coming back afterwards?"

"Good question. Why?"

"I don't want to stop. Would you bring me something to eat?"

"I was in the kitchen earlier. Rachel was making sandwiches for a noon meeting. Call her. She'll make an extra."

"You don't want to take care of me?" Sal stuck her lips out in a pout.

"I don't know how long I'll be gone."

"Fine. I'll make Rachel take care of me. She's pretty good at feeding the ravenous beast."

"Keep up the good work, beast," Polly said. "When's the city council meeting?"

"Not for another two weeks. I have time to prepare. Thanks for listening. I needed to say it all out loud."

"I love you, too." Polly waved and headed for the Suburban. The drive to Beryl's didn't take long and Polly hoped she'd given her friend enough time to pull herself together. A few words from Rebecca and she moved forward to change someone's world. Or at least someone's day. The girl had no idea how much power she wielded.

When Polly pulled into Beryl's driveway, she sent a text. *"I'm here. Are you coming out or am I coming in?"* It occurred to her that life had changed in her lifetime. And she had adapted. When she was younger, sending a text like that wasn't a reality. You simply went to the front door. Now, a text was expected. No one wanted to have their privacy invaded without notice.

In answer, Beryl opened the front door and waved to Polly to come inside. Then she disappeared.

Polly smiled to herself and headed for the house. She opened the door and said, "Hello? Where are you?"

"Come on in. I'll be there in a minute," Beryl called back.

May and Hem, Beryl's two youngest cats, had been curled up on the sofa together, but when Polly entered, they scattered.

"Not used to having company, huh?" Polly asked the empty room. "That's going to change once Rebecca gets to town. Good thing she already loves you."

"Who are you talking to?" Beryl asked.

Polly's eyes went wide. Beryl was dressed in a pair of wild lemon-yellow flowing pants. She had a bright multi-colored blouse, mostly oranges and yellows, with a belt around the waist. To top off the outfit, she'd wrapped a scarf around her head that came close to matching her pants.

"When I told you to get dressed," Polly said. "I wasn't expecting this."

"I needed to send grumpy away. Yellow always does it for me." Beryl did a quick spin. "Am I presentable? Nothing hanging off my body that shouldn't be hanging off my body?"

"You look fantastic. You look like Beryl."

"Perfect." When Polly moved her feet to stand up, Beryl gestured for her stay seated. "I want to show you something. It's a little unnerving. Don't tell Lydia or Andy, okay?"

"I'm not comfortable hiding things from your friends," Polly said. "You have to trust them."

"I'm old and grumpy. I don't trust so easily these days. Andy is forever trying to get me to change my behavior so that ..." Beryl shook her head in frustration. "I don't know why. It's getting old and makes me question myself."

"Tell her that."

"It will start a whole thing. She'll get defensive and then she'll cry, and I don't want to start in on it."

"And Lydia?"

"Lydia has always been that way about me. She is protective like a mama-bear. It's always driven me nuts, but I've been able to tell her to back off. Lately, it feels more difficult to say that to her."

"I'm sorry. You do know that you need to clear the air so you don't isolate yourself from your best friends."

Beryl flopped onto the sofa beside Polly. "Is that what I'm doing?"

"What do you think?"

"That's what I'm doing."

"You've trusted those two women with your life for decades. Now is not the time to stop," Polly said.

"You're a strange woman."

"That isn't new news. What is it that you want me to see?"

Beryl took out her phone. "I want to get rid of all outside communication in my life."

"That would be bad."

"This is an email I got the other day." Beryl held out her phone, then took it back. "You don't need to read the whole thing. Sorry. It's from my admirer. Ever since you told me that I needed to keep some of these things, I stopped simply deleting them. Before, I'd send it to the trash without looking at the content. That might have been a mistake."

"What did the email say?"

"That I need to rethink my artwork. That this person is watching everything I do."

"That's creepy."

"It gets worse," Beryl said, slumping against the back of the sofa. "If I don't do what they want, they're threatening to contact my galleries and inform them that I'm a fraud."

"No one will believe that. The gallery owners know you. They know your work."

"It gets worse," Beryl said again. "They know where I live."

"Are you sure?"

"No. It was implied."

"Is it someone who lives in Bellingwood?"

"I don't know. I don't know anything. But they told me that I couldn't hide from them. And then they finished the email by telling me that they'd see me soon."

"Is this a male or female?"

"The emails are signed with only two initials, J. W."

"How long have these emails been coming to you?"

"A few years. I don't remember when it started. I truly just ignored them, thinking it was nothing."

"How often do they show up?"

"It used to be every few months. This last year the pace increased and over the last three months, it increased again to once a week. Now, I'm seeing them every three or four days."

"Have there been threats in past emails?"

"I don't know."

"Will you talk to Anita Banks at the sheriff's office? Let her dig into it? They can usually identify a sender through their IP address."

"Their what?"

"I love you, Beryl Watson. For as brilliant and talented as you are, technology is not your thing, is it?"

"It's Rebecca's thing. I'm going to hire her and keep her forever and ever."

"She will love that. A good hacker like Anita can find out more information."

"Good thing she works for the sheriff."

"Exactly. She'd be dangerous if allowed to be on her own."

"Nah, she's too nice."

"You need to tell Lydia and Andy what's going on," Polly started.

Beryl scowled at her. "I don't want to."

"Yes, you do. If you need help, I'll always be there, but so will your best friends. They are friends because, no matter what, they support you."

"I'm properly scolded," Beryl said. She drew Polly into a hug. "And I needed to hear it. I don't know why I've stopped telling them everything, but it needs to end."

"Are they meeting us for lunch?"

"I told them we'd be at Sweet Beans. Should we hustle our buns?" Beryl stood up and wagged her bottom. "I'm hustling. You need to get with the program."

When Polly stood, Beryl pinched her bottom. "Waggle your tailfeathers, girl."

"Leave my tailfeathers alone. They waggle for no one."

Beryl hugged her again. "You are good for me. Don't tell anyone how much I love you."

"That secret I will keep." Polly headed for the front door and waited for her brightly colored friend to follow her to the Suburban.

Arriving at Sweet Beans, Polly parked beside Lydia's Jeep.

"Lunch is on me," Beryl said. "I owe you for more than just straightening me out."

"You don't owe me a thing. This is what friends do. Rebecca was grateful to have a vehicle during her last week of school. She's been able to slip out at any hour of the day to pick up coffee or chocolate. No asking for help, just going. That's meant a lot to her."

"She said that to me. If I'd thought about it, I would have given her my car earlier."

"She has a car," Polly said, "but there was no reason for it to be in Des Moines. Next year will be different. Rebecca needs more independence. She's really fighting the idea of not being available when people need her. She wants to be able to drive to Iowa City on a whim or come home without bothering one of us to pick her up. It's her senior year. It's time."

Beryl opened the door and held it for Polly, who went straight in. "No time for taking in the ambiance?"

"I'm taking it in as I walk." Polly waved to Lydia and Andy, at a table near the side door. The place was busy today.

"Is it crazy that I'm nervous?" Beryl asked.

"A little. Who are these women who have you so intimidated?"

"My best friends. Keep reminding me of that. This is all in my head. It's not real." Beryl pranced, yes, she pranced over to Lydia and Andy, then threw her arms around Andy's shoulders. "I've missed you both."

Lydia looked surprised. "Missed us? Where have you been?"

"Locked in my own little brain, thinking about only myself. Polly came over and insisted that I stop it. So, I dressed in my best and here I am."

"Now, I'm curious," Lydia said.

"You have a right to be. I need to tell you about things in my life, but you have to promise not to judge me or criticize my decisions or try to fix me or any of that." Beryl laughed. "How is it that at our age, I'm still trying to figure out how to be myself without worrying about the implications?"

"If I ever say anything, it's because I worry," Andy said.

"And you need to stop. I'm a big girl who has traveled all over the world. If I need help, I'll ask. If I don't ask, I will figure it out."

Andy looked as if she might cry. "I'm sorry if I upset you and made you feel uncomfortable."

"Don't do that," Beryl said, wrapping her arms around Andy again. "Don't get all empathetic and Andy on me."

"Andy on you?" Lydia asked. "Is that a thing now?"

"Look at her," Beryl said. "It's a very real thing. Now, let me tell you ..."

Polly interrupted and pointed at the chalked menu blackboard. "I'm going to order our lunch. Tell me what you want and while I'm gone, Beryl can fill you in on her life."

This conversation was between Beryl and her friends. Polly didn't need to be part of it. She took out her phone, made sure that she had their lunch orders, and left them to their business.

Because she'd been focused on getting Beryl to her friends, Polly hadn't looked around to see who else was here. When her eyes landed on Kayla, in a booth with Nan Stallings, Kayla gave a little wave.

"Hello there," Polly said. "What are you two girls up to?"

"Miss Stallings is treating me to lunch. This morning she started training me," Kayla said.

Nan shook her head. "It's Nan. Just call me Nan."

"I can't do that when I'm talking to your clients. Stephanie says I should be professional."

"When we're alone, I'm Nan. Otherwise, you can use the honorific."

Kayla tried not to let her confusion at the word show, but her eyes gave her away.

"The title before her name," Polly said. "It shows honor and respect when used. Calling her Nan is casual."

"I've never heard that word before."

Polly laughed. "I wouldn't be surprised if you learn a lot of new words while working for both Nan and Mr. Gardner. Are you excited?"

"I'm nervous," Kayla admitted. "There's a lot to learn."

"Think about how you'll feel in a year. Even in three to six months," Nan said. "You'll know more about how we work and feel more comfortable."

"I guess." Kayla shrugged. "I thought I was getting comfortable in my job at the grocery store, but it was like it got harder as I went along."

"Was that the people or the job itself?" Polly asked.

"The people. I never fit in. I don't know if I'll fit in here, but I'm going to try."

"You don't have to fit in," Nan said. "You need to be yourself. If I've learned anything in my life, it's that fitting in is giving up to other people's expectations."

Polly smiled. That was exactly what Kayla did. She adapted herself to her friends, to her job, to her family. Anything to keep from standing out. "Sounds like you're going to learn a lot from Nan. When do you meet with Mr. Gardner?"

"I'm meeting him tomorrow afternoon. He says that I will learn how to love tea. I'm supposed to choose my favorite mug from his shop and that will be mine to use."

"That's fantastic," Polly said with a laugh. "I'm happy for you, Kayla. I'm glad that you're going to be back in Bellingwood all the time, and you'll have a regular schedule. That will make it easier for you to spend time with your friends."

"Rebecca said we are going shopping on Saturday with Cilla and maybe even little Fiona," Kayla said. "She told me they're going to upgrade my wardrobe."

"Won't that be fun?"

"I haven't really bought new clothes in, like, over a year. Hopefully, they won't make me spend too much money."

"Are you starting with thrift stores?"

Kayla nodded. "Cilla knows how to sew. She said that if I needed things altered, she'd help. She learned a lot about fixing costumes while she was in college. Rebecca said that you sew, too."

"I don't sew clothing," Polly said. "I'm not that talented."

"Yet," Nan said. "Not that talented yet. If you need to learn, you will. Nothing can stop a girl from doing whatever she wants."

Polly shook her head. "Sewing clothing is nothing that I want to do. Quilt tops and pillowcases, curtains and other décor are enough for this girl. But you are right. There is nothing that can stop us from doing whatever we want. Good luck, Kayla. I hope you two have fun."

"You should stop in sometime," Nan said.

"Maybe I will." Polly smiled, tapped her hand on the table, and walked to the counter. The last of a line of customers had just been handled by Camille as she walked up.

"Coffee?" Camille asked.

"I have an entire order for you," Polly responded. "My friends are changing the world. I'm supplying lunch." She was startled by a tap on the shoulder.

"Remember I said that I was buying today?" Beryl asked. She handed Camille a credit card. "Make sure she doesn't pay for a thing. It's on me." With that, she walked away, her wild pants fluttering in the breeze she created.

"I love her," Camille said. "You never know what's coming next."

"That's the best part about Beryl. She will always surprise you." Polly showed Camille the order that she'd saved on her phone. "Is Sylvie back there?"

Camille nodded. "She's not busy today. At least she wasn't planning to be when we talked this morning. Sometimes I don't know if that makes her nervous or happy. Sylvie thrives on being challenged."

"I'll be back to pick this up." Polly pointed at the baked goods display. "We're going to want treats, too. Ring the food and drinks up. I'll take care of dessert."

"Beryl will yell at me."

"Or me." Polly walked away and down the hall to the bakery where Sylvie was sitting in front of her laptop. "Hello there," she announced, standing in the doorway. Walking into that space was asking for trouble. You just didn't startle these women when they were working.

"Polly!" Sylvie came over and gave her a quick hug. She whispered, "Can you believe it?"

"Which part?"

"We're going to be family. I knew it was coming. Why was I surprised when they told me?"

"Because they're still our little children," Polly said. "Nine years old without a care in the world, other than what was happening in the next few minutes. It's hard to see them as adults, making adult decisions."

"I'm more excited than I should be," Sylvie said. "When or if Jason and Charlie get married, it won't be quite the production that Andrew and Rebecca will create. They'll have the wedding at the Bell House, won't they?"

"I hope so. I've imagined Rebecca coming down that staircase on Henry's arm, with a long train flowing behind her since the day we moved in," Polly said.

"She'll be beautiful." Sylvie gripped Polly's hand. "Of all the decisions Andrew has made in his short life, this is the best one I could hope for. Your family is so important to us. You've been there for him for years. I would have hated for him to be attached to anyone else."

"I love that boy," Polly said. "I will always love him."

"That's what makes me happy."

CHAPTER EIGHTEEN

Excitement was in the air at breakfast. Rebecca would be home this afternoon for an entire summer. It didn't matter how many kids lived at the Bell House, she connected with each of them, and they loved her. Having Rebecca home also meant that Andrew was around more often. The kids loved him just as much.

Since it was Thursday, Polly headed for the hotel to spend her morning with June Livengood. She could only hope enough time had passed since she discovered Ethan Jenkins' body. Maybe June would have moved on from that topic to something that didn't involve Polly. The woman had a great memory, though, so anything was on the table.

The parking lot at Sycamore Inn had emptied. By this time of day, most of its overnight guests had already checked out. Polly pulled into a spot across from the front door and steeled herself for whatever might come. At least there was coffee.

Instead of seeing June behind the desk, Polly was surprised to find Skylar. He waved and smiled as she crossed the room.

"Where's June?" she asked.

"Her aunt fell last night and they took her to the hospital. She may have broken a hip. They'll know more today. I told June not to worry. I can cover for her for the rest of the week. How are you?"

"I'm good," Polly said. "I had myself all geared up for whatever stories she wanted to tell me and now … nothing. I'm not sure what to do with myself. I'll be in and out in only a few minutes at this rate."

"I hear that Rebecca comes home this afternoon. Kayla is excited to spend more time with her."

Polly nodded. "My kids were excited about it this morning, too. Can you imagine being the person who is so wonderful that your family and friends can't contain their joy at your return?"

"I have Stephanie. That's enough."

"Dang, that's sweet," Polly said.

"Did I do it right?" Skylar laughed.

"Especially since she isn't around to hear you say it." The computer she used was already turned on, the programs were open, and everything was set out for her. "Did you do this for me?"

He nodded. "The only thing missing is your coffee. I'll be right back."

"I can get my own coffee. You spoil me."

"I have to clean the tables, so let me." Skylar walked away and Polly settled in.

June never had things this well prepared. Polly would be in and out in less than an hour. What was she supposed to do with the rest of her day?

As she worked, Skylar moved around the lobby, straightening books on the shelves, re-setting the coffee maker and taking notes on the stock in cabinets. He hummed along with the overhead music.

The bell on the front door rang and Polly looked up. "Tonya! Good morning."

"I was heading to the gym when I recognized your Suburban," Tonya said. She nodded and smiled at Skylar. "You don't go anywhere without people knowing it's you, do you."

"Nope. If someone needs me, there I am. I haven't seen you nearly as much as I expected."

"Because you haven't gotten yourself into anything exciting. For that, we're all grateful."

Skylar let loose a laugh.

"He knows me," Polly said. "Everyone knows me. How do you like Bellingwood so far?"

Tonya shrugged. "It's good. I don't know anyone, which shouldn't be as big of a deal as it is. It isn't like I walked down the streets of Boston and saw friends everywhere I went. Ray knows all his neighbors up town and people talk to him like he's their friend. It's weird."

"If you live in town, that will soon happen to you," Skylar said. "I was a stranger and now I can't go anywhere without someone stopping to talk to me. It feels strange at first, but I like it now."

"Do you still plan to find a place in one of the cities?" Polly asked.

"Ray thinks I should suck it up and move to Bellingwood. He tells me that I'll be much happier. But how am I supposed to meet people? It's a small town."

"More people our age than you think," Skylar said.

Polly looked at him in surprise. She never really thought about how old he was. She knew quite a few people in Tonya's general age group. Maybe another party was in order this summer.

Skylar continued. "Stephanie and I are homebodies, but if we wanted to go out, we have plenty of friends we could call." He huffed a laugh. "Of course, they'd wonder if we'd lost our minds, but they'd meet up with us to make sure."

"How would I meet them?"

"You know Polly. She knows everyone. Come to a single one of her parties and you'll never be lonely again."

Polly shrugged. "He's right. Ray will be at Rebecca's twenty-first birthday party next week. If you're still in town, you should come with him."

"I need to find a place to live. I can't stay here at the hotel until I find a house to buy."

"We're giving Ray the friends-of-Polly discount," Skylar said.

Polly smiled. "Thank you. But Tonya, you could move in with Ray. He has plenty of space in that upstairs apartment."

"No, thank you," Tonya said. "I love the man like a brother, but living with him would send me right over the edge. He is OCD about the weirdest things. It's better for me to have a place to escape from his world."

"I'll tell him you said so."

Tonya shrugged. "I've told him. He did invite me to stay. I'd rather be in a hotel room on the main highway through Bellingwood than do that."

"Have you had a chance to visit the winery?" Polly nodded toward the southeast.

"Not yet. I work remotely most of the day if I'm not at the gym. Even there, I still work from my laptop. Has Ray talked to you about when he's opening the gym for regular customers?"

"Not yet. It's still not ready?" Polly asked.

"Oh, it's ready. Your son, Caleb, has been a real help. Cleaning and setting up equipment. He's a good kid. Ray has him lifting weights. Caleb is strong."

Polly nodded. She knew Caleb went to the gym after school, and she loved the fact that he was spending time with Ray. He wouldn't tell her about what he was doing, though. Caleb was so private about his life. Not because he was afraid of her or Henry, but he'd learned in his early childhood that it was safer to keep quiet and not talk about things. That way no one could make fun of him or take away the things that he loved. He'd grown since coming into their home, but his privacy was still important.

"He is a good kid," Polly said. She was proud to be able to say that about her children. After Caleb's close call with the law because of Ariel Sutter, he'd worked hard to bring his life together. "Where do you plan to look for a place to live?"

Tonya glanced around. "I want a cheap apartment until I figure out what I'm doing next."

"What do you mean, next? I thought you were in the Midwest for good."

"I am. Do I want to rent or buy a house or what?" she shook her head. "I thought I had my whole life figured out and then it went bam, straight into the toilet."

Polly had assumed something had happened to cause Tonya to want to leave Boston. "I'm sorry."

Tonya's eyes filled with tears. "We were married for nearly ten years. She died last year. I've been coping as best I can, but it's impossible sometimes."

"I'm so sorry." Polly hated that she was on the wrong side of the counter. She wanted to hug Tonya. "Did you two have a good group of friends?"

"Yes, but I isolated myself from them after Meg died. It was too hard. They moved forward while I stayed stuck. They lived the same lives as before, but Meg wasn't part of it. I hated myself for hating them. They went on with their lives while I grieved the loss of part of my heart." She shrugged. "I'm still not there, but I'm better than I was. I had to get away from it all and start again where Meg wasn't part of my life. When Ray asked if I wanted to come with him to Bellingwood, I leaped at the chance."

"I understand running from difficult things."

"That Joey guy."

"The thing is, I needed to have something good to fill my life. Otherwise, I was just running away."

"To save my heart," Tonya said. "That's why I ran."

"Your family?"

"They all still live in Massachusetts. They tried to be there for me, but I wasn't much good to anyone. The only thing I was able to manage was working every day."

"What was Meg like?"

A brilliant smile broke through the shadows on Tonya's face. "She was amazing. A psychiatrist and a talented pianist. She played nearly every night. I had my own personal concert space."

"Do you play?"

"Not in the least. That's the farthest thing from any of my talents. She dragged me to concerts and museums and plays. I learned about a different world from Meg."

"She sounds amazing."

"She really was. It took most of this last year, but I finally dealt with personal things that I don't need to keep. It was hard to find a home for her piano, but once that was out of our house, her clothing and other items were easier to pack up."

"It's difficult to not want to keep everything," Polly said. "When my father died, I had it all packed up and put in storage. I didn't have it in me to go through anything. It wasn't until I came to Bellingwood that I finally emptied the storage unit into my garage at Sycamore house and started dealing with it. And by dealing with it, his entire woodshop has been integrated into Henry's world. Dad's furniture wasn't a big deal, though I wish now that I'd kept his favorite chair. It wasn't all that comfortable, but it was his."

Tonya glanced at the smart watch on her wrist. After tapping it a few times, she smiled. "Ray is looking for me. I should go. It was nice to talk to you, Polly. Please stay out of trouble."

"You know me," Polly said. "I try, but it finds me all by itself."

~~~

Polly was surprised to see Henry's truck in the garage when she pulled in. What was he doing here? She went inside and when no one greeted her, stepped into the kitchen and listened for house sounds. They came from the foyer. She opened the foyer doors to find Henry and Lexi setting up tables.

"Thank you," she said. "I was going to ask the boys to help you tonight, but this gives me extra time while Rebecca is around to decorate and set up."

"It's been bugging me," Henry said. "Tomorrow will be busy enough moving pianos and doing the rest of the setup.

Sunday afternoon, they were hosting a piano recital for Jeanie Dykstra's students. It had grown enough that families no longer fit in the family room. Tomorrow, Len and Brandon were coming over to move the pianos into the foyer. They'd come back on Saturday to ensure they were still in tune.

Rebecca's idea of decorating for the recital was to turn the foyer into a garden party. They had everything necessary. The archway that had been used for different events would sit between the two pianos underneath the balcony, between the double staircases. Rebecca planned to wrap greenery with small white lights around the arch and the banisters. Flameless candles seated in wreaths of green would become centerpieces on the tables.

They weren't serving a meal, but trays of meats, cheeses, and crackers would be served alongside cheesecake and cookies. Lexi had it all under control.

Polly needed to bring down the decorations from the attic. Even if all she did was get them to the second floor, her big family would take things to the foyer. Having a large family of helpers spoiled Polly. It wasn't that many years ago, she'd hauled hay bales by herself. She made a fist and looked at her arm muscles. Not quite the same strength she'd had in those days.

"What are you laughing at?" Henry asked.

"Myself."

"Showing off your muscles?"

"Showing myself how much they've deteriorated since I quit hauling hay. Now that I have a house filled with children, I let them do the heavy work while I supervise."

"It is nice," Lexi said. "I get so much more done when I don't have to lift and carry things from place to place."

"Small brains, big muscles," Henry said. "Then they grow up and figure out that someone younger than them can pick up the slack. It all works out."

"You should see Rebecca ordering them around. She's a master," Lexi said. "I strive to be like her."

Henry pointed at Polly. "She learned from the master."

"Until you get them on your side, you can't order them around," Polly said. "I start with asking. Once they're on board, we move to the orders. They're good kids and know that if I'm setting up for something, fun is about to happen. Everyone likes to participate in fun experiences."

The dogs, who had been quietly waiting for attention from

anyone, jumped to their feet and raced through the open foyer doors to the kitchen, barking and wagging their tails with joy. Someone was here.

Polly followed them to find Rebecca coming into the house.

"You're earlier than I expected. Hello there."

Rebecca nodded and yawned. "I need a nap. The professor allowed us to take our final as early as we wanted this morning, so I dragged myself out of bed, drank a load of coffee, and was in his office by nine o'clock. The semester is over and all I wanted to do was come home. Cathy helped me pack most everything into Beryl's car last night. It's weird living in an empty room. She took all her stuff home this week. Nothing was left in there except my clothes for today and my toiletries." She nodded. "And my backpack and phone and stuff. But that was all. What are you doing?"

"Setting up tables for the recital on Sunday."

"That's right. I'm helping. Please tell me I have until tomorrow. I'm tired."

"Your room isn't conducive for a nap. Do you want to use our bed?" Polly looked back at Henry, who shrugged his agreement.

"Would you mind? I could go over to Andrew's house."

Polly laughed. "Uh huh. What do you want to do about Beryl's car?"

"I told her that you and I would get it to her tonight. Is that okay?"

"Good idea. When the kids get home from school, they'll unpack it all for you. Everything in there should go to your room in the basement?"

"I don't care where it goes."

"They're excited about you being home for the summer. Now's the time to take advantage of that."

"After I'm awake." Rebecca smiled. "It's good to be here, and I'll be up before they're home. I promise to be more alert and pleasant by then."

Polly gave her a hug. "You're fine. Finals are finished, your junior year is over, and you just keep heading for a big life.

Sometimes big lives require big sleep. Take some dogs and cats with you. They help fill up that big bed."

Rebecca held on and then broke away. She set keys on the island. "In case I'm not awake. Everything can go to my room. I'll tear into it later. Or maybe I'll call Kayla and ask her to help me."

"Amalee would help," Polly said.

"I should invite both to the chaos. It would be nice if they got to know each other better. Kayla barely remembers her from high school."

"That's not surprising. Now go sleep. We have all summer to talk and spend time together." Polly gave her another quick hug. "I'm glad you're home."

Henry headed for the door as Rebecca went upstairs, Obiwan and Han trailing behind her. The two smaller dogs, Georgia and Angel, didn't know her as well and would wait forever for their favorite boys to return.

"I'm going back to work," he said. "Don't want the boys and girls to think I'm a slacker."

"No lunch?" Polly asked.

"Maybe I already have a date for lunch."

"I hope she's pretty."

"One of the beautiful and brilliant women in town."

Polly blinked and then laughed. "You're having a lunch meeting with Sal."

"Such a smart wife I have. She's putting numbers together and I have information she needs." He walked back toward her and gave her a kiss. Not one of the spine-tingling, heart melting, stop her in her tracks kiss, but she didn't mind. It was enough.

"What are you having for lunch?" Polly asked Lexi once Henry was out the door.

"I hadn't thought about it. If you all aren't around, I usually snack on whatever I'm cooking for dinner. Or I just snack on whatever I find in the fridge. Did you have something in mind?"

"I can snack," Polly said. "I got home early today because June wasn't at the hotel. Usually when I finish there, I can make myself believe any excuse to head to Sweet Beans."

Lexi laughed. "That sounds good too. Would you like me to run up and order something for us?"

"We have lunchmeat and bread, right?"

"And leftover spaghetti. We also have that cashew chicken I made the other night."

"I didn't say anything, but that was amazing," Polly said. "What did your friends think of it?"

"I got good feedback. I haven't tried many Chinese food recipes. It makes me want to do more."

"The kids loved it. But then, you've trained them to learn new flavors. I appreciate that. Hot dogs and hamburgers would get old in a hurry. I'm going up to the attic, but I'd help you finish the cashew chicken." She looked at the clock. "An hour?"

Lexi smiled. "Maybe Rebecca will be up by then."

"Nah. That girl can take a three-hour nap like no one's business. She'll be starving when she comes downstairs, but don't expect to see the whites of her eyes for quite a while. She's releasing all the stress of the last week, along with the transition from college to home. When we see her, we see her."

"Okay. I planned for meatloaf and mashed potatoes tonight."

"You are so good to her," Polly said. She wasn't going to pester Lexi about today being her day off. With Rebecca's return to the household, Lexi had already expressed an interest in being here to welcome the girl home. "See you in a bit." She headed for the stairs and went up and then on up to the attic. It had been a while since she'd spent time in her craft room and gave it a longing gaze before looking for the boxes of foyer decorations. She had to move aside boxes and boxes of Christmas décor. How long had it been since she was up here? This place was a mess. Henry needed to build utility shelves in here so they could be better organized.

By the time she found what she was looking for and a few other things, Polly was tired of traipsing up and down the attic steps. She took one box and headed for the main level. Yes, her kids would help to finish that project this evening.

"Brownies, brownies, brownies," she muttered to herself over and over.

"What are you saying?" Lexi asked.

"Brownies. If I'm going to ask the kids to help move boxes to the foyer, I should reward them with brownies."

"Those won't take long to mix up," Lexi said. "If you want to heat up leftovers, I'll whip up a pan. That's a nice treat. I never think about it."

"One of these days, you should make a two-layer brownie recipe." Polly chuckled. "It isn't really a recipe. One layer of brownies, the other layer is chocolate chip cookies."

"In one dessert? That's sinful."

"We like sinful desserts. It's the only way to live."

CHAPTER NINETEEN

It wasn't always like this, but here she was, in the kitchen alone on a Saturday morning. Henry had to run out to the shop to do something or other, so he'd dropped Noah, Elijah, and Caleb off at their favorite spots. She would have gotten up to make them breakfast, but one of their favorite things to do together was go to Joe's Diner. Who was she to interrupt that tradition? As long as the boys were up and moving on time, off they went. Henry wasn't above leaving one or the other to their own devices if they weren't ready to go when the truck left the house. It wasn't like Bellingwood was such a big town that the kids couldn't get where they wanted to be in a few minutes, but they all enjoyed feeling special while sitting with their father amidst his friends and associates.

Polly also credited her peaceful Saturday mornings to Lexi. She wasn't a morning person, but she was always awake because her daughter was up and ready to go. Delia had learned that on Saturdays, if she knocked on Gillian's apartment door, she could hang out in her pajamas with the older girl and watch television while snacking on fruit that Lexi kept upstairs for the girls. By the time they all came downstairs, they were ready for the day to start. If Polly remembered to set out clothes for Delia the night before, her youngest daughter would dress herself at some point in the morning. It was good to train children into independence. Especially when so many lived under one roof.

She was glad to have Rebecca home. Yesterday had been a fun day at the Bell House. Rebecca hadn't gotten out of bed until after ten o'clock, but that was normal behavior for the girl. Fortunately for her, Beryl ran on a similar clock, so Rebecca would rarely be expected to show up for work early in the morning.

Len and Brandon arrived at one o'clock to move pianos from the living room to the foyer. Thank goodness for double doors. It made things much easier when it came to those big pianos. Henry had wanted to be home for the transition, but something came up with a client and he was required to intervene. The pianos were on rollers, so it hadn't been difficult for two men to do the work. Len would be back this afternoon, bringing Elijah with him, to ensure the pianos were tuned for tomorrow's recital.

After they left, Rebecca went to work on the foyer's décor, transforming the room into a beautiful space with garlands of greenery and white lights hung around the room. Rebecca had a terrific eye and it occurred to Polly that she should be paid for the work. She'd make that happen today. Especially since Rebecca was taking her friends shopping. The trip was mostly for Kayla, who, as Rebecca said, desperately needed to upgrade her wardrobe for the professional world. Cilla and Amalee were going along for a fun day.

Last night, Rebecca invited Kayla to help clean and organize the mess that had been dumped in her bedroom. Amalee was asked to be part of the event as well. They spent several hours sorting, doing laundry, taking out trash, and organizing Rebecca's room. Rebecca said she felt like she was finally at home.

Polly remembered the days of going back and forth from college to her home. Since Boston was a long flight from Iowa, she didn't carry everything home each summer, but she grew weary of feeling like a nomad.

She looked around and laughed. No more nomadic life for her. She was well settled into her home. Even going to the vacation home they shared with Mark and Sal Ogden for a long weekend didn't disrupt her sense of home. They had filled the place with blankets and pillows, artwork and family treasures, toys and games.

Sal had taken to going by herself just to find some quiet in the midst of her newly chaotic life. She generally took Patrick and Betsy-Kate, knowing that Mark and his two oldest boys had fun together. With Alexander and Theodore both in school during the day, it was easy for him to pick them up, take them to the vet clinic, or out with him on a call.

The Sturtz kids were too busy with their lives to really enjoy spending time in the country. They had friends and activities. Leaving it all behind wasn't something they enjoyed. It would come. Heath and Ella, Hayden and Cat with their family, and even Marie and Bill had found time to escape this last year. The home was well-used and well cared for.

Polly heard footsteps coming up from the basement and glanced at her phone to check the time. What in the world?

Rebecca walked in, her hair mussed from sleeping, wearing shorts and a t-shirt under a robe, and rubbing her eyes.

"What are you doing up at this hour?" Polly asked.

"Texts from everybody. Kayla should know better. Cilla should know better. They want to get started on the day. Are you kidding me?" Rebecca dramatically draped herself across the island. "Are they kidding me!"

"Sounds like they aren't. Would coffee help?"

"It's my only hope."

Polly chuckled and walked over to the coffee pot. They heard footsteps on the stairway coming down from the second floor and soon, Amalee was with them in the kitchen.

"You're awake," she said to Rebecca. "What is it with your friends and Saturday mornings?"

"They grew up better than me," Rebecca said. She hadn't yet lifted her head, but stuck her hand out across the island for the coffee. "Help me, please." Then she looked at Amalee, who was showered, dressed and ready for the day. "Who are you and why do you live in my house?"

Amalee laughed. "I'm your worst nightmare in the early hours of the morning. I don't mind mornings as long as they don't start before six o'clock."

"That hour only happens for me once a day," Rebecca said, "and I'm usually eating supper."

JaRon and Zachary were the next two down the steps, followed by Cassidy, who ran right to Rebecca and gave her a hug.

"Good morning to you," Rebecca said. "What's going on today?"

"Mrs. Agnes is planting more flowers, so a bunch of us are going to help her. I had a lot of fun last night. I love looking at all your stuff. You are such a good artist. Do you think you could paint something for my room?"

"Of course," Rebecca said. "What do you want me to paint for you?"

"I don't know. Flowers? Anything? I just want something made by you hanging on my wall. Mrs. Agnes says you're going to be a famous artist someday and I should make sure to keep everything you ever draw. You know I have things of yours, don't you?"

Rebecca peered at her. "What do you mean?"

"You know, when you doodle on a napkin or a piece of paper or stuff. I pick it up when you leave it, then stick it in my folder."

Polly wanted to grab Cassidy into a huge hug, but Rebecca did it for her. "That's the sweetest thing ever," Rebecca said. "Thank you. I never think those things are important, but I love that you do."

"Everything you make is important," Cassidy said. "That's what Mrs. Agnes tells me. Whenever people are creative, you make sure to pay attention. Like, you know, JaRon and his cooking. I can't keep his cooking creations, but when he's famous and making cookbooks, I'll have those to remind me."

"What if I don't become a cook?" JaRon asked.

"Then I'll remember you for what you do."

"What about French toast and bacon for breakfast?" Polly asked.

"French toast?" Cassidy said. "You never make that."

Polly grinned. "We have bread that needs to be used."

"We never have extra bread in the house," Rebecca said.

"I might have gotten a little excited and bought too much this week."

Amalee took off for the back stairs. "I'll tell Teresa and Kestra to move faster."

"Keep an eye out for Gillian and Delia. I'm texting Lexi that breakfast is moving forward."

With a nod, Amalee took off.

"She's much too cheery in the mornings," Rebecca said. She turned to Cassidy. "If you all would help Polly set the table and make breakfast, I need to take a shower. Can you do that?"

Cassidy gave Rebecca another hug. "We will. I'm so glad you're home."

~~~

"Do you think that's enough?" Polly asked JaRon.

He looked at the spread in the dining room. "It's a lot."

JaRon and Zachary had helped her prepare supper. Tonight, Will was taking Gillian and Lexi to dinner and a movie. It was hard to get Lexi to leave the house. She took responsibility for everything. When Polly realized that it had been too long since Lexi had a night off, she bullied the poor girl into making a plan that didn't involve caring for the Sturtz family. Polly also wasn't above texting Will to ask him to get the girl out of the house for something other than picking up kids or shopping for the household. It hadn't taken that much this week. Lexi had been busy and was ready to spend time with her little family.

Lexi had everything ready for tomorrow's recital. Once Polly realized that, she insisted that Lexi and Gillian leave the house for a few hours.

While Polly didn't want to spend time baking, she was more than happy to put together a fun meal. And she had a surprise dessert for her family that hadn't taken her any time to prepare. Those were the best kinds of surprises.

Dinner was a taco bar. She taught JaRon how to bake tortillas into salad shells. He thought that was a brilliant idea. The kids wouldn't eat salad, but all the lettuce they'd shredded, the tomatoes she'd helped him dice, and the heaping bowls of cheese, along with a few sliced onions and red peppers, filled the sideboard in the dining room. She'd marinated diced chunks of chicken and had a huge platter of ground beef they'd cooked with taco seasoning. Polly had to ask Lexi for instructions on cooking Spanish rice, but once that was in hand, she was ready.

At the last minute, Polly called Ray, inviting him to bring Tonya to dinner. Ray never said no to her. She couldn't imagine how lonely those two might be, new to town, with only a few people they knew. Once the gym opened, that would change, but even then, she needed to stay aware. Ray was used to spending downtime at his mother's house. He was there every Sunday. One of these weekends, she wanted to ask him to make Ragu like Mama Renaldi made.

Agnes Hill and Andrew would also be at dinner. The Sturtz dining room table was never empty.

Music flowed from the foyer as Elijah practiced the pieces he planned to play tomorrow. He was performing the song he'd written as a surprise for his family last Christmas. She smiled as she heard familiar themes. Once he'd explained which passage was hers and how it fit into the lines of Henry's theme, she'd been so proud. He hadn't created motifs for everyone in the family, but had integrated himself and Noah into the piece. That was enough. It was his interpretation of how the two boys had found a new family and fallen in love with their parents.

The girls had enjoyed a wonderful day of shopping. Polly made sure that Rebecca knew anything she put on her credit card today would be paid for, giving her daughter permission to purchase clothing for Amalee if she saw something she loved.

Amalee wasn't much for purchasing things for herself, so Rebecca had paid close attention and when the girl longingly touched a blouse or an outfit, picked it up and put it into the cart. She was going to expand Amalee's wardrobe this summer if it was the last thing she did.

Rebecca had been proud of Kayla. Rather than buying clothing that made her look dumpy, she allowed Cilla, Amalee, and Rebecca to help her find clothes that accentuated her attributes. They'd picked out new outfits which would make Kayla more comfortable when working with Nan Stallings and Simon Gardner. The first of Rebecca's list of tasks to accomplish this summer was complete.

"Dad wanted me to ask if you needed any help." Caleb was talking to Polly as he walked in from the hallway.

"We're nearly ready. If he'd send everyone to wash their hands, I'll finish in here."

Caleb nodded and smiled before heading back down the hallway to the living room where Henry had taken Ray and Tonya. Caleb had come to idolize Ray's strength and his caring nature. If the boy she worried about the most set Ray Renaldi on a pedestal, Polly was fine with it. He was a terrific role model.

By the time Polly had the last of the meat on the table, the chairs surrounding it were filled with her family. She took a place between Henry and Delia, and after Elijah offered grace, she sat back. They knew how to feed themselves.

"I was thinking about college days today," she said to Henry.

"Yeah?"

"About how nomadic we were back then. Home was in the dorm room, and it was also in our old bedrooms."

"What brought that up?"

"Rebecca moving home for the summer. She has everything put into its place, but in a few months, she'll have to find ways to create a new nest for herself."

He nodded.

"Then I look around here and realized what a great big, oversized nest I've created."

"And lined it with people," he said with a laugh.

Suddenly, the dogs flew out of the dining room, barking and barking.

Polly looked around. Everyone was here. The doorbell hadn't rung, there was no one knocking. She jumped out of her seat and followed them. Han raced back and forth between the patio doors and the porch.

When she backed away from the patio doors to head for the porch, she nearly ran into Tonya. Ray was already moving for the door.

"What's going on?" she asked.

"I saw someone streak across your back yard," Tonya said. "The dogs reacted faster than I could get out of my chair."

Ray growled. "I thought we put a lock on that gate."

By now, everyone was in the kitchen, making movement nearly impossible. Polly pointed at the dining room. "Please, go back to your seats. We need to find out what's going on."

"I need to," Ray said. "Tonya, don't let her out of your sight."

Polly glared at the two of them. "My house, my yard ..."

"My best friend," Ray said. "Why would someone come into your yard?"

Polly's phone rang. Since it wasn't in her pocket, it took a minute for her to remember where she'd left it. The incoming call was from Andy Specek.

"Hello?" Polly asked. Ray was out the door and gone before she heard Andy's voice.

"Someone broke into the Jenkins' house. Len and I thought at first it was Bailey's family coming to pick up things she needed, but then I realized it was a young man. Not Bailey's father. When I stepped out onto the back deck ..." She sighed and then said, "Don't you dare tell Beryl I did this. She will have my head on a platter."

"Nope," Polly said. "I'm not getting in between you ladies. You tell me stuff; it might go anywhere. What did you do?"

"I yelled! I haven't yelled like that since I had high school kids at home."

"You never yell."

Andy chuckled. "Oh, you should hear me when I'm all worked up. But you never will because when I do that, I save it for the times when I'm home alone and in my basement where no one can hear me. Anyway, I yelled. Whoever it was, bolted out of the house and took off for your place. Tell me you saw him."

"I didn't," Polly said. "Ray and Tonya are here. He's gone after the guy and Tonya is being protective. Sounds like she should come to your house and protect you. How long was this person in their house?"

"I have no idea. I didn't notice anything until I heard a crash in their back yard. He'd pushed over the grill and dumped the contents out of their storage bench."

"Have you called Aaron?" Polly asked.

"I didn't know whether to call him or Chief Wallers. This probably has something to do with the murder, though."

"Yes."

"I'm still having difficulty accepting that a man was murdered right next door, and I didn't hear it happen."

"You call Aaron. I'll call Tab. They need to get into that house right away. If this person was looking for something and didn't find it, they'll be back. Or," Polly said, "they'll go looking for Bailey, hoping that she knows where her husband put whatever it is."

"She and her family don't need that while she's trying to recuperate," Andy said.

Polly didn't know if Bailey had said anything to Andy about the trouble she'd experienced with Ethan before moving to Bellingwood. Bailey needed more than just recuperation for her body. She needed years of caring to recuperate from the abuse he'd handed to her.

Ray came back inside, disheveled from running. He shook his head. "I missed him, but I saw cameras on your neighbors' house at the end of the block." He pointed toward the Gordon's home. Polly didn't realize they'd put a camera out there. In this day and age, it probably was a necessity for an elementary school principal. Either that or Jody was a curious sort who didn't want to answer the door if she wasn't sure who was there. That was more likely.

"I'm calling Tab Hudson," Polly said. "Thanks for noticing that. It will help her."

"I hope. He was going like wildfire."

Polly realized she was still talking to Andy. "You call Aaron," she said. "Right now."

"I don't want to tell him that I yelled at a thief. He'll yell at me."

"Tell him that you are a grownup and get to make your own decisions in life. It works so well for me," Polly said.

"I've heard that. Everyone is okay at your house?"

"Absolutely. We were just sitting down to dinner. Have you and Len eaten? You could come up and have tacos with us."

Tonya just looked at Polly and grinned.

"We've already eaten," Andy said. "Thank you, though."

"We're having a treat for dessert later on. I'm surprising everyone, so I won't say what it is out loud."

"We're good," Andy said with a laugh. "I'd better stick around here so I can speak with Aaron when he and Lydia show up to read me the riot act."

"Tell him I'm calling Tab. Maybe he'll let her handle it."

"Lydia never gets the opportunity to tell me that I've done something silly. She'll want to be here for this."

"You all are funny," Polly said. "I'm grateful to you. Thanks for calling."

The questions from her family were incessant until Henry put his hand up to stop the noise. "Your mother has another phone call to make. We don't know anything except that someone ran through our back yard. Give her time, please."

CHAPTER TWENTY

"So, do you want to take a walk with me?" Polly asked Henry. The kids were all in their rooms, with the exception of Noah, who was still in the library working on a paper that was due tomorrow. Today had been a long day. It had been a great day, but still … long.

"Either that or I fall asleep," Henry replied. "What were we thinking, having all these kids to take care of?"

"That we'd love them, and they'd love us back."

He chuckled. "We do have that going for us."

"It's that whole going and going thing that's killing us," Polly said. "I was proud of Elijah and Teresa today."

"She's a good little piano player."

"All I want is for her to enjoy herself. I don't think that she's as committed to it as Elijah is …"

Henry put a hand up. "Elijah is special, that's for sure. He was so excited to wear his tuxedo."

"It makes him look so much more grown up," Polly said. "All this growing up is hard to handle. I want them to mature, but never age."

He shook his head. "Rather than a walk, is there anything left of that strawberry shortcake from last night?"

"You sneaky husband, you," Polly said. "Get the kids off to bed and then steal their leftover dessert?"

"My leftover dessert. Your leftover dessert. We're the king and queen of this castle. We get to eat whatever leftovers we want. One of the privileges of parenting."

"How about a walk and then dessert?"

"You really want to get out of here."

"I've been moving so fast these last two days; I just want to stroll somewhere with you and the dogs."

"A trip through the cemetery?"

"It sounds peaceful."

"You really are blitzed."

"If we walk, I'll sleep better. My body is wound up."

"Then, let's walk."

"Thank you. It's a beautiful evening."

"Polly," Henry said. "If you want to take a walk with me, you don't have to justify it."

"Okay." She held her hand out so he could pull her up from the sofa. "See, I'm a mess. Everything hurts. How is it that I feel like an old lady?"

"You've had a lot going on. Let's go. I really want a piece of that strawberry shortcake."

"You nut," she said. "It was the easiest thing in the world. I cut up the strawberries while everyone was busy with something else, doused them with sugar, then cut up those angel-food cakes I bought from the grocery store. Top it with spray-on whipped cream and everyone is happy."

"Including the dogs." Henry laughed. "Homemade pup cups for the win."

"One of these days, I'll make real strawberry shortcake and we can serve it with homemade ice cream."

"But we'll still get to have whipped cream, right?"

"That's why Lexi and I don't keep any in the house," Polly said. "We'd never keep little hands out of it."

"And then there wouldn't be any in the house."

"Exactly." Polly sent a quick text to Lexi and Rebecca that they were going to take a walk. She stopped in the doorway of the library. Georgia was curled up at Noah's feet while her son was madly typing away on the laptop he used at home.

Noah looked up, his eyes bleary. "I'm almost done."

"You're fine. Henry and I are going for a walk. I only wanted to let you know. We're only going to the cemetery."

"Okay." Noah held up a book he'd been using as a reference. "I love this stuff. I love looking things up and then writing about them."

"You're a weirdo, my son," Henry said. "I love you very much and I'm proud of you, but that's just plain weird."

"I loved it too," Polly said. "Words on a page are the coolest thing ever."

Noah's eyes showed his excitement. "They are. They tell you everything. I wish I could read everything on all the shelves. Then I'd know it all."

"You already know a lot," Polly said.

"There are so many things to learn. Do you think that I could figure out how physics works just by reading books?"

"I think you could," Henry said. "But why don't you take a physics class in high school, so you get a good understanding from someone who already knows how it works."

"No one knows for sure how it all works," Noah said. "There just isn't enough time to learn everything. Sometimes, when I think about it, I wonder if I were to read every book out there, would I know everything? Could I save the world just by knowing things?"

"You do understand that you'd have to talk to people and interact with committees and organization and ..."

Noah stopped Henry from continuing. "I know. It all sounds terrible, but learning is just so exciting. I don't want to stop reading."

"Finish your paper and get some sleep," Polly said. "I hate to be a wet blanket, but for that gorgeous brain of yours to keep working, it needs rest. That's my job. I will tell you how amazing you are and then I will tell you to eat good food and get good sleep."

Noah smiled at her. "I'm glad you're my mom. At least you don't tell me that I'm too dumb to learn."

"I would never. Did you hear that from someone?"

"Before we came here. It was a long time ago. But sometimes, it creeps back into my head, and I wonder if I really know what I'm doing."

"You're a brilliant young man," Polly said. She'd crossed the room to stand beside him. "Don't ever wonder whether that's true or not. If you do, come find me and I will point out all the amazing things that you know."

"Thanks." Noah yawned. "My body is trying to tell me something. It won't take me long to finish this."

"I love you."

"Love you too." Noah took a breath, then put his hands back on the laptop's keyboard. His fingers were flying across the keys as she met Henry in the hall.

"It scares me sometimes," Henry said as they walked into the kitchen.

"What's that?"

"How incredible those two boys are – Noah and Elijah. What would have happened to them if we hadn't adopted them into our family? Would they have been able to find their talent?"

"I'd hope that Roy Dunston saw something in them and would have kept them safe from a world where they did nothing more than exist."

"And they tried to stay alive. I remember those nights when the two boys needed Obiwan in their beds simply so they could sleep." He opened the patio door, letting Han and Obiwan go first. "I'm glad they've had a safe place to find themselves."

Henry laughed as they approached the back gate. "How am I supposed to tell Ray that the kids are in and out of this gate all the time. He was unhappy that it wasn't locked."

"Ray is overprotective. While this is all going on, we could lock the gate, but come on. Life is too short to live in protective custody all the time." Polly made sure the gate was latched closed once they went through.

Polly didn't want to admit that she wanted to check out the Jenkins' home. He wouldn't let her get close, but her curiosity had been killing her since everything erupted last night. She hated it when people wouldn't give her all the details. Though, she didn't always need the details. Sometimes they were overwhelming. Which was why Tab carried a notebook. Once things were written down, she could line them up to make sense of what she knew. Even when she didn't feel like she knew enough.

This murder had been frustrating for Tab. Bailey wasn't able to give her any more information and that had them stalled. They were waiting for authorities in the Quad Cities to uncover details about what Ethan was involved with, but that wasn't bringing in quick results.

When Polly called Tab last night to tell her what had happened, she was surprised to hear a sound like jubilation. This might finally be a break. If the man had used gloves, they wouldn't be able to pull a print, but maybe she'd find something new. Tab also planned to go back through the house with a fine-tooth comb. What had Ethan Jenkins been into?

Those thoughts had Polly stopping outside the back yard of the Jenkins' residence.

"What are you doing?" Henry asked.

She looked at him in surprise, not realizing that she'd stopped walking. "Sorry. I was thinking."

"No thinking. Only walking. We're not breaking into this house."

"I would never do that."

"Yes, you would. Don't kid yourself. If you thought you could find a clue, you'd break in without a second thought."

Polly looped her arm around his. "You're mean to me."

"I am the worst."

"Yes, you are. And I'm glad you're all mine. You don't need to make life difficult for other women."

"Hello there!" Andy called from her deck. She and Len both walked to its edge. "What are you doing out this evening?"

Polly waved. "We're out taking a walk."

"Spying on the neighbor's house," Henry said. "I can't keep this woman away from crime scenes to save my life. Even when it's something as innocent as walking the dogs, she finds a way."

"Stop it," Polly said, elbowing her husband. "Thank you, Len, for all your work the last few days. We appreciate it."

"It wasn't much," Len said "The recital today went well. Your boy has a load of talent in those fingers. And that piece he composed shows potential. I hope you're ready to follow him around the world when he starts touring."

Polly looked at her husband and smiled. "That would certainly be a different life than what we're living now. Fortunately, we have a few years before that happens. It was nice to hear you and Brandon play, too. The kids should know that piano lessons are bigger than just their parents telling them to practice and prepare for recitals. You always show them that music is essential to life."

"Brandon is kind of a different fella to be showing off his piano skills," Len said. "I like the boy, but girls like him better. Big ole handsome boy like that playing the piano with all those skills. They don't know what to do with him. They're more used to his type playing football. But he takes great joy in music. I don't know what I'd do without him. Those muscles of his help a lot. Say, are you going to be okay with me taking Elijah out to tune pianos this summer?"

"Whenever he has time, that would be wonderful."

"He enjoys playing baseball," Andy said.

"It's fun to see you at his games. He's pretty proud that you show up for him," Polly said. "I don't know how many more years he'll want to play, but as long as piano and baseball don't collide, I'm all for having him do both."

"Would you like to come in for a minute?" Andy asked.

Polly looked at Henry. He wanted strawberry shortcake, but he would do whatever she wanted. "Not tonight. I promised Henry ..."

Len put an index finger in each ear and said, "Nah, nah, nah, nah. I don't want to hear what you promised Henry tonight. That's too much information."

"It was strawberry shortcake, but if he's a good boy ..." Polly allowed the sentence to fade away.

"Like I said, too much information."

"Good to see you folks," Henry said. "I'm going to scurry her along on this walk so we can get back to the previously planned promises."

"Alliteration," Polly whispered. "Good night, you two. Enjoy your evening."

As they walked away, Henry chuckled. "We know such good people."

"It feels like Len loosens up whenever we spend time with him. We should invite them over for dinner more often." Polly tucked in closer to Henry as they walked. "I'm glad Elijah has him in his life."

"Our kids find their own mentors, don't they?" Henry said. "And Caleb has found two, well, two locations. The guys at the garage enjoy spending time with him. Every once in a while, Kirk stops me to let me know what a good job Caleb does there."

Polly nodded, her mind wandering from Kirk to his daughter Cilla, and the apartment she might rent. Then, she trailed off to Tonya who was trying to find a place to live in Bellingwood.

"Now what?"

"Just thinking."

"About? Tell me it's not about murder and mayhem."

"No, building nests. You mentioned Kirk and I thought about Cilla. She needs to get out of the house, or her mother will smother her in her sleep."

"That's graphic."

"I know. But those two are like oil and water. Andrea still isn't certain that Cilla made the right decision by not giving up Fiona for adoption."

"The decision was made. Surely, she can understand that."

"You'd think, but Andrea is used to getting her way. She raised a daughter who is much like her and insists that she gets her way. It's a cycle."

"And Tonya?" Henry moved Polly's arm so he could take her hand instead. "I like her. She's a nice girl. Ray's lucky to have her around. She's not so caught up in the big city stuff that she can't relax into small town Iowa."

"Because you know so many people like that."

"Sal."

"Once she met Mark, it was all over. Sal would have gone to the ends of the earth to be with him."

"Good thing. I didn't want to have to fight him for you."

"It was never a fight. It was never a thing."

"I had to pull out all of my moves."

"You have pretty great moves." Polly ran her shoulder into him. It must have surprised him because he stumbled. "Oops, sorry."

"No, I tripped on something. Henry stopped to pick up a rock. Daylight was waning, so he set the chunk of stone off to the side. "That's odd. I'll call Charlie in the morning."

"About a rock?"

"I can't tell what it is, and you never see rocks on his sidewalks. He'll check the monuments to ensure there hasn't been any damage." He took her hand again. "I need to push the city council."

"I'm sorry, what?"

"You were talking about places for people to live. They need to approve a bunch of things so we can get moving on Sycamore Acres."

"Is there a problem?"

"Other than slow thinkers? No. There will be a few protests from people who don't think we should be adding more developments."

"Then they'll be upset when Sal and Eve announce the new development they're planning north of town."

"We exist simply to drive those poor people crazy."

"That's funnier than it should be," Polly said with a laugh.

They turned the corner at the top of the cemetery and headed back to the break in the hedge. The dogs knew exactly where they were and stood in front of the gate wagging their tails. Nothing like coming home to your own yard.

Henry locked the back gate. "I don't like doing that."

"I don't either. But maybe it's for the best until they find the murderer."

"I'm just going to say it again. It's weird that these things happen around us. I'm thankful they don't happen to us, but ..."

"It's still weird." Polly took his hand back and pulled him in for a kiss. "I'm thankful that you seem to forget all the things that do happen to us."

"I suppose," he said and smiled at her. "But they don't devastate us. I appreciate your attitude. With everything that's happened in the last ten or eleven years, you never sink down into the grime and guts of it. You pull us all back out with a smile and the knowledge that it's one day or one week – it's never forever."

"We're forever, though. Love is forever. That's what matters."

"We haven't talked much about Andrew and Rebecca."

Polly slid the patio door open and waited for the dogs to bound inside. "We have time. It won't happen for at least a year. Is there something that concerns you?"

"Not really. You were talking about how love is forever and I thought ..."

"Now *you're* thinking?" Polly interrupted. "You hate it when my brain wanders off."

"Only because I lose track of where you're going if you aren't talking out loud. No, I can't imagine those two married to anyone but each other, but I want them to understand the enormous impact marriage has on two people. That the only way to get through it some days ..."

"Careful," Polly warned. She laughed. "I'm sorry. Go on."

"Is to know how important it is to love each other. Not just to be in love, but to truly love."

"They passed the infatuation stage when they were still only nine or ten years old," Polly said. "Andrew loves Rebecca without hesitation. He would climb the highest … well, you know. The whole thing. Rebecca's love goes deeper than what we see on the outside. She has a deep well of love that will never run dry."

"She gets that from you."

"And her mother. I watched those two love each other until Sarah died. And then I watched Rebecca continue to love her mother, all while she learned to love me. She realized that it wasn't one or the other, that love could look different for each person you associate with. You love based on how they respond, not how you want them to respond."

"You're thinking deeply now. It must be painful up there in your head."

"Brat. So, strawberry shortcake?"

"You promised."

"What if there is only enough for one person?"

"You like ice cream sandwiches."

Polly laughed out loud. "And I like you. I don't have these kinds of conversations with everyone, you know."

"You have pieces of them with your friends and family."

"But when I talk to you, I am able to think through all the words and ideas floating around in my head. I get to put them together before they're out in the world."

"Strawberry shortcake," Henry said, pointing at the refrigerator. "Please? With your special topping of love on it?"

"Oh, for heaven's sake." Polly took out the containers. "The least you can do is get plates and forks."

"And napkins." Henry snagged one of the whipped cream containers, tipped it up to his mouth and squirted. "I can't do that when the kids are around. Want a hit?"

Polly opened her mouth. Not only did he squirt it there, but managed to get it all over her chin and her cheeks. Once she got enough swallowed so she could talk, she said, "Brat."

"All of that and more. Should we take one of these cans upstairs?"

"I have no more words."

CHAPTER TWENTY-ONE

Gusts of wind blew through the sycamore trees lining the creek at Sycamore House. Polly was glad to be inside. The wind hadn't blown this hard earlier when the kids left for school, but wow, things had picked up. Blue skies were dotted with fluffy white clouds moving east. She wondered what this wind might bring. Spring weather was far from predictable. Polly hoped it wouldn't bring a thunderstorm, if for no other reason than that Caleb's dog, Angel, melted down in spectacular ways. They'd tried everything from specialized clothing to a mild tranquilizer to taking her to the basement in order to save her from feeling and hearing the thunder. Nothing worked. The dog did her very best to climb inside Caleb's skin. He was the only one who could comfort her, which meant that during the days that he was in school or working at the garage, she was a mess.

None of the other dogs liked stormy weather, but at least they didn't lose control. For a long time, Delia made herself a hideaway whenever thunderstorms arrived, but one day, Henry held her in his arms at the back patio doors and showed her how to count between lightning strikes and the sound of thunder. He talked to her about how the pouring rain filled lakes and rivers, bringing water to animals and people. He allowed her to experience a storm from within the protection of his arms, not only once this spring, but several times.

During one rainy, but not stormy day, Henry took as many of the kids who would go, outside in the rain and played with them, showing Delia and her siblings how much fun it was to be okay with getting drenched. They'd come back inside, went upstairs to change clothes, and when they returned, he had a fire going in the living room fireplace. Polly and Lexi had brownies and milk ready for them, and a vacuum to clean up the inevitable mess left by a houseful of kids. Only under certain circumstances were they allowed to have food in the living room. It was always a treat.

Polly turned to look at the pasture. The donkeys were having fun with a big blue ball that seemed to be playing with them all on its own. They'd chase it across the pasture, but before either Tom or Huck could get to it, the wind blew it in a different direction. She laughed when Eliseo tried to track it down before it blew out of the pen.

"Branches down in the back yard," came Lexi's text.

"Big bad ones or normal-sized branches?" Polly sent back.

"One big one and lots of little limbs. Kind of becoming a mess."

"We'll deal with it when we have kids at home. Nothing hit the roof there, did it?"

"The big one came close to the gazebo, but I watched it come down and it missed."

"I'll tell Henry to bring home a chain saw. Looks like we can set in wood for next winter."

Lexi sent her a laughing emoji.

Polly didn't want to go back to work, so she called her husband.

"Hey," he said. Henry sounded tired.

"You okay?"

"Chasing the wind today."

"Lexi said we have a big branch down in the back yard. Can you bring home a chain saw?"

"Figures. Any damage?"

"Other than the tree itself, she said there was none."

"Good. Chastain's had a big tree drop onto the corner of their house. I'm heading out there to see what I can do to close it up until we can fix it."

"Whoa," she said.

"James called me first. I appreciate that my clients feel comfortable reaching out, but if the wind doesn't calm down, this won't be the last call I get."

"Did you get a chance to call Charlie about that piece of rock?"

"I'm sorry, no," he said. "This morning has been one thing after another."

"That's okay. I'll take care of it. Don't think about it any longer."

Henry chuckled. "It was already gone from my mind. Thanks. Anything else?"

"Let me know if you'll be late. I'll save food for you."

"We're out of strawberry shortcake by now, right?"

"But we still have whipped cream." Polly had tried to use her most sultry voice, but it didn't work so well when he was stressed about work, and she was distracted by high winds blowing through the yard.

"Okay," he said.

"You're distracted."

"Traffic. Sorry."

"Talk to me later when you don't feel so stressed. I love you."

"You too," Henry said and ended the call.

Polly leaned back in her chair to watch the donkeys and Eliseo in the pasture. When life got stressful, animals helped lower the blood pressure.

Her phone buzzed with a text from Rebecca. *"Beryl got another one of those weird emails and she won't call Aaron. What am I supposed to do with her?"*

"Tell her that if she doesn't call him, I will. I thought she was going to give the emails to Anita Banks so they could find out where the emailer is from?"

"Yeah, she didn't. When I asked if Lydia knew, she said that she didn't make a big deal of it. What is it with people? Protect yourself."

"Beryl's been around a long time. Long enough to think that since she's been safe all these years, nothing should change."

"Like those elderly people who get caught up in scams. Just because someone tells you that they will fix your computer for you over an email or the phone, doesn't mean they're trustworthy. Or just because you get a call that your grandson needs bail money, doesn't mean it's true. For heaven's sake, doublecheck first."

"I love you, Rebecca. Older generations grew up trusting people because we're all human beings."

"Some people are ruthless human beings," Rebecca wrote. "Tell me, what am I supposed to do with this woman?"

"I wasn't kidding. Tell her that if she doesn't call, I will. She knows I don't just mouth inanities. I'll do what I say I will. Give her an hour. I'm calling back to find out if she's followed through."

"You're hard to get along with. I appreciate that about you."

"Good. How's the first day going?"

"I have so much work ahead of me. I'm going to clean up her website and show her how to use apps on her phone. I have to dig into her paperwork and all her financial stuff."

"You're kidding me."

"She wants me to do it. I'm going to learn Excel this summer if it kills me."

"You can always ask Edna or Mason for help." Polly's two financial people were two of the most wonderful people she'd ever known. Edna especially. Kind and thoughtful, never derogatory about what people didn't know, Edna loved to dig into financial reports to simplify them. She was fine with the deep intricacies of the various companies' finances, but when those reports hit Polly's desk, everything was easily understandable.

"I might have to. First, I have to buy Beryl a new laptop. This thing is old, slow, and miserable to work on."

"I'm sorry. Okay, you talk to Beryl. Call me later."

"Thank you for listening … or reading my insanity." Rebecca sent a hug emoji.

"I'm always here for you."

Polly hadn't thought much more about it, but after talking with Henry, she wanted to make sure that Charlie knew what they'd tripped on last night. Sure, it was their problem. He hadn't put the piece of stone in the middle of the sidewalk, but if someone had vandalized anything, she wanted to talk to him.

His was a contact that she didn't often reference, so it took a couple of tries for Polly to find Charlie's phone number. When she sent the call through, he responded immediately.

"Polly Giller. How are you, my friend?"

"Hello, Charlie. I'm doing well. How about you?"

"Can't complain. What can I do for you?"

"Last night, Henry tripped over a piece of rock on the sidewalk over by Marion Nevins' grave."

"Oh yeah? I'll check that out. Sorry."

"No, I'm only telling you so you know it's there."

"Piece of concrete maybe?"

"I don't know. It was dusk and we weren't paying attention. Henry just wanted to let you know."

"I've been picking up bits and pieces of broken concrete all over the cemetery. Maybe the wind blew it in. He didn't think it was marble from a gravestone, did he? If so, I need to check for other damage."

"We really don't know," Polly replied. "You'll know when you look at it. What's up with the other stuff in the cemetery."

"I don't know. Last week there was concrete debris everywhere. Like someone scattered it. I haven't found all the pieces if what you're telling me is true."

"You know the boys would be glad to help you clean up the cemetery when something like that happens."

"I know, but I take my time. Don't get around as fast as I used to, but it still gets done."

"You're a good man, Charlie Heller. Thank you for what you do."

"Aww, you make me blush."

"That's perfect, then. I'll let you go. Don't get blown away."

"That wind is fierce today, that's for sure. Surprised we don't have a storm coming in. Just wind, though."

"Good to know. Wind is enough. Let us know if tree branches come down and get in your way. Henry's always looking for more firewood."

"Good idea, that. He keeps an eye on us. Heard that he's got some house damage to deal with."

"Now, how did you hear that?" Polly asked, astounded. It hadn't been that long ago that she'd talked to Henry.

"Word gets around. Say, what do you know about that murder?"

"Not enough," Polly said. "What have you heard?" Charlie was as integrated into the local rumor mill as June Livengood. They probably had a phone chain going when something new hit the wire.

"That he was an SOB, beat his wife. Do you think she hired someone to do him in?"

"No. The poor girl was so cowed by him that she wouldn't have come up with that on her own."

"Maybe her family did it then. Trying to rescue her and all that."

"Maybe, but I don't think so. Sounds like the guy was involved in something that he shouldn't have been."

"Probably drugs. That's what everything comes down to these days. Don't think Bellingwood would have much to do with weapons transportation. You know, funding armies in countries preparing an overthrow."

"I hope we don't," Polly said.

"Your new friend in town would know more about that than anyone."

"You mean Ray Renaldi?"

"Doesn't he run a security business with his brother?"

"Something like that," Polly said. "He's in Bellingwood to open a gym."

"Saw that going in. Don't think it will do much for an old guy like me. Best if I just keep walking the cemetery. I can do it as slow as I like without anyone rushing me through machines that I don't understand."

She laughed. "Mr. Charlie Heller, if you decided you wanted to understand how those exercise machines worked, you'd do it. It's okay if you aren't interested."

"Then I'll just say it. I'm not interested. Too old to show off my body in order to catch a young sprite."

"You're a nut."

"Someone has to do the job."

"Let me know if you come up with an idea about where those concrete pieces came from," Polly said.

"Around this place, it could be for any reason. People dump their trash here when no one's looking. They drop weird things off to keep their loved ones company. Would you believe that last week I had to rescue a fish tank full of turtles? I called the family, and they thought the turtles would do fine in the weather. They didn't want them back, so I took the poor beasts to the humane society in Boone. What do people think when they do things like that? Ask questions, please. We have rules."

"That does sound odd," Polly said. She was grateful her boys hadn't been around when Charlie discovered the turtles. They'd have created an entire turtle empire before the evening was over.

"I've seen stranger things."

"I can't imagine." Polly was grateful for Rebecca's incoming phone call. "Rebecca is calling me. I'll let you go."

"Thanks for the chat, Ms. Giller."

She tapped to open the second call. "What did you find out?"

"I made the call to Anita. Beryl told me I could after no small amount of fussing and fuming. I might have pulled the poor little worker bee on her."

"What does that mean?"

"I told her that if she's under threat, that means I'm under threat too since I work here now and will be the one opening those emails."

"That's mean."

"It worked. As soon as she quit thinking that everything was only about her, she relented without a whimper. I've sent everything I can to Anita. I'm going to dig deeper into Beryl's emails to see if I can find things she hasn't destroyed. The woman has never emptied her email trash."

"I thought the program only kept things in trash for thirty days."

"Oh, she clicked some button that made the trash never empty. Good grief. I'm going to buy a new laptop for me to use and I'm going to make her learn how to use a tablet. Maybe she'll stay out of trouble that way. I still can't believe that some maleficent robot hasn't stolen her identity or all her money. Nothing is protected on this laptop."

"Have you placed the order for the new hardware?"

"Not until I talk to Andrew. I want to make sure I'm smart about this. I don't want to be in a rush."

"Good girl. You could always ask Anita."

"She's too busy."

"Doug Randall then."

"Ooh, that's a good idea. Any excuse to go to Boomer's. I'll do that in the morning before I come over here. Oh, Polly. My summer is going to be busy."

"I'm glad for you."

"It sounds like I'm complaining and maybe I am, but only a little bit. Beryl needs me so much. If I can get everything together for her before I go back to school, I can work on her stuff remotely. She said she'll keep paying me if I do that."

"You have a lifetime of taking care of Beryl ahead of you."

"It's pretty cool. I'll learn all about the business and get to spend time with her in the studio painting and drawing and learning. Who else do you know that is that lucky?"

"Not many people."

"What are you doing?"

"Watching the wind blow."

"That doesn't sound productive."

"I was productive before you were out of bed, Miss Thing."

"Right. I forget. People really do work at abnormal hours. I'd

224

better go. I've placed a grocery order and need to pick it up. Beryl has nothing in the kitchen. Nothing at all except coffee. And thank goodness for that. Again, I had to pull the poor little worker bee on her and tell her that I needed to be able to eat, even if she didn't."

"She does, though."

"You know that. I know that, but Beryl gets caught up in her work and forgets. I promised to make her eat during the day. We talked about the foods she likes. I can handle all of it."

"You know Lexi cooks for her friends."

"Oh!" Rebecca exclaimed. "I forgot about that. I need to get on Lexi's mailing list so I can ask Beryl if she's interested in any meals. What a great idea."

"I'm full of 'em," Polly said.

"You're full of something. I'm hanging up now. I just wanted you to know that I've talked to Anita, so you don't have to get involved."

"Thank you. See you tonight."

"I might be a little late."

"What does that mean?"

"Like six o'clock. It won't be this way every day, but I have to take care of this woman today."

"We eat at six thirty. You'll be fine."

"Thanks."

This morning had turned out to be less than Polly expected. She looked at the open reports on her laptop, closed them, and decided that today was over for her. Tapping the intercom button, she said, "Kristen, I'm going home."

"Okay. Things are quiet here today. No need to hang around, I guess."

"If you need anything, you know how to reach me."

"'Kay. Bye."

Polly needed to do some planning for Rebecca's birthday party this weekend. With all that had been going on, she and Lexi had yet to sit down and ensure everything was in motion. She'd ordered a cake from Sylvie, but now she needed to check the weather and make sure they'd be able to host people outside. Today had her a little worried. Not that it meant anything. Weather forecasts changed in a flash. Right now, Saturday looked to be a beautiful day.

Everything was where it needed to be, so Polly picked up her tote bag and headed for the side door.

Sal walked in before she reached it. "Leaving so early?"

"Things in my head," Polly said.

"And in your back yard."

"That's one of the things in my head. Everything okay in your space?"

"The goats are hiding in the shed. Some furniture has been tossed around. We'll pick it up once the wind dies down. The forecast said it should get better this evening. Once Mark is home, we'll have an outside party and clean up the yard. This is nuts."

"Henry's bringing home a chain saw. If you need it, let me know."

"You okay?" Sal asked, touching Polly's arm.

"Yes. I don't know what bit me in the soul, but I need doggie love and kitten purrs. Nothing is wrong, I'm just out of sorts."

"You'll let me know if you need me to do anything."

"I love you, Sal Ogden," Polly said, giving her friend a quick hug. "You're the best friend ever."

"I know that. I'm glad you recognize it. If you need dirty diapers and a slobbery baby fix, I have that available too."

"Aren't you the generous one."

"I'll give you anything I have."

"Thanks. I'm going home for more coffee, lunch, and naminals."

"Animals."

"Or naminals," Polly said.

CHAPTER TWENTY-TWO

Only Polly. She really did try to spend time in her office, but Tuesday morning brought more outside activity.

When Tab Hudson walked into her office, Polly tipped her head and smirked. "What do you want?"

"I want you," Tab said, pointing straight at Polly. "Are you deep down into it here today or can I take you away?"

"A person would begin to believe that I never work," Polly said. "I'm always gallivanting off."

"The benefits of hiring good people?"

"That's the gist of it. Henry hires good people. He always works. I'm just a slug."

"No, you're the woman who puts everyone else's needs above her own. Especially since it's safe to do so." Tab pointed at the main building. "Because you hired good people."

"What do you need from me? Where am I going?"

"To Boone. To see Bailey Jenkins."

"Really," Polly said, sitting back in her chair. "What's up?"

"Every time I talk to her, she mentions you. Somehow you make her feel safe."

"It's my big muskles." Polly flexed her arms. "I'm a kick-butt and take no names kind of a girl."

"Or it's because you don't push, but you show empathy all the same. I want to ask questions about her husband's life outside his work. She's more likely to talk if you're there."

"This case has dragged on for a while, hasn't it," Polly said.

"Too long. I want to be done with it. If I have to drag you away from your business to make that happen ..." Tab chuckled. "Well, I'd beg and plead first, hoping that you'll agree, and I don't have to get tough."

"I'm coming, I'm coming," Polly said. "Can I follow you?"

"That would be best. I'll text you the address so if we are separated, you can find me."

"Bailey knows I'm coming?"

"I set the appointment with her and once I told her that you would be with me, she relaxed."

"Weird," Polly said.

"You in a nutshell."

Polly pressed the intercom button.

"Are you leaving us again?" Kristen asked.

"How did you know?"

"It's the only time you ever use the intercom."

"I'm heading to Boone with Tab Hudson. We'll see how the rest of the day goes."

"I'll let Jeff know that you're leaving him alone again. He'll like that. He makes trouble when you're gone."

"I like his brand of trouble," Polly said. "You know how to reach me."

"She's not arresting you or anything, is she?"

"That's funny," Tab said. "Not yet. You never know, though."

"That's what I thought. Talk to you later, Polly. Bye, Deputy."

"Shall we?" Tab asked, gesturing to the door.

"Two minutes." Polly closed the programs she had opened, pushed the laptop lid closed, and took one last long drink from her coffee cup. There was never enough of that stuff. Especially on days like today.

"Do we need to stop for more coffee?" Tab asked.

"Maybe on the way back to town. I'm ready to go." Polly snagged her tote bag from a chair inside the door and made sure her office was locked. It was startling to realize that people who were here for meetings and events wandered through the building, hoping to discover something interesting behind closed doors.

"I sent the address to your phone," Tab said as she veered to her vehicle. "Meet you there."

Polly climbed into the Suburban, sent the address to her GPS, and backed out of the parking spot. She knew the general area of the Houseman home. Funny how familiar even Boone had become. It took ten years for that to happen, but it finally did. She was glad to live in central Iowa. This was home.

Her phone rang as she drove down the highway toward Boone.

"Hey, Henry. How are you today?" He'd not been in a good mood last night. Some of that was because he hadn't been able to get home in time for dinner. It wasn't that he said or did anything. It was that he didn't say or do anything. He just sat in their home office in the dark. The only light came from his tablet and the laptop. Things were bad when he had both pieces of technology going.

"I'm better. A crew is working on the Chastain house, so I can stop thinking about it. If we're getting rain this week, I want them to be covered. I'm sorry I was such a grump last night."

"Don't worry. You were exhausted and hungry. That would make me a grump, too."

"You sound like you're on the road."

"Going to Boone with Deputy Hudson. She wants me there when she talks to Bailey Jenkins."

"Why?"

"I'm the good cop."

"Is that true?"

"Kind of. Bailey trusts me. Tab is going to drill down on what her husband was doing in the Quad Cities."

"It must have been something nefarious."

"I don't know for sure what it was, but we'll soon find out."

"Do you think you can get her to talk?"

"It's been two and a half weeks since her husband died. By now, some of the shock and awe should have worn off. Hopefully, she'll give us enough information so Tab can move forward. This case is frustrating her."

"If she's calling you in to help, it must be frustrating."

"Hey."

"You aren't law enforcement. You're her friend, and oh, you're the one that keeps her busy with dead bodies."

"Not my fault."

He laughed. "I would never imply that. I saw Charlie at breakfast this morning. He said you two talked yesterday."

"He has a lot to say."

"We made him concerned about all the chunks and bits of concrete in the cemetery. Now he's worried about where it came from."

"Worried or curious?"

"Interesting. I would have said worried, but you know Charlie. His curiosity runs deep."

"I'm pulling in behind Tab's vehicle. Will you be home at a normal hour tonight?" Polly paused. "I'm not pushing, only asking."

"It's all right. I'll be home as early as possible. We have a week and a half before the Memorial Day weekend and crews are pushing to have things at a stopping point by then."

"At least they're thinking about that now and not next Thursday."

"They hope to be able to leave early on Friday. Gavin and Heath are the ones who remind them of deadlines."

"You're lucky to have them."

"Yes, I am. You go. Let me know what you come up with. And please be careful today."

"You think a woman in a full leg cast plus a hole in her shoulder is going to take me down?"

"Polly Giller. Who are we talking about?"

"Apparently Polly Giller."

"Yes. All I'm asking is that you stay aware of your surroundings and do everything you can to be careful."

"No trust," Polly said.

"I love you, too."

She smiled and waved at Tab, who was waiting near the front steps of the house. A hastily erected ramp had been set up where banisters had been removed from the front porch. With all the disabled and elderly people in Polly's life, she wondered if it was time to have a chat with Henry about how construction companies could make it easier to get into a home. For some people, even a single step was an insurmountable obstacle.

"What were you doing?" Tab asked Polly.

"Talking to Henry. He told me to be careful."

"The man knows his wife." The two walked up the steps to the front door. Though the banister had been removed from the porch, it was a pleasant spot with chairs and a table, flowerpots hanging from the eaves, and rugs on the floor. The front door had stained-glass set into the arch at the top.

"I like front porches," Polly said. "It was a shame when they started building homes without them."

"Privacy. Everyone likes the privacy of a six-foot fence around the back yard so they can sit on their deck and drink without judgment."

"If you sit on the front porch and drink, people will join you."

"And who wants that?" Tab pressed the doorbell. She poked Polly. "I forgot. You want that."

"Then I invite them to my big back yard with the six-foot fence."

An attractive woman opened the front door and smiled. "Welcome. You must be Polly Giller. Bailey has said some very nice things about you. Come on in. Would you like coffee or tea?"

"I'd love a cup of coffee," Polly said. It was easy to see that Mrs. Houseman wanted to do something productive. "Tab?"

"Honestly, a glass of water would be wonderful. I never seem to get enough during the day. Thank you."

"Bailey is right in here. She's doing much better on her own these days. My girl is an independent sort, you know."

That didn't sound like the Bailey Jenkins that Polly had met, but if that's what her mother thought of her, then that would be the constant positive support that Bailey would receive.

The young woman used the lift chair to bring herself to a standing position. She snagged the crutches standing beside the chair and hopped toward them. "I'm going to walk on this leg if it's the last thing I do. Please, have a seat." She nodded toward the sofa. "Mom's getting you something to drink?"

Polly nodded. "You look much better than when I saw you in the hospital."

"That's what happens when your mother gets you into her care. Washing my hair was the best thing ever. Since I'm more mobile, now we can wash it in the kitchen sink. It's pure heaven having her scrub my head. We need to go back to the house and get my makeup and some more clothes one of these days, but we make do."

Mrs. Houseman walked back in, carrying a tray filled with drinks. A plate with different types of cookies took up the center of the tray. "I'll just set this here. Bailey, would you like a refill?"

"I'm good, Mom. Thanks." Bailey thumped back to her chair, sat in it, then adjusted it for comfort. "Oops. I'd like one of those frosted pumpkin cookies. Sorry."

Her mother smiled and said to Tab and Polly. "Help yourself."

"Did you bake all this?" Polly asked.

"It's what I do when I need to turn off my mind," Mrs. Houseman said. "Helps me focus again."

"She's a transcriptionist for several doctors in town," Bailey said. "I couldn't do that to save my life."

"You'll do a lot of things to save your life," Mrs. Houseman said. "When I need to tune all the voices out, I bake." She patted her stomach. "Probably not the best choice, but it makes me happy."

"She shares with the neighbors all the time," Bailey said. "So much baking goes on in this house."

"I'll let you three talk," Mrs. Houseman said. "Unless you want me to stick close."

Bailey shook her head. "Go on. We'll be fine."

Her mother pointed at the tray. "Please, help yourself. Don't be shy on our account."

Polly had heard *frosted pumpkin cookie* and found herself yearning for one. There were chocolate chip cookies, snickerdoodles, lemon, and what looked like chocolate cookies with macadamia nuts. She wanted one of everything. But first, coffee. She took a sip and smiled. It wasn't Sweet Beans, but it had been brewed well.

They talked for a few minutes about Bailey's recovery, and Polly asked, "Do you think you want to live in Bellingwood?"

Bailey sat up straighter. "I don't know. Ethan paid cash for the house, so I don't have to come up with house payments. That would be nice. I could sell it and move anywhere."

"The woman who lives next door, Andy Specek, is a wonderful person. She'd be a great neighbor."

"What would I do with myself in that big house?"

"If it's paid for, you could do anything," Tab said.

"That nursing home is right next door. I always wanted to work in geriatrics. I'd also like to get my RN degree."

"It's a wonderful place to work," Polly said. "I have a few friends there. My kids love spending time with the residents."

Bailey looked surprised. "Really?"

"Really. Not all of the kids, but a few enjoy spending time with those people. It's good for everyone."

"That would be awesome to see."

"We don't want to take your time," Tab said. "Would you mind talking to us about Ethan?"

Bailey's face went blank. "Okay."

"We need more information on what he was involved in when you lived in the Quad Cities."

"I don't know that much. He never talked about his work."

"How did he save enough money to buy your house with cash?"

With a huff, Bailey shook her head. "I have no idea. I didn't dare ask. I was only glad that we were moving closer to my family."

"You really had no idea what he was involved in," Polly said quietly. "I know that my husband has a lot going on that I don't pay attention to, but if I was curious, I'd find things out."

"You'd just ask him. He's an open book," Tab said.

"Ethan was never an open book."

"Where did he work?"

"John Deere. He was some kind of foreman there."

"That doesn't explain large amounts of money," Tab said.

"He had something else going on. When he wasn't at work or at home scolding me, he was out doing stuff. Sometimes he'd come home drunk or high. Sometimes he'd come home happy, like he'd scored the winning touchdown. Sometimes he didn't come home at all. But he always kept an eye on me, calling if I wasn't doing what he thought I should be doing."

"Did he travel much?"

"He always said it was for work. He'd come over to Des Moines. You know, John Deere has plants and offices all over."

Tab nodded. "When you moved back to central Iowa, where did he work?"

"He said he got a job with the railroad. That made sense. He worked there when he was in high school. Some of his buddies work there, too. But he never came home dirty like he did when he was younger."

"Did he work regular hours?"

"He left the house about eight thirty every morning. I figured it was a mid-day shift or something."

"Do you believe Ethan might have been involved in transporting drugs?" Tab asked.

Bailey shrugged. "Wouldn't surprise me. Those are the people he hung out with in high school. They weren't dealers or anything, but you could tell they thought it was an easy way to make big money."

"Did he bring drugs to you?" Polly asked.

"No way. He wanted me to be perfect. You know, the sweet girl he knew in high school who was always perfectly dressed and ready to do whatever he wanted to do. Drugs would have messed that up for him. It was like he had an image of the perfect wife in his head."

"Did you know his mother?" Polly wondered if he'd dreamed something up because of the woman who raised him.

"She died when he was in elementary school. His dad and his dad's sister raised him. That old bat was a mean one. She should have been happy that she had a place to live. She never got married, never had kids, never had anything until Ethan's mom died. Then she moved in and acted like she owned everything. I think she's still alive. Ethan doesn't talk about her, but oh, he talked about his mother and how perfect she was. I was never as wonderful as she was."

That made sense to Polly. Ethan Jenkins had internalized his mother's loss and his aunt's nastiness, and it came out in abuse.

"Did you find his address book?" Bailey asked. "I know he had one in a desk at the house."

"It was gone," Tab said. "How long did the man who shot Ethan spend in the house that morning?"

"I don't know for sure. I was in the kitchen making Ethan's breakfast. I didn't even hear the man come in. They could have been talking for a while. Ethan had music playing really loud." She looked at the two on the sofa. "Because he intended to shoot me. He didn't want anyone to hear. I didn't think about that."

"There was no music on when I got there," Polly said.

"Then the guy must have turned it off so neighbors wouldn't complain. I'll bet he took the address book, too."

"Can you remember names of Ethan's high school friends?"

"I should," Bailey said. "They were always hanging around. I need to think."

Polly took a bite from the chocolate macadamia nut cookie and tried not to moan. She must have made a sound because Tab glared at her. "Sorry," she whispered. "Bailey, do you want another cookie?"

"Because sugar will help me think?" Bailey asked with a laugh. "No, I'm good. Mom stuffs me with food all day long. She said I lost too much weight while I was married. Ethan wanted me thin and perfect, you know. I remember two names. Dillon Anderson and Freddy Mayburn. Do you know those names, Deputy Hudson?"

"I'm afraid I do. Mayburn is in jail on drug trafficking charges. Anderson was released two months ago."

"Which would have been when Ethan was in an all-fired hurry to move back to the area."

"But Anderson is a go-fer. He's not the big guy."

"If Ethan wanted to make connections, he would have used Dillon to do it. They go back a long way. Did you find Ethan's phone?"

"It wasn't anywhere in the house or on his person."

"You checked his car?"

"We did. Nothing."

"You should check the back end of the car with a drug-sniffing dog. I'll bet the dog would go crazy. Ethan drove it everywhere."

Tab nodded, taking yet another note in her notebook. She looked at Polly.

"Did Ethan do anything else strange when you moved into the house?" Polly asked.

"Like what? I don't even know how to determine if something he did was strange."

"Did he do any remodeling?"

"A lot," Bailey said. She pondered, lost in her thoughts. "He built shelves in the attic and more storage in the basement. I don't know why. It wasn't like he let me keep things. He dug holes for trees because he said that neighbors wanted to see a new house get upgraded. A few of those retaining wall pavers were broken and cracked. He replaced them. Man, he hated that job. Told me that the next time he was just going to hire someone to do the work. He didn't need to sweat just to keep dirt in place. That was a bad night. He started drinking while he worked and by the time he came inside it was dark. He was in a horrible mood and nothing I could do or say made it better. I thought for sure he was going to hurt me, but because he'd been drinking all night, he passed out on the sofa. Man, I had a terrible time getting all that mud and dirt cleaned up the next day before he got home from work. But I did it."

"Anything else?"

"He hated the back patio, but he bought nice furniture for it. Said we had to at least look good for the neighbors. That was another weird night. He came home with the furniture in a rented truck." She looked at them. "You know what? Dillon was with him to help unload the furniture. I hadn't seen him in years. He looks like hell. I barely recognized him. After unloading, they spent the rest of the evening drinking on the patio. I had to stay up until Ethan got back from taking Dillon home. At least I had time to put cans in the recycling bin and clean up after them. I had the house sparkling clean."

"You've been really helpful," Tab said, sitting forward. "Thank you."

"I'm sorry I was so out of it before. My concentration was nonexistent," Bailey said. "Thank you for being patient with me. Just a second." She took up her phone and typed something, then set it back down. "Mom will be right here."

"If you consider moving back to Bellingwood," Polly said, "you'll have a community ready to support you."

"Mom has the number of that lady counselor you recommended. When I'm more mobile, I'll call her."

"Good. Coming out of a life of abuse isn't easy, but please know that I'll be there for anything you need. If you live next door to Andy Specek, she'll be there, too, along with some other wonderful people in town."

"Andy's best friend is Sheriff Merritt's wife," Tab said. "Now, that woman will take care of you. She's the sheriff's best advocate in the county."

Mrs. Houseman came in carrying two plastic containers. "I know you'll protest, but taking these cookies off my hands would be a blessing."

"Because then she gets to make more and not feel guilty," Bailey said. She triggered the lift chair to help her stand and put her crutches under her arms. "Thank you for coming. I feel like more of the fog is lifting from my mind."

"It will take a while, sweetheart," Mrs. Houseman said. "We can be patient."

CHAPTER TWENTY-THREE

Looking up when she passed Pizzazz, Polly smiled and stopped abruptly in front of Renaldi Fitness. Today was the first day she'd seen outdoor signage. She pulled into a parking space and went to the front door. It was locked. A sign on the door announced they would open June 1. She shook her head in frustration. People might want to sign up. Polly rapped on the door and when she didn't get a response, texted Ray.

"Hey there. Let me in!"

"In where?"

"Into the gym. I'm standing out front feeling exposed. Your signs are amazing."

"Tonya will let you in. I'm in the basement."

"Working on secret stuff?"

"Something like that."

"Like what?"

"Like secret stuff. Leave me alone. If you want a tour of the gym, Tonya's your girl."

"She's a good girl," Polly sent back.

"Weirdo."

"Yes, I am. And I'm proud of it. I do have questions about Ethan Jenkins. What did you find out?"

"What have you gotten yourself into?"

"Come upstairs and find out."

"SMH."

Polly was a full sentence texter. She was about to ask him what he meant when Tonya unlocked the door.

"Out and about?" Tonya asked.

"I saw the signs are up. They look great." Polly pointed at her phone. "What does SMH mean?"

Tonya shook her head as if trying to clear out cobwebs. "SMH? As in texting? It means shaking my head."

"Look at me. I learned something new," Polly said. "Anyway, Cool signs."

"Nan Stallings helped with the design. Ray is happy with the work. They were installed this morning."

"Am I the first person to knock on the front door?"

Tonya nodded. "Since the sign in the window says we don't open until June 1, people are respecting that. It's strange. No one would care in the city. Barge right in whenever you want."

"People will barge in around here, but a gym isn't like a coffee shop or pizza place. You have to really want to go exercise to randomly walk into a gym."

"Is it outside your norm?"

"You know it," Polly said. "I'm more of a walk around the cemetery kind of girl."

"Would you like me to show you around?"

Polly pointed at various types of equipment one by one. "Machine I don't understand. Another machine I don't know how to use. The treadmill there would probably kick me off the back end and then I'd have a bruise on my backside. Oh look, another machine that would beat me up."

"You're hilarious," Tonya said. "And a little pathetic. All it would take is one time and you'd have everything figured out. Caleb would be glad to tell you about all the machines. He helped hook them up and I think he's worked out on every single one."

"That's amazing," Polly said. "I should let him teach me. That would help his self-esteem. We'll talk about it."

"You mean in three or four months after we've battered you with shame?" Ray asked, striding across the room. He pulled Polly into a hug. "What are you doing today?"

"Tab and I just met with Bailey Jenkins," Polly said. "Sounds like Ethan was trafficking drugs across the state."

"Sounds about right. We did more digging into his work at John Deere in the Quad Cities. Asked questions of some of his co-workers. No one liked him."

"Really. That sounds bad."

"A couple of people were willing to talk to us since we aren't the police. They bought from him and said he had a ready supply whenever they asked."

"Any information on his connections?"

"Maybe, but it's vague and shadowy. I've told Sheriff Merritt what we discovered. He's been talking to law enforcement over there."

"But nothing on a contract killer."

"Nothing yet, though it sounds like he's not left town."

"Which is dumb," Tonya said. "Do your job and get out."

"Maybe his job isn't finished yet," Polly said. "If there is that much money attached to Ethan Jenkins, his suppliers want it back."

"Or the drugs he had on hand," Ray said. "He'd have been a fool to stash them at his house."

"I asked Bailey about renovations on the property after they moved in. Ethan was a busy boy. Everything from shelves in the attic to backyard patio furniture."

"Like I said, the man would have been a fool to stash things at his house."

"But criminals are generally not all that smart. They're focused on only one thing, keeping themselves safe and keeping their contraband close," Polly said.

Tonya smirked at Ray. "It's strange that she knows that."

"You need to spend more time with her," Ray said. "Polly's

intuition and understanding of the human experience will surprise you until it doesn't."

"Ten years of looking for murderers has proven to me that criminals are basically idiots. Especially when it comes to drugs," Polly said. "It's not like a criminal mastermind is sitting in his office, overlooking the city and making plans that no one can comprehend. The last one that tried to do that around here was murdered by his own son."

"Who was that?" Tonya asked.

"Frank Mansfield. You met his daughter, Eve."

"The woman with the disabled son," Tonya said.

"He's pretty abled," Polly countered. "He's a musician and he doesn't let much stop him. His mother didn't raise him to feel sorry for himself. This is what he lives with, and he's learning how to live his best life."

Tonya chuckled. "The other day, I saw a pitiful comment on a cool post about friends getting together. This old dude commented that he didn't have any friends because he was a cripple. His life was miserable because no one ever paid attention to him. All I could think was, Buddy, your life is miserable because you aren't a nice person. No one wants to spend time with you because all you think about is your disability. You want everyone else to make your life better, while all you do is whine and complain."

"I'm not much for whining and complaining," Polly said. "Though I've been known to do plenty of it when life gets too overwhelming."

"Not even then," Ray said. "Anyway, I've been in touch with Sheriff Merritt and Deputy Hudson about what we found regarding the Jenkins' case. Tab didn't tell you?"

"Tab has been busy trying to find a break in this case. When she picks me up to talk to someone, I know that she's frustrated. We did get the name of one of Ethan Jenkins' high school friends who welcomed him back with open arms."

Ray's phone rang. When he looked at the face of it, he smiled. "It's my brother."

"Jon?" Polly asked.

Ray scowled. "Do I have another brother?"

"Whatever."

"Let me walk away and take this. If it's business, we'll be a few minutes."

"I can leave," Polly said to Tonya as Ray walked toward the back of the building.

"There's more to see. Come on. Wander with me."

Before they got further than another piece of equipment that made no sense to Polly, Ray was back, holding out his phone.

"Tell her, Jon."

"Polly, I can't believe you're there. I was going to call you next."

"What's up?"

"We have a baby! Chloe and I are going to be parents."

Polly felt tears in her eyes and did her best to hold them back.

"Are you still there?"

"I'm trying not to cry," Polly said. "This is wonderful news. When is your baby coming to you?"

"The birth mother is close. She's been holding out on signing paperwork because she needed to make sure the baby's father didn't want to intervene. They finally got him to sign away his parental rights. It could happen in the next two weeks."

"Two weeks!" Polly exclaimed. "I don't have near enough time to get everything ready."

"I'm sorry," Jon said with a laugh. "Get everything ready?"

"All the things that I plan to send to you. Baby clothes, baby toys, more baby clothes, meal gift cards so you can spend your time oohing over the new baby. Do you know the gender?"

"It's a girl. Can you believe it? I'm going to have a baby girl to raise."

"That's frightening," Ray said. "You'd better do right by that child or I'm stealing her. A little girl? Mama must be ecstatic."

"Mama is insane," Jon said. "She, Chloe, and Drea have planned an all-day shopping trip on Saturday. I have to drive. And then I have to lift and carry because I'm nothing more than their drudge. We don't have anything at the house. Chloe and I looked at cribs and nursery items, but didn't want to set ourselves up for heartbreak, so it's all still at the store."

"You need to hurry. You know two weeks isn't a firm number," Polly said.

"I don't care if the baby has to sleep in the drawer of our dresser," Jon said. "I just want her home with us."

"If you put her in a dresser drawer, I want pictures."

"You will be so overloaded with pictures, you'll have to tell us to stop. Ray, will you come home to meet her?"

"If you and Chloe don't come to Bellingwood first." Ray laughed. "You tell me when that baby is in your hot little hands, and I will be on the next plane to Boston."

"Polly? Will you come with him?"

Polly closed her eyes. All she saw was her calendar.

"I'm kidding," Jon said. "I know what your life looks like. I'd never ask that of you."

"But you should be able to," Polly said. "I have too many kids in my house."

"Graduations, birthday parties, summer activities. I get it. What about a weekend in June after the baby is used to us?"

"That's not a bad idea. The next problem would be that all my kids would want to travel with me."

"We'll be in Bellingwood soon."

"Do you have names?" Tonya asked.

"Is that you, Tonya?" Jon asked. "How do you like Bellingwood?"

"It's growing on me. I'm considering living here."

"No way. That would be terrific. Want to babysit when we're in town?"

"Hey!" Polly said. "You all can come to my house and babysitting will be taken care of by multiple people. Tonya asked you a question. Do you have names yet?"

"We have a plethora of names," Jon said. "We're going to wait until we meet her. Chloe says that she'll know which name fits the little girl when she's in our arms."

"You're killing me," Polly said.

"On purpose. Speaking of killing. How come you haven't found the murderer of that drug guy yet?"

"I've been busy. Don't bug me about it. If I could end this mess, I would. I have a feeling that things will come to a head soon, though. Jon, I'm so happy for you and Chloe. I can't wait to see pictures and I can't wait to meet your baby girl."

"I can't believe you were at Ray's place today so I could tell you both. Ray, take her out for coffee to celebrate." Jon laughed. "I know that it's early to start drinking, but a toast of some sort is necessary. I'm about to be a daddy."

"You'll be a great daddy," Ray said. "I'm happy for you and Chloe, too. Mama needs this in her life."

"She misses you, big brother," Jon said. "She misses you a lot. But Drea and I understand your need to leave the city behind. Always know that we support you."

"Thanks." Ray smiled at Polly and Tonya. "Give Mama a kiss for me and tell your beautiful wife how happy we all are. I'll see you soon."

"Thanks," Jon said. "Talk to you later."

The call ended and Ray turned to Tonya and Polly. "Coffee sounds good. Who's up for something from Sweet Beans?"

"There is never a time that I'm not ready for coffee from Sweet Beans," Polly said. "I haven't had nearly enough to get me through the rest of the day."

"Tonya?" Ray asked.

"I'm going to stay here. I have more work to do in the office and I was on a roll."

"Before I unceremoniously knocked on your front door," Polly said.

"It's been a nice break, but I should go back to work. Ray, would you bring me coffee?"

"It might be a while. Polly and Sweet Beans are inextricably entwined. It's hard getting her out of that place."

"I'm in no hurry." Tonya smiled at Polly and headed to the back.

"You didn't really get a good tour of the place," Ray said. "Do you want to see more?"

"If you don't mind, I'd like to ask Caleb to show me around."

"That's a great idea. Coffee it is."

As they crossed the street, Polly said, "Do you think they'll name the baby with a family name or something unique and interesting?"

"We have unique and interesting in our family history, but I don't know. They wouldn't talk about it since they were terrified it would never happen."

"It was always going to happen. Just a matter of when."

"That's what we told them, but after you are messed with a couple of times, you begin to think there's a problem."

"Problem?"

"None at all, but Jon can make stuff up in his mind if we don't pay attention. It's good for the business because he thinks through most problems that might crop up, but it's not good for his personal life. He worries too much. And it's gotten worse since the day they started the adoption process."

"I thought you were the worrier."

"I'm pretty good at it." Ray opened the door of Sweet Beans and waited for Polly to enter. "When it comes to you, I'm a master worrier. You have so many people who depend on you. What would they do if something happened?"

"Nothing will happen," Polly said. "If it does, we deal with it."

"I don't want to deal with something happening to you. So there." Ray pointed at Doug Randall and Billy Endicott, who were eating lunch. "Those are friends of yours, right?"

"Billy and Doug," Polly said. "My Jedi heroes from years ago. They're all grown up now. Both are married, and Billy has a two-year-old daughter. I'm surprised they're here. Those two are more like the diner set. Excuse me." She had caught Billy's eye, who waved at her. Doug turned around and grinned when he realized who had come in.

"Polly," he said, standing up to greet her. "And Mr. Renaldi. Right? How are things coming at the new gym?"

"Close to opening," Ray said. "You own the comic book store, don't you?"

"You should come in sometime. We do more than comic books. Video games, board games, all sorts of things."

"What are you two doing here rather than the diner?" Polly asked.

Billy shook his head. "The place was packed. It was as if every single person in Bellingwood decided they needed ..." He put his head back and a look of understanding crossed his face. "They needed chicken and noodles over mashed potatoes. I saw the email this morning."

Ray blinked. "What?"

"It's a thing," Doug said. "It's the best thing, but Joe only cooks it a couple of times a month. He sends an email to anyone who wants to know and then the diner explodes all day long."

"I'm surprised Henry didn't say something. He loves that meal," Polly said.

"Lexi could make it," Doug said. "She's good at cooking. We really appreciate her."

"Noodles over mashed potatoes?" Ray was still processing. "That sounds like a lot of carbs."

"Heck yah," Billy said, patting his stomach. His skinny, young man's stomach. "It makes you want to take a nap, but it's the best thing ever. I'm kinda sorry we didn't get there in time, but this comes in a close second. If Lexi wanted to make everyone happy, she'd cook that up one of these days."

"Tell her," Polly said. "Better coming from you than me. She knows that our family will eat whatever she serves, but if you want something special, tell her."

"Anita can't believe Lexi even exists," Doug said. "When she comes home wiped out from work and I have dinner set out for her, well, it's a very nice evening."

"Dude, stop it," Billy said. "Innocent ears here."

"Where?"

"Everywhere. We don't want to know what you and Anita do during your evenings."

Doug grinned at Polly and Ray. "He's so easy. Polly, tell Elijah that his comics are in."

"Anything else there for my family?" she asked.

Ray looked at them. "Your family likes comic books?"

"We have a bunch of families with standing orders," Doug said. "Makes it fun. Some people, like Polly, trust me to not let their kids get out of control."

"I don't care about control," Polly said. "I like the idea of them reading words. Whatever words they will enjoy. I even order some that Noah likes to read to Gillian and Delia." She thought for a moment. "Cassidy isn't an adventurous reader, but I wonder about Teresa. I need to ask Elijah to take her with him some day this summer. He'd introduce her to the wonders of graphic novels. She took a dragon novel off the shelf in the library two weeks ago. I'll bet that girl will fall in love with fantasy."

"You're always thinking," Ray said. "It's nice to meet you."

The two nodded. Doug said, "I'm not much of an athlete. Don't know if I'd join a gym, but Billy needs to build up his muscles."

Billy rolled his eyes.

"I'll be offering a discount to local business owners," Ray said. "You can use it or pass it on to someone who will."

"Anita would," Doug said, shaking his head. "She could beat me up if she had a mind to. Good thing I treat her like the princess she is. I'll talk to her."

"She probably works out in Boone," Ray said. "It's not a big deal. If she's interested, have her stop in."

"She doesn't like to work out in Boone," Doug said. "It's one more hour that she isn't home with me. But if she could do it here in Bellingwood, I could hang out sometimes. That would be cool."

Ray smiled. "If I don't put another mug of coffee in Polly's hand, she might fall asleep. Nice to see you."

"They're good kids," Polly said. "Doug still has a sense of innocence that the world hasn't destroyed. It's nice to see."

"Anita is the tech wizard who works for Sheriff Merritt, right? I've met her a few times. Those two are married?"

"They are a perfect match. Doug didn't want to believe it, but she wrangled and roped him until he agreed that she was right about everything. They belonged together. Anita was patient. Very patient. It all worked out."

He didn't reply, but put his hand on Polly's back as they walked toward the counter.

"Hello, again," Josie said, beaming at Ray. "You are turning into one of our best customers."

"It's a nice place to spend a few moments," Ray said. "Polly needs coffee. I need a matcha tea and we both need to look at the baked goods."

"You look, I'll pour, we'll meet back here in a few minutes," Josie said. "How are you today, Polly?"

"I wondered if you were going to ignore me for the gorgeous man at my side."

Josie laughed. "Sorry. He is all that. Good thing I'm married, or I'd be a terrible flirt."

It was good to see Ray blush. With his hand still on Polly's back, he moved her to the display. "You're horrible," he said in low tones.

"It's my thing."

CHAPTER TWENTY-FOUR

Driving home from Sweet Beans, Polly was surprised when her phone rang. She shouldn't have been, but it still made her jump.

"Rebecca, hello," Polly said. "Do you miss me?"

"Can you come over to Beryl's house?"

Polly braked and turned at the next corner. If Rebecca was asking, she was going. "Why? What's happening?"

"Another email. I've already called Anita and she's sending Deputy Decker."

"What did the email say?"

"That it was time for them to meet. Polly, whoever this is, either came to central Iowa today or already lives here. Who would be this nuts?"

"I can think of a lot of people. Have you told Beryl?"

"No. She's finishing something in her studio that has her on edge. I don't want to bother her unless it's absolutely necessary."

"How scary did the email sound?" Polly asked. She didn't want to tempt Chief Wallers or Bert Bradford with catching her speeding through town, so she held herself back. Moving through Bellingwood wouldn't take that long. Except for the little old man in front of her who must have been out for a lazy drive. Polly turned at the next corner to get away from him, only to run into street reconstruction and one-lane traffic.

"What is it with this?"

"What?" Rebecca asked.

"Slow drivers. Construction. I am trying to get there. I really am." Polly had dealt with this type of annoyance all the time in Boston. It was part of living in a city, but she didn't like dealing with it in Bellingwood. When they put new blacktop on the highway going through town, she'd learned to duck off the highway as soon as possible. The only problem was, everyone else had the same idea. Traffic had been out of control for those two weeks. Scraping off the old, laying down new, adding new curbs, on and on. It had seemed like the project would never end.

Since there was a big hole in the street, Polly figured this one must be a water main break. Infrastructure in places like Bellingwood had been allowed to languish. If you couldn't see a problem, there was no problem. Until something broke. Then, it was all hands on deck. She took an annoyed breath and waited. How many cars were there that had chosen to come down this specific street? Too many. And she was the third car back on the other side.

The person with the sign looked back and then turned the sign from stop to slow. Like she could drive any faster than the person in front of her. Whoops. She was annoyed. She needed to get over that right now. Rebecca was worried and a snarky Polly was the last thing the girl wanted to deal with.

Then Polly realized the phone call was still open. "Sorry. I'm being annoyed at traffic," she said.

"I'm watching out the front window. I wasn't paying attention to you anyway."

"Did you hear back from Anita about the email sender?"

"Yeah. Sounds like they can find the person."

"She didn't give you any information?"

"You mean, like who they are or where they live?" Rebecca asked. "No. I'm not you. I don't have a personal relationship with everyone at the department. I'm not best friends with the sheriff's wife either."

"But you're my daughter."

"I'm still a kid to them."

"It's important that they are only sending one deputy," Polly said. "If they were worried about it becoming dangerous, they'd send more people."

"That's good to hear. I just hope this person isn't as crazy as they sound."

"What did the email say?"

"Just that Beryl hadn't responded and so they were coming to meet her. To make her understand their demands. Because ... Okay, I see you in the driveway. I'm going to open the front door when you get here. Not before. Hurry. I don't want to put you in danger, too."

Polly wasn't going to argue. She ended the call, looked at her tote bag, wondering if there was anything in there she needed. Then, she got out and tripped the lock on the doors. No use tempting someone to steal her car in an attempt to get away.

Rebecca was peeking through the window of the front door. After all these years of living with Polly, she still worried about the smallest things. Polly hurried to the door. Rebecca opened it and practically pulled Polly inside. She didn't wait for the screen door to close, and pushed the heavy wooden door shut, locking it once it latched.

Without a word, Rebecca went back to the wall beside the window and peeked outside again. "I want Deputy Decker to be here before this person shows up."

"It will be fine, honey."

"How do you know that? Whoever it is wants Beryl's attention and is mad that she won't give it to them. It could be a deranged killer."

"Or a pathetic fan," Polly said. "Someone who needs to be seen and heard. You're on social media. You see how important it is for those people to make their voices loud enough that others pay attention to them."

"I also watch the news. And stalkers abound."

"Beryl isn't that famous."

"It doesn't matter," Rebecca said, clearly frustrated with Polly's low-impact responses. She was ready to amp this up. "If someone is obsessed, they'll do whatever it takes to get attention. Did Mark David Chapman need to kill John Lennon? No, but he did it anyway, just so the world would pay attention to him."

"How in the world do you know that name?" Polly asked. She certainly hadn't remembered Lennon's assassin.

"Something Andrew was researching. We were talking about murderers and how their names go down in history, when it should be their victims who are remembered."

"Rebecca, your mind is taking you down paths that aren't helpful. You need to push those thoughts aside and focus on what can be done."

"Nothing," Rebecca barked. "Nothing."

"You've already done something. You called Anita. You called me. That's something."

Stu Decker's vehicle drove past the house, slowing as he looked around. He turned south at the corner and backed up, then drove past the other way.

"What's he doing?" Rebecca asked.

"He's looking for anything out of place," Polly replied. "Do you not trust him to do his job?"

"Right." Rebecca looked at the floor. "I'm being dramatic again, aren't I?"

"A little. It's understandable, but not helpful."

"I worry so much about Beryl."

"Beryl has been taking care of herself for many years," Polly said. "You can't come in here and place your concerns on her life. She hired you to help her, not control or protect her."

Rebecca frowned. "What do you mean?"

"How many times have you seen adult children taking over when their parents try to make decisions?"

"I don't know. That's a thing?"

"It's a big thing. Trust me, if any of you try to tell me and

Henry what to do when we are older, you'll find yourself in a snowdrift somewhere. It's rude and irresponsible. Treating older adults as if they're incapable of managing life is ridiculous. Even if they move slower or take longer to make decisions. The thing is, they have decades of experience that tells them to slow down and make good decisions rather than fast decisions.

"You don't do that to Grandma Marie or Grandpa Bill, do you?"

"I hope not. I hope someone would tell me to stop it if I did."

"I'll tell you."

Polly laughed. "I know you will. But I'm telling you right now. Do not treat Beryl as if she's a slow-thinking, poor-decision-making old lady. She won't insist on her own way, but she will lose respect for you. As will her friends."

"I hadn't thought of it that way."

"That's why I'm here for you."

They both jumped at a knock on the door.

"I wasn't paying attention," Rebecca said. "Who is it?"

Polly was already moving toward the door.

"Don't open it," Rebecca demanded.

"It's Stu. I think I'll open the door," Polly said.

She unlocked and opened the door, then gestured for Stu Decker to come inside.

"Hello, Polly. I wasn't at all surprised to see your Suburban in the driveway. Trust you to be where the action is."

"I called her," Rebecca said. She looked outside. "Where's your car?"

"On the next block north. There is no sign of anyone wandering through the area," he said. "Where's Ms. Watson?"

"In her studio."

"Can a person get to the studio without coming through the main house?"

Rebecca's eyes grew wide. "What was I thinking? If they know so much about her, they know where she works. They wouldn't come to the house." She took off.

Stu gave Polly a look of surprise and raced after Rebecca. They tore down the steps to the basement and toward the back door. While Polly didn't run to catch up to them, she moved just fast enough to arrive at the back door when Stu pushed Rebecca back into the house.

"Why?" Rebecca asked.

"If it's not safe for Ms. Watson," he said, "it's not safe for you. Stay put."

He put his hand on his gun, not drawing it, but making sure he was prepared as he approached the steps leading to Beryl's studio.

Beryl opened the door at his knock and stepped back, shock apparent on her face. "Deputy Decker, what are you doing at my studio door?" She looked around him to see Polly and Rebecca. "What is going on here? Rebecca, is everything okay?"

"I guess," Rebecca said.

"Has something happened that I should know about?"

"Would you come inside the house with us?" Stu asked. "And can you lock the studio door when you do?"

"It will take a minute to find the key, but I can do that," Beryl said with a laugh. "You're scaring me. Is this about my stalker? I was in the middle of something."

Stu walked with her back to the safety of the basement, his eyes darting around the yard.

When they got inside, Beryl started to sit on a sofa, but Rebecca took her arm. "Let's go upstairs. It's safer there."

"Why?"

"I'm a nervous Nellie. That's why." Rebecca locked the sliding glass doors before drawing the curtains closed.

"That seems like overkill," Beryl said. Then she stared at Rebecca. "Was there another email?"

"This one said the person was coming here today," Rebecca said. "I called Polly and Anita because I didn't want to bother you. I know you are trying to get your work done."

"You can always bother me, dear. I'm on schedule. If I have to take time for a stupid stalker, I can find it. Deputy, have you found out anything about the person?" Beryl dropped onto her sofa, pulling one of the two cats, May or Hem, into her lap. The other cat showed up from heaven knew where and climbed to the back of the sofa, laying its head on Beryl's shoulder.

Stu smiled at the scene and sat in an overstuffed chair. He had to move a quilt and a pillow, but he got there. "We know a lot more," he said. "The person uses Wi-Fi in a variety of locations in town. The library, Sweet Beans, the comic book store, even Pizzazz."

"That means they're local," Rebecca said.

"But they haven't moved until now," Beryl countered. "The strange thing is that I haven't done anything abnormal lately. Nothing to draw this person's attention. I haven't changed my style or sold paintings to evil cabals."

"You have become more public with your art," Stu said. "Anita tells me that your artwork is everywhere."

"Of course it is," Beryl said. "I want my friends to have a part of me in their lives."

"It's hanging in shops now. That's new in the last few years. You have an immense piece in the front lobby of Sycamore House."

Beryl put up a finger. "That has been there for over ten years."

"There is more upstairs at Sycamore House, and even more is hanging at Greene Space."

"You know where I am," she said.

"You've been generous with your paintings. Is there anyone you refused?"

Beryl huffed a laugh. "The only person I flat out said no to was Cyrus Wagner. He wanted me to donate a piece so he could hang it at the General Store. He told me that it would generate sales. Umm, Cyrus, I don't need to generate sales. He became annoyed that I wouldn't just give him a painting out of the goodness of my heart, but he's not foolish enough to stalk me. He'd call me out in front of his cronies."

"How long ago was that conversation?" Stu asked.

"It's been a couple of years," Beryl said. "He hasn't brought it up since then, though that surprises me. He isn't one to let people get away with saying no to him." She grinned at Stu. "Don't tell me that I'm wrong about him and that Cyrus Wagner has been stalking me. That would be creepy. Wait. Maybe he's interested in me. Hah, I wouldn't date that snake if he was the last man on earth."

"Cyrus at the comic book store?" Polly asked. "Sweet Beans? The library? He might take his family to Pizzazz, but the other locations would hold no interest for him."

Stu nodded. "I know him well enough to know that he wouldn't do something like that."

"Then who?" Beryl asked. "I've been wracking my brain for months." She shrugged. "For weeks. Before that I simply ignored the emails. No use responding to the crazies out there."

"That means we have crazies in Bellingwood," Rebecca said. "And just when I thought it was utopia."

The other three stared at her.

"Utopia?" Beryl asked.

"It's pretty close," Polly said. "You only have to ignore a certain subset of people."

"What does that mean?"

"The negative grumpy subset that is determined to bring everyone else to their level. My goodness, they'd rather be sarcastic and mean than be happy. I ignore them. Just as you ignored that negative grumpy emailer."

A knock at the front door caused everyone to tense up. Beryl pulled the cat closer to her chest, Rebecca moved over to sit beside her friend, and Polly stood, ready to take on whomever might walk through the door.

"I'll answer it," she said.

"Why you?" Rebecca asked.

"I'm not about to let it be you," Polly said. "Beryl doesn't need to be part of it, and if Stu answers the door, the person might run before we find out why they're doing this. It has to be me."

Stu closed his eyes. "I understand why Deputy Hudson drinks antacid by the gallon."

"She does not," Polly said.

He smiled. "No, she doesn't. I'll be right behind you."

"Out of sight, though."

"Right behind you," he repeated.

The person knocked again, this time with a little more force.

Polly ignored the thumping of her heart and walked down the short hallway to the front door. She looked through the window, then motioned for Stu to look as well. The person on the other side of the door was a young, quite overweight man. He carried a sheaf of papers in one hand and his other hand rested on a large messenger bag.

Cyrus Wagner's grandson, Jebediah. He was the same age as Rebecca, but everyone ignored him. The boy was strange. When Noah dated Cyrus's granddaughter, Millie, he told Polly stories about how Jeb lived in the basement of their parents' home, never coming out except to get food. His parents couldn't get him to join them for activities, much less meals.

He obviously knew enough about the internet to not log in to his computer from home. She'd seen him a few times at Sweet Beans. It made sense that he spent time at Boomer's Last Stand. Even the library would feel comfortable to him.

Stu nodded when she placed her fingertips on the door handle. "Go ahead. He's not dangerous."

Jeb knocked again, more insistent. As he pulled back to hit the door with a fist, Polly opened it. He stopped himself before punching her in the nose. "What are you doing here?"

"Better question," Stu Decker said. "What are you doing here?" When Jeb tried to back away, Stu took his arm. "Come on inside. I have questions for you."

"I didn't do anything," Jeb protested. "I'm here for a scheduled meeting with Ms. Watson."

"Funny," Polly said. "She knows nothing about any scheduled meeting. In fact, she's upset that you are bothering her while she's in the middle of completing a project."

"That isn't my problem. I told her I was coming. If she doesn't know about it, that's her issue." The boy tried defiance, but it came out more like whining.

Rebecca stood behind Polly and said, "Jeb Wagner, what in the world?"

His eyes grew wide, not expecting to see her. "Why are you here?" he asked.

"I work for Ms. Watson. Are you the one who has been sending her threatening emails? What a fool you are. I always tried to be nice to you, but you didn't want that, did you? You wanted to feel sorry for yourself and act like the world was against you. In fact, you set yourself up for failure. This is disgusting." Rebecca gave her head a quick shake and turned away.

When she turned, Jeb's face fell. "I didn't mean to be threatening. I only wanted to talk to Ms. Watson. She should have given us a painting."

Rebecca walked back into the living room and out of his sight.

"You admit to sending emails to Ms. Watson," Stu said.

Jeb shrugged. "You got me. Better call my grandpa. He'll get me out of this."

"With the number of harassing emails that you have sent and the fact that you showed up here today to harass or intimidate Ms. Watson, you are looking at a felony charge, young man," Stu said. He took the sheaf of papers from Jeb's hand and gave them to Polly to hold. Then, he removed the messenger bag and set it on the floor. "What is in here?"

"My laptop and other stuff," Jeb said.

"Turn around." Stu pushed the young man's arm and Jeb turned.

When Stu pulled his arms to his back and snapped a zip tie around Jeb's wrists, the boy burst into tears. "What are you doing to me?"

"I'm arresting you for harassment."

"You can't do this. You know who my grandfather is."

"I can do this. I don't care who your grandfather is."

"He'll have your head on a platter."

"Are you threatening me?" Stu asked.

That was the moment when Jeb decided that it would be best to stop talking. He shot Polly a furious look and kicked toward her, making contact with the messenger bag instead. "Grandpa is going to hate you for this."

"I didn't do anything wrong," Polly said. "I'm only here to make sure that a friend is safe."

"He'll still hate you. You can't do this to me."

"Looks like I already have," Stu said. "I'm about to read you your rights, but the first thing you might do is choose to be silent. You do not need to talk to me, so please don't." He picked up the bag, then opened it, motioning for Polly to put the papers she held inside. When she looked at them, she realized they were printouts of many of Beryl's paintings located around town. The boy had done his homework.

"Now, you get to walk with me," Stu said. "My patrol car is on the next block. Won't it be fun to show all the neighbors how we deal with someone who harasses our residents?"

"I can't walk very far," Jeb whined. "My knees are bad."

"Imagine that." Stu pushed him to get the boy to move. Sure enough, Jeb made a scene, limping down the sidewalk.

"This is abuse," he cried. Then he shouted. "Police abuse! Police abuse!"

Polly watched Stu turn Jeb onto the front sidewalk. All the while, the young man cried, whined, and complained. She didn't envy Stu his task today. He was speaking to someone on his walkie as the boy continued to complain.

When she closed the door, Beryl peeked around the corner. "Is he gone?"

"Poor Stu has to put up with him all the way back to Boone," Polly said. "That won't be pleasant. Thank you for not coming out."

"He wasn't going to have the pleasure of meeting me face to face," Beryl said. "Though he has seen me plenty of times when he's been in Sweet Beans. What a little brat. Why would his parents let him get away with being like that?"

"It's easier to ignore them when they get weird," Polly said.

"You don't take the easy way."

"I have plenty of bad parenting ideas," Polly said, "but I won't allow my kids to hide from me or the world. They can be introverts and still participate as functioning members of society."

"Like me," Rebecca said.

"You are one of the most extroverted people I know," Beryl said, wrapping an arm around Rebecca's shoulder. "Thank you for standing between me and the crazy today. I wish it hadn't been necessary, but it's over. Polly, would you like to stay and have something to drink with us?"

"Drink?"

"Iced tea or coffee," Rebecca said with no small amount of disdain in her voice.

"No. I was on my way home. It's been a busy day." Polly hugged Beryl. "I'm glad this is over for you. Will you be able to go back to work?"

"No," Beryl said. "My concentration is blown to pieces. Maybe Rebecca and I will go for a drive with our cameras. See what we can see. That will bring me peace."

CHAPTER TWENTY-FIVE

Everything in the forecast changed this morning, sending Polly's frustration level up. Rain this afternoon. Great. Any effort she put into setting up the back yard would become a mess. It didn't look like tomorrow would be much better. Rebecca's party would have to happen in the foyer. That didn't sound awful, but she hated forcing people into one room when the Bell House had such a great back yard. Children could play, and people could mill about without bumping into each other.

"Stupid rain," she muttered.

"What was that?" Lexi asked.

"Mad at the weather, that's all," Polly said.

"We aren't going to be able to have it outside, are we?"

"Nope. Stupid rain."

"Stupid rain," Lexi agreed. "I need to go to the grocery store in Boone. Do you need anything?"

"You're leaving me?"

"For less than an hour. I promise. Do you want me to pick something up for you?"

"Kahlua, vodka, rum, whatever you want."

"Are you serious?"

Polly grinned. "No. I'm being dramatic. My mind has been whirling about with plans for this party. I can't let go of what happened with Bailey Jenkins. I really want to figure that out so we can put it behind us."

"Seems like this would be a great day for you to wrap up that whole thing."

"Any day would be a great day to wrap it up."

"If you did, you would be able to enjoy tomorrow's party. Everyone that you love will be here. You don't want to carry your worries with you."

Polly laughed. "You sound like me now."

"All that teaching has been ingrained in my soul," Lexi said. "Do you want me to stop at Sweet Beans on the way back and buy you some treats?"

"No. I'll suffer in silence."

"At least you don't hide your feelings."

"Suffering in silence is hiding my feelings."

"So far there hasn't been much silence." Lexi smirked and picked up her bag and keys. "I'll be back before you have a clever retort for me."

"Sassy girl," Polly said under her breath as Lexi left the house. "She's right. I need to do something proactive to solve this stupid murder." She swiped her phone to Tab's phone number and placed the call.

"Polly. How are you?"

"Frustrated."

"By me?"

"Yes, but not really. Did you go through the Jenkins home again after Bailey told you about the different things that Ethan had worked to replace and fix?"

"We went through it with a fine-tooth comb," Tab said. "With all the rain, we didn't dig around outside much. We'll do that once the weather calms down. I don't know where to start, though. It won't be fun digging up freshly planted trees. It seems mean. Once the storms pass, we'll be back."

"That makes sense. And nothing from Dillon Crane?"

"At least we have him off the street again. He'll be busy in jail for quite some time."

"Or not busy."

"He has enough friends that he'll find a way to keep himself busy. What are you up to today?"

"I want to solve this thing."

"So do I. We'll get there. We always do."

"I want to solve it before tomorrow's party."

"That's specific. Why?"

"Because I want it out of my head. It's been one of those niggly little things that shows up when I'm trying to go back to sleep. Between that and the stupid weather, I'm grumpy."

"A grumpy Polly is no fun. You're not able to use the back yard tomorrow, are you?" Tab huffed. "Of course you aren't. The forecast says it will rain all day. Do you need help getting the house ready for people? I can be there after work."

"You're amazing. No, I have plenty of help. We'll spend more time cleaning tonight than I planned, but I have Rebecca, Lexi, and Amalee to guide the rest of the family."

"It's nice having Rebecca home, isn't it?"

Polly smiled. "I love having her around, and I can't wait until next week when all the kids will be home. There will be more things I'm required to manage, but I love it when they're here."

"Is Amalee eighteen?"

"Non sequitur," Polly said. "Yes, she turned eighteen last November."

"I saw her at the grocery store last week. That doesn't seem like a good job for her. Did you know that Dani is looking for help at the winery?"

"I didn't," Polly said. "Amalee would be great at that."

"I'll say something to Dani, but Amalee needs to stop in and apply for the job. Dani will be there tonight. Would she be comfortable working there?"

"I won't know until after school. This is her last day since she graduates next week. If I can scoot her out the door, I will."

"She might work on the floor and in the gift shop. There are a million things to do there. JJ tries to stay away from hiring, but it's becoming a necessity. I didn't even think about your family until you mentioned them just now. What do you think?"

"I think he better bonus her with wine for me," Polly said.

"If she takes the job, he'll say thank you. Trust me. This is stressful for him. He wants to do so many things, but he needs employees and he hasn't found the right person. When I'm required to work the floor for parties, you know things are bad."

"We should talk to Nan about setting up a board on the Bellingwood website for companies to tell the town what employees they need."

"That's a good idea. Make yourself a note. You'll forget."

"It's like you know me. Okay, this conversation got bigger than I expected," Polly said. "I shouldn't keep you."

"It's nice to talk to you about things other than murder and crime. We both have lives and I like being part of yours."

"I like being part of yours, too. Henry and I need to make more of an effort to go to the winery."

"With your underage children?" Tab asked with a laugh. "That's like me saying that I need to …" She paused. "I don't know how to end that sentence."

"You go back to work," Polly said. "I'm going to take a walk before the rain hits."

"It's funny to me that the cemetery is your favorite place to walk."

"It's convenient. People go there to visit their loved ones. Any conversations they have are with the people they miss, not me. That means it's usually quiet. I might stop to talk to Charlie, but I like him, so that makes it nice."

"You are a good person, even when you're grumpy because of the weather. I will talk to you later. I was serious about stopping by to help you clean and get ready for tomorrow. Don't hesitate to call." Tab paused. "Maybe I should tell Lexi the same thing. She'd be more likely to ask for help than you."

"We'll be fine. I have kids galore in the house. Since Lexi and I constantly push them to pick up after themselves, that part won't be bad. We have dusting and vacuuming to do, but even that isn't awful. Lexi is the best person in the world. She takes good care of me."

"Let me know," Tab said. "JJ is working tonight, so I'll be home with nothing to do."

"If you're looking for entertainment, you're always welcome. We'll talk later."

"Be good. No more dead bodies. We don't have time for that this week."

"Got it. I'll be on my best behavior."

"And ... now, you've jinxed it."

"I really did. Sorry," Polly said. She laughed. "We don't believe in superstitions, right?"

"I believe in superstitions. You be careful out there. I'll keep my phone close in case you need me. Talk to you later."

"Okay." Polly ended the call. All four dogs looked at her, hoping for something ... anything. "I'm going by myself today. I can't manage all of you."

There was enough wind blowing that Polly took a jacket. She wanted to enjoy the walk and calm her inner being, not shiver and shake while rushing back to the house.

She passed through the back gate and the hedge separating their property from the cemetery, then walked to the left instead of toward Andy and Len's house to the right. This was a new pathway for her brain. Funny that she always took the same route. Today would be different.

As she walked, she breathed in and out, slow enough to lower her stress level. Charlie wasn't here today. His shed was closed. No one else was around. She had the entire cemetery to herself and could take as long as she wanted to bring herself back to center. Lexi would be home in an hour. If Polly wasn't home by then, something else had happened. But an hour would be a good amount of time to wander through the grounds.

She drew close to Charlie's shed – and shed wasn't the right word for the small building he used as his home base. It was painted a beautiful dark gray, with white trim on the windows and door. He'd planted flowers around it and installed a pretty bench on the east side. Today, in front of the bench were pieces of concrete that Charlie had picked up. She didn't know why he hadn't discarded them yet. You never knew when it came to Charlie's habits. He kept things that made no sense. But that was his thing.

Her mind flashed back to the morning she'd spent with Tab and Bailey Jenkins. One thing that Ethan had done was work on retaining wall pavers. What if these bits of concrete had come from one of those? Polly's imagination ran wild as she veered off onto a walkway that cut across the middle of the cemetery. He could have easily ... No, that would have been too much work. But was it? Why wouldn't he scatter the concrete pieces he broke off the back of a paver and hide something behind it. It would have been a big task, but anyone with strong enough intent could do that work. Depending on what he was hiding, Ethan Jenkins would have been highly motivated.

She stopped before entering the Jenkins' back yard. She should call Tab. But what if she was making this up? Tab didn't need to spend any more time here. Ray would scold Polly for wading in without anyone knowing what she was doing. Instead of Tab, she called Tonya. Unless she was busy, Tonya would come over. She'd also tell Ray that Polly had asked for help, which would earn Polly goodwill points with him.

Swiping through the contact list, she landed on Tonya's number and tapped the call button.

"Hey, Polly," Tonya said. "What can I do for you?"

"Are you busy?"

"I'm always busy, but never too busy for you. What do you need?"

"Backup."

"I'm sorry, what?"

"I'm being responsible and calling you rather than wading into a potential situation without anyone knowing where I am."

"Would you like me to join you?"

"You'll get here after I start, but yes. That way, Ray won't get mad at me."

"He is protective of you. I'm heading out the door to my car. Tell me where I'm going."

"Do you know where I found that body?"

"Sure."

"That house. Front yard. Retaining wall pavers. I think Ethan Jenkins hid something in one of them."

"I'm not going to ask why you think that. I'm simply going to get in my car and come over. I will ask why you think that digging out a paver will get you into trouble."

"Because it's the way things work in my world," Polly said.

"And you called me because?"

"I'm not going to bother Deputy Hudson unless it's real. They've been over this house a lot and found nothing. She's busy with other cases. I won't call Ray because he won't let me do anything on my own. Henry is at work, Lexi isn't made for this stuff, and you are my badass friend."

Tonya laughed. "I have tools in my trunk if you're digging a paver out of a retaining wall. What did you think you were going to use?"

"I was going to ransack their garage." Polly laughed. "That's a lie. I hadn't actually thought that far in advance. Something always comes to me, though. Today, it's you and your toolbox. Thank you."

"I'm almost there," Tonya said. "Nothing like being in a small town to get places in a hurry. I've never lived like this."

"It's a good life." Polly walked around the gated back yard. When she got to the driveway, she had to either walk all the way to the end and back up, or sit on the retaining wall, then jump down. She sat and jumped to the driveway, thankful this driveway wasn't how she had to get in and out of her garage. She'd surely hit something while backing out.

Tonya's vehicle pulled in and the back hatch opened. "There is a lot of rock here," Tonya said. "How do you plan to uncover which he pulled?"

"He wouldn't have gone any lower than the second or third row. After that, it would be impossible to pull the paver. The top row might be too obvious. I'm looking for one that looks like it was disturbed in the last month."

"Second or third row. Got it. I'll take this side, you take that side. Anything out of place, we'll dig it out."

"Thank you for coming," Polly said.

"Any time. I'm proud of you for asking." Tonya strode to the garage and then, using her hands, traced the pavers as she walked toward the end of the driveway.

Polly did the same thing on the other side, peering at each one, hoping to find something that looked different than everything else.

"I think I found it," she said. A paver in the second row, about halfway down the driveway was chipped on one edge. Dirt had settled, but something had happened here.

Tonya arrived at her side with a shovel, a hammer, and a tire iron.

"One of those should dig this out," Polly said with a laugh.

"He already did the hard work," Tonya said. "He wouldn't have made it difficult to pull it back out."

Polly pushed and felt the paver give. Then, she put her fingers on both sides of it and gave a short tug. Tonya was right. Ethan Jenkins had made it easy to take it out of the wall. When she pulled it out, she realized that it was only a four-inch façade. He'd broken the rest of it off to leave space for something in the back.

"I can't believe it," Tonya said. "You did it."

"Now, I need to call Tab."

A deep voice growled at the two of them. "You need to back away."

Polly still had the paver in her hand. "Who are you?"

"The person who is willing to shoot you both if you don't do exactly what I tell you to do."

"Really?" Polly asked. "You're wearing a balaclava in this weather? Like people in Bellingwood won't notice something like that?"

Tonya made an audible gulping sound.

"If you see my face, I'll have to kill you," the man said. He had raised the gun in his right hand, his finger on the trigger. He didn't hold it like others Polly had seen, who had no idea what they were doing with a gun. If this was the man who killed Ethan Jenkins, he knew what he was doing.

"Where did you come from?"

He shrugged. "I've been watching the house. We knew Jenkins had hidden this somewhere; we didn't know where. Now that you've found it, I can be on my way. Back off."

Polly lifted her shoulders as she took a breath, hoping that Tonya was ready to deal with whatever came next. As she took a step back, she made it look as if she were stumbling. In that same moment, she tossed the paver at the man, not at all surprised that it missed him. It took him off guard. He wasn't expecting pushback from two girls. Men should know better than to underestimate women.

His eyes were drawn to the paver, and Tonya unleashed on the man. She'd dropped the shovel and hammer when Polly stumbled. Using the tire iron as a weapon, she moved past Polly and knocked the gun out of the man's hand. When she brought it back around, she smacked him in the shoulder before kicking him in the groin. It all happened in a matter of seconds.

He dropped, holding his nether region with both hands. Tonya dropped the tire iron. With a closed fist, she rapped his temple, driving him further to the ground. He was whimpering by the time she finished.

"Front seat," she said to Polly. "Zip ties. Get two."

Polly was stunned by the show of power from the woman and ran toward the front of Tonya's car.

A black duffel bag in the passenger seat was the only place the zip ties could be. Polly unzipped it and found a slew of various non-lethal weapons and other items. Did this girl travel with these things all the time? She pulled out two zip-ties and raced back to Tonya. Within seconds, the man was moaning because he couldn't protect his poor aching groin any longer.

"Who are you?" he asked.

"Better question," Tonya said as she pulled off his balaclava. "Who are you? And don't give me the, I'm your worst nightmare, crap. Honey, I'm *your* worst nightmare."

"I'm not talking to you."

"Fine," Polly said and took out her phone. She called Tab.

"Did you reconsider my offer?" Tab asked.

"No, but I'd like to inform you that I have your murderer moaning in the Jenkins' driveway."

"You what?"

"Yeah. I also found what he was looking for."

"You what?"

"Are you on your way to Bellingwood now?"

"You what?"

"Not by myself."

Tab sighed. "Who is with you? Lexi?"

"Nope. I called Tonya Adkins. She's badass."

"I've met her. She isn't someone I'd want to encounter in a dark alley if she was angry with me. I can't believe you asked for help."

"I know me. This guy had a gun and because I had an idea where to find the contraband ..." Polly looked at the gaping hole in the retaining wall. They still hadn't pulled anything out. "Anyway, I assumed that my luck would be at play. I was about to get myself in trouble. If I was wrong, I didn't want to waste your time. If I was right, I needed help. And besides, Ray would kill me if I waded into one more thing without thinking."

"So would Aaron. It's a good thing you have two men on your conscience."

"Are you on your way?"

"With Will. I'm already driving. When we hang up, I'll call Alan Dressen. Where did you find what we were looking for?"

"In the retaining wall. Charlie Heller couldn't figure out why pieces of concrete were scattered in the cemetery. This was one of the things that Bailey said her husband had worked on after they moved in."

"And I hadn't gotten there yet because of all the rain," Tab said. "Trust you to make it happen."

"Call Alan. Tonya has control of the situation here. I'm safe."

"I can't tell you how much that means to me."

"You know I'm about to ask the man questions," Polly said.

"Be sure to video tape the conversation. It will give me a starting point when he gets back to the shop."

"Thanks for not being mad that I didn't call you."

"You called Tonya. She's not law enforcement, but I trust her. Thank you." Tab ended the call and Polly looked at the man curled into the fetal position, still moaning on the ground.

"Good thing it isn't raining yet," she said. "Deputy Hudson is on her way. She's the one who has been searching the house for whatever it is that you thought was important enough to kill for."

"He asked for it," the man said. "And then he went and shot his wife. I wasn't sure if I was going to kill him until he did that. I think he waited for me to show up so he could blame an intruder for what happened to her."

"He knew you were coming?" Tonya asked. She had already started a video on her phone.

"Sure. It was supposed to be a simple hand-off. At least that's what he thought. Little did he know that I'd been hired to get rid of him if he made trouble. Stupid idiot. He thought he could establish a new territory over here. Iowa isn't that big of a state. Did he think we wouldn't know?"

"Let me get this straight," Polly said. "You work for a drug dealer in the Quad Cities. You scheduled a meeting with Ethan Jenkins at oh-dark-thirty on a Saturday morning. When you showed up, you had a silencer for your gun so you could assassinate him. He also had a gun, but used it on his wife instead of you."

"Because he's that much of a jerk," the man said. "We knew he was beating her, but that wasn't our business. As long as he did his job, we didn't care how he lived. But when I saw him shoot her, I wasn't having it. He actually grinned at me, thinking that I'd approve."

The metal box that Polly tugged out of the hole was heavy. "What's in here?" she asked.

"Open it. I can't change the course of things now."

She set it on the ground, then thought better of opening it. That should be something that Tab or Will Kellar did.

He shook his head. "Fentanyl and Oxy. Close to a quarter million worth of pills. He bought it over here and we planned to distribute it out of the Quad Cities. Idiot Jenkins thought he could pull a fast one and keep it for himself, opening his own distribution network. Sounds like he had some low-class high school friends who were willing to work for him. I asked him nicely to turn it over. He said he'd never gotten the shipment. The man was not a good liar."

"But you're a good talker," Polly thought to herself. Out loud, she said. "Where's the gun he used on Bailey?"

"Gone."

"What does that mean? Why would you get rid of it?"

"Just muddied the story. She's better off without him."

"No doubt about that," Polly said. "Where's your car?"

He glanced toward the east, then shook his head. "Find it or not. I don't care."

"What kind of car is it?"

"Black Subaru Outback. Scott County plates. You'll find his book and phone in the back seat."

"You're awfully talkative."

He shrugged and tried to come to a seated position. Tonya pushed him back to the ground. "Look, I'm going to prison. Might as well be honest. Once I'm in, I'm not coming out. Besides, you aren't law enforcement. I'll get a lawyer and he or she will do what they can for me. Right now, this whole thing is on me. I'm going to keep it that way and keep my life intact."

Two Boone County sheriff's vehicles drove into the cul-de-sac. Tab was the first one to reach them. She shook her head while she grinned. "You really did it."

"If you give me your email," Tonya said, "I'll send you the video of the last few minutes. He told Polly everything."

"Of course he did," Tab said. She took out her notebook, wrote on a page, tore it out, and handed it to Tonya. "Thanks. People tell Polly things they would never consider telling me." She pointed at the box. "Did you open it?"

"No," Polly said. "That's your job. He tells me there are fentanyl and oxy pills in it."

"Well, isn't that pleasant. Just what we need in Boone."

She pointed at the man on the ground. "Does he have a name?"

"Not yet," Polly said.

"Deputy Kellar? Would you read him his rights and take him back to Boone? I'll wait here for Dressen and his crew."

"Nice to see you, Will," Polly said. "You coming to the party tomorrow?"

"Wouldn't miss it." He smiled at her.

Things had gotten much easier between them the more they got to know each other. He was good for Lexi and Lexi was good for him. She softened his demeanor.

"Do you want me to give you a statement now?" Tonya asked. "Or can I come down to the station?"

Tab smiled. "Thank you. It's going to be crazy for a while. I'll give you a call. If you want to get out of here before the crime scene tech arrives, go ahead."

"Thanks." Tonya flipped her keys in her hand, and then picked up the hardware she'd deposited on the ground. She packed things up, waved at Polly, and backed out of the driveway, waiting for Deputy Kellar's car to drive off.

"You're something else," Tab said to Polly.

"At least I keep you busy."

CHAPTER TWENTY-SIX

Nothing could stop them now. The house was ready. Everyone had gotten involved in cleaning the main level last night. When Rebecca started handing out orders, no one balked. Especially since the party was for her. They set up tables in the foyer and in the living room. The dining room and kitchen would hold the food, and for those that needed time away from too many people, the family room was in better shape than it had been in months. Polly felt good about it all.

"I'm so ready to wear my ring," Rebecca whispered to Polly. "It feels like I've been waiting forever to tell people."

"What? Two weeks?" Polly asked.

"Andrew and I have been talking about it for months." Rebecca smiled. "He chose the ring, but at least he asked questions about what I wanted. I can't wait to have it back on my finger. Did you like it? I never asked."

"I love it, honey," Polly said.

The ring was a beautiful platinum setting with a center diamond, emerald cut like Polly's mother's ring. On each side were two small emerald baguettes, Rebecca's birthstone. The wedding band had two matching emerald baguettes with a third emerald that nestled the engagement ring's diamond.

"I didn't want something busy because I use my hands to work all the time. I'm nervous enough that I'll catch the diamond somewhere and tear it out of its setting. All those busy extra stones around the band would definitely catch on stuff. I'd probably run around with threads hanging off my hand."

"You probably wouldn't," Polly said with a smile, but she understood. During the first months she wore her mother's rings, she hadn't been able to stop fussing over them. She'd finally gotten used to having them on her finger and now, it was as if they'd always been there.

"It's a little intimidating that everyone in town is going to know about this engagement in a matter of hours," Rebecca said. "I'm not ready for that."

"That's because nearly everyone will be here watching it happen."

"Again, intimidating," Rebecca said. "I have to be on my best behavior, and I have to keep looking nice until he does the whole thing and ..."

Polly put her hand on Rebecca's right arm which was flailing about as she thought through all that was about to happen. "And it will be fine. Then it will be over, and you'll go back to your normal life."

"Nothing is going to be normal once that ring is on my finger. Everything changes. Am I ready to be married? Am I ready to be a full-grown adult making decisions all by myself?"

"You have been ready to be a full-grown adult for a long time," Polly said. "As for making decisions by yourself, that's a fallacy. You will still have me and Henry around to help when you need it, and Andrew will be part of the big decisions."

"Unless he's in front of his laptop with stories pouring out of his fingers. Interrupting him isn't awful, but I know it takes time for him to get back to it, so I try not to do it very often."

"Things can usually wait until his brain is focused on the real world again."

"You know me," Rebecca said. "I like to have my questions answered right now."

"Then, it's a good thing Andrew loves you."

A warm smile crossed Rebecca's lips. "He really does love me. When I think about it too much, I cry."

"Oh, honey," Polly said. "I understand. You wonder how you got so lucky."

"Not everybody does, you know."

"I know. And sometimes, loving someone requires you to work hard at overcoming what you see as their flaws."

"And sometimes their flaws will destroy you. Like that guy who was murdered. Did his wife really love him before they got married or did he tell her that she did and would never find anyone else who would love her?"

"I don't know."

"It scares me how many people get into relationships with others who are so broken that they will do anything to protect themselves, including abuse."

"Today is not the day to talk about that," Polly said. She opened a drawer in the desk where she sat. Rebecca was in the comfortable chair with her cat, Wonder, in her lap. "I do want to ask you about this, though."

Rebecca stared at the envelope in Polly's hand. "Not today."

"When?"

"I don't know if I ever want to know what's in there. Did Mom tell me about my father? Did she leave last minute instructions on how to live my life? What was her purpose in giving it to you and not me? Did she not think that I could handle it on my own? I don't want to handle it at all. If it's about my birth father, well, who cares? He didn't. Why did we run away and move so much? Because he was one of those broken people who threatened Mom with abuse? I don't want to know that."

"I'll hold it here until the day you're ready to open it."

"I'd rather just burn it so I never have to think about it."

"When you decide to take it out of my hands, you can make the choice to read it or burn it."

"You've never looked at the letter?"

"I don't even know if it is a letter from your mother. It could be a hundred different things. Maybe it's a check for two million dollars."

"We wouldn't have lived like we did if Mom had two million dollars."

"Maybe it's her life insurance policy."

"She didn't have the money to invest in one of those either. It's not money. She'd have given that to me right up front."

"You're right," Polly said. "Are you sure that you don't want to read this today?"

"Today of all days – no," Rebecca replied. "Maybe when I turn forty. Maybe never. As much as I hate secrets and unopened boxes, that thing makes me cringe. Mom was up front and honest about our lives. About everything. That she had something she needed to keep a secret isn't something I want to know."

Polly slid it back into the drawer. It had been with her for years. Her curiosity didn't matter today. No one but Rebecca mattered when it came to whatever was in that letter. The thing was, because Rebecca wouldn't look at it, the thoughts in her head were bigger than whatever the reality was. "It's put away again."

"I'll remember that it's there. I think about it a lot. Sometimes I think that it would be easier to just get it over with. Then I think about how much it would hurt if I found out something terrible about Mom or the man whose genetics I carry. Maybe he was a murderer. Maybe he was a drunken idiot that she had sex with in a parking lot. Maybe he's a wealthy executive who was married and they had a fling. How would any of that help me live a better life?"

"Maybe you should go down to your room and get ready for the party. People are going to show up within the hour."

Rebecca's eyes grew wide. "I'm not ready!"

"Like I said …"

~~~

The one thing about parties at the Bell House was that once people were there, Polly stopped worrying if it would be successful or not. Between conversations that moved around the room, food, and the fact that they were celebrating birthdays today, there was plenty of entertainment.

Sylvie had approached Polly about adding Andrew's name to the birthday cake. Why she hadn't thought of it herself bothered Polly, but of course it should happen. He turned twenty-one in April. Family had celebrated with him, but college made it difficult to throw a big party. Today was his day too.

He'd been surprised to find a banner with his name hanging opposite Rebecca's banner. He'd been even more surprised to find his name on the cake beside the girl that he planned to propose to today.

It didn't matter that Rebecca had begged for there to be no gifts, the gift table was filled with presents and cards for both young people. Polly had fielded many questions about what Rebecca might want. She wanted to tell people that cash for travel was Rebecca's greatest desire, but that would turn into something bigger than Rebecca wished to deal with.

Rebecca's college roommate, Cathy South, had come up for the party. She planned to spend the night. Thank goodness Rebecca and her friends had cleaned and organized the room. Not that Cathy didn't know exactly what Rebecca's living space was like.

"When is he going to do it?" Cathy whispered to Polly.

Polly chuckled, thankful that she hadn't jumped since the girl had come up from behind her. "I have no idea. Have you seen either of them?"

"That's why I asked. Are they downstairs making out or preparing for the proposal?

"Making out," Polly said. "That's my guess."

"You're weird."

"I know. It's what makes me who I am. How was your first week at home?"

Cathy shrugged. "Dad is doing his thing. You know, I never realized how much Mom held us all together. She was, like, the glue in the family. I know Dad loves me, but he's so busy with his life that he probably doesn't know I'm living in the house again. One more year and I can move out and be on my own."

"Are you still okay with living in a dorm your senior year?" Polly asked.

"When you talked about the expenses of living in an apartment, both of us realized we weren't ready. We'll take one more year of a coddled lifestyle and save as much as possible. I love the idea of my own place without all the rules of dorm life, but I also like the fact that I'm on campus and don't have to go far to get to my classes. I don't have to drive every day and then look for a parking place. The dining hall is easy; it's all easy."

"It sounds like you two have thought this out."

"Rebecca thinks about everything."

"Yes, she does."

It felt like the foyer had gotten smaller. People were coming in from the living room, the kitchen, and the kids who had been playing video games in the family room ran in to find their parents.

"Something is going on," Cathy said.

"I wonder who is behind all the moving around."

Cathy turned a flat stare to Polly. "Rebecca. No one is going to believe that this proposal is a surprise."

"We'll let the two of them live in their dream world." Polly had no idea what Rebecca and Andrew had planned for today, but she wasn't surprised when Rebecca came out onto the balcony from the second floor.

It took a few moments for people to stop what they were doing and look up, but when she had their attention, Rebecca said, "Thank you for coming. Celebrating my twenty-first birthday with family and friends is amazing."

She took the first step down on the kitchen side of the room, still talking. "When Polly and Henry asked if I wanted a party, my first thought was to say no. But then, I realized that there is nothing better than seeing everyone I love in the same place. Polly taught me that."

Rebecca paused halfway down the steps to look over the crowded room. A collective intake of breath was heard around the room. Though her friend, Cilla, might be the actress in the crowd, Rebecca knew how to draw and hold people's attention. "It's hard to imagine that next year is my last year of college. I'm sure Polly will have another party when I graduate." She walked down three more steps, paused, and looked across the room again. "I look forward to having many parties in this room with you all."

Andrew walked through the door from the kitchen, and up the steps. He gave Rebecca a quick kiss on the cheek, then stepped up one step from where she stood, his back to the main part of the room. When he went down on one knee, she smiled at him. Silence fell. Rebecca didn't feign surprise, she simply waited, giving people enough time to move so they could watch.

The two of them had chosen the perfect position. They weren't so high that people would have to strain to see, but were high enough on the steps that very few wouldn't be tall enough to watch them.

Hayden lifted Lissa to his shoulders. Noah hauled Delia into his arms and pointed.

"Rebecca!" she cried out.

Rebecca glanced at the little girl and smiled again.

Andrew opened the ring box, held it out to her, and said, "Rebecca Heater, the one person I have always and will always love, will you marry me?"

"Yes, Andrew, I will. I love you more than I will ever have words to express." Rebecca trailed her fingers along his cheeks, tears flowing from her eyes. She bent to kiss him, then allowed him to remove the ring from the box and place it on her finger.

Applause rang out as the two walked down the rest of the steps to the main floor of the foyer. Polly couldn't help it. She'd known what was coming, but felt tears in her eyes. It was real now. Her daughter was engaged. She stepped back out of the way. Though people would want to congratulate her or tell her how happy they were, today wasn't about Polly Giller. Today was about Rebecca and Andrew.

"How are you?" Henry whispered as he slipped an arm around her waist.

"Proud. Happy. Emotional. Glad it's real. Scared that it's real." She took his hand. "You know, all the regular emotions that show up."

Sal and Mark Ogden walked over. "Did you know this was happening today?" Sal asked. When Polly nodded, she continued, "And you didn't tell me? What kind of friend are you?"

"The kind of friend who knows how much you love a good romantic surprise," Polly said. "The best kind of friend."

"That was too sweet for words. Have you made plans for the wedding yet?"

"Not even a date," Polly said. "It will happen next summer, and that's all I know. Oh, and it will happen here."

Sal swooned a bit, and said, "What a beautiful scene that will be. Rebecca coming down the steps in her wedding gown, preparing to marry her sweet boy. You okay with that, Henry?"

"I'm happy for them," he said.

"That's all you've got?"

"For you, that's all I've got."

"Come on, Sal. Give the guy a break," Mark said. "He's about to invest an enormous amount of money in order to see his daughter get married. The man has a lot on his mind. Let's congratulate the couple and then help ourselves to some cake. The party is just getting started."

It felt like everyone in the room stopped to talk to them about the upcoming wedding. And to a person, they talked about how beautiful Rebecca would look coming down the grand stairway on Henry's arm.

"You're going to have to build them a little house next to mine," Agnes said.

"What?" Polly asked.

"Where else are they going to live? In your basement? They need some privacy."

"Maybe you should move into the basement, and we'll rent your house to them." Henry grinned at her.

"Maybe you should bite your tongue. I'm not giving up that house until they drag me out of it feet first. You built me a masterpiece and I plan to enjoy it as long as possible. So there." Agnes stuck out her tongue and then hugged him. "I can hardly wait for this wedding." She turned to Polly. "Will you let me help? I want to be part of everything."

Polly's eyes filled with tears again. The thought of Agnes being part of it hadn't occurred to either her or Rebecca. "Of course."

"I will grow all the flowers she wants to use," Agnes said. "I will help you plan a menu. I will do anything that I can do, even if it's corralling little girls before they become a menace."

"Rebecca and I already talked about the possibility of having you grow some of her flowers."

"I'll grow roses. I'll grow anything for Rebecca. All she needs to do is tell me what she wants. If we have a terrible spring, I will talk to Judy Greene, and we'll make sure the flowers safely grow in her greenhouse. Let me do this for you."

Polly nodded. "That will be an amazing gift."

"You're paying for the seeds. I'm just doing the work."

"Got it," Polly said with a laugh. "You do know that you are my problem child, don't you?"

"And doesn't that make me happy." Agnes turned and looked at Marnie and Dave Evans, who stood behind her. "Other people want to talk to you. I need to love on the young'uns before I get a piece of cake. What a party this has turned into."

As Mark Ogden's assistant at the veterinary clinic, Marnie had become a close friend of Polly's. Once her daughter, Ella started dating Heath, both families had gotten to know each other better. Their son, Barrett, was a friend of Rebecca and Andrew's from high school. It was amazing how many people Polly had in her life these days.

Marnie gave Polly a quick hug and said, "This is probably a lousy time to talk to you about a different wedding, but I have a couple of questions."

"Are you telling me that Heath and Ella are planning a wedding?" Polly asked. "That brat hasn't said a word to me."

"He wouldn't," Dave said with a laugh. "Ella is pushing him now that she's nearly finished with her education. He wants to make sure everything is in place before they make a decision. Since they haven't built a house or done any of that, he keeps trying to hold her off."

"Ella is stronger than that," Polly said.

"Speaking of Ella finishing college," Marnie said. "We're celebrating next weekend with just our family. Hay and Cat will be there with their kids. Would you and Henry come, too?"

"At your house?"

"No," Dave said. "We couldn't hold everyone. We made a reservation at Davey's. I would have done something in Ames, but graduation weekends are nuts over there. Davey's will be nice. Friday evening at six-thirty. Will that work?"

"We'll be there," Henry said. "Now, what's this about a wedding? Where are they planning to have it?"

Marnie gave him a sheepish look. "Here? What would you think about that?"

"I would think it's the best location in town," Polly said. "When?"

"We need to look at your calendar. Whenever it works out for you. They don't want a big wedding." Marnie gestured to the large crowd of people. "This would be too much, but they have college friends and Ella has high school friends. The people Heath works with every day, and any family of yours that will come."

"Everyone will be there, then," Polly said. "What month are you thinking?"

"Early August before kids go back to school." Marnie shrugged "It could be late August, I guess. I know this is last minute, but those two have been going back and forth. They are trying to make each other happy about everything. It was time for me to stick my nose into the process. If nothing else, the process needs to kick into gear. Ella will kill me for talking to you, but if we wait for her and Heath, we'd still be thinking about it next year."

"Give me a call," Polly said. "We'll find a date. Then the chaos will begin."

Marnie shook her head. "You have no idea. At least Rebecca is giving you a year to plan."

"Rebecca has been planning her wedding for the last six months without telling me," Polly said. "My job is to go along with everything she's dreamed up."

Henry clutched his heart. "Good heavens."

"These girls of ours," Dave Evans said. "They find the love of their life and it's all over."

"You found the love of your life," Marnie said. "Look how far it's gotten you."

He nodded. "Pretty far, that's for sure."

~~~

After the party ended, Andrew and Rebecca left the house with their friends. He promised to come back tomorrow afternoon to help with cleanup, but Henry brushed him off. Today was not a day for those two to be responsible for something as simple as cleaning up the foyer. They had plenty of help.

Food was stowed and trash bags were hauled to the back of Henry's truck. He'd deal with those tomorrow. While the foyer wasn't completely clean, most of the mess around the house had been dealt with. The kitchen was back to normal, and kids had found their way to their rooms or at least to a quiet spot away from their parents.

Lexi leaned on the island. "This was a fun day," she said. "I didn't expect the proposal, but I should have. You knew before it happened."

Polly smiled. "Andrew asked Henry's permission."

"Not really," Henry said. "He wanted us to be part of it, so he came to us first. He's a good kid."

"He's a young man, you know," Polly said. "They stopped being kids a long time ago."

"I'll never see him as anything else, no matter how old he gets."

Lexi set her chin in her crossed hands, elbows on the island.

"They're starting something that we won't be part of. That's hard to imagine. Those two will have such fun together." She smiled. "Kind of like you two. You're good role models for them. *How to love each other and have fun in life,* by Polly and Henry. Sounds like it would be a great book to read.

THANK YOU FOR READING!

I'm so glad you enjoy these stories about Polly Giller and her friends. There are many ways to stay in touch with Diane and the Bellingwood community.

You can find more details about Sycamore House and Bellingwood at the website: http://nammynools.com/ Be sure to sign up for the monthly newsletter.

For news about upcoming books: https://www.facebook.com/pollygiller

There's a community for you! Bellingwood Readalong for discussions about the books Bellingwood Cooking & Recipes (free recipe book PDF download)

For information on Diane's other writing projects, https://www.facebook.com/dianegreenwoodmuir

Watch for new releases at Diane's Amazon Author Page.

Recipes and decorating ideas found in the books can often be found on Pinterest at: http://pinterest.com/nammynools/

And if you are looking for Bellingwood swag, https://www.zazzle.com/store/bellingwood

Made in the USA
Middletown, DE
29 May 2024

55029884R00166